TRUST IS A DEADLY GAME...

I0451662

Solo Publication, LLC.
Email: solopublication@gmail.com

Copyright © 2021 By, Hector L. Rodriguez

All rights reserved. No part of this book may be reproduced in any forms or by any means, including graphic, electronic, mechanical, photocopying, recording, taping, or by any information storage retrieval system without the consent of the publisher.

This novel is a work of fiction. Any resemblance, references, or similarities to actual events, real people, livin or deceased is intended to give the novel a sense of reality. Any names, characters, places, and incidents are entirely coincidental and part of the author's imagination.

Library of Congress Control Number:
ISBN: 978-1-7370285-0-5
Cover Design: Vida Oddball Graphics Washington DC
Editor: Carla M. Dean
Publisher: Solo Publication

PROLOGUE

Three wise men founded this empire: Sam, Will, and O-Dawg. They had the reputation and brains to build a multi-million-dollar drug empire. At the time, the Feds marked them as the biggest drug distribution ring in the tri-state area, with power ranging to Puerto Rico and other Latino countries. The business, its political connections, man-power and money were the glue that held together this mob-like structure.

These wise guys held ranks within the organization, and they always paired the hierarchal order with a lump sum of cash. They took all possible measures to protect their operation from snitches, informants, and anyone with bad intentions; only close friends and associates were the ones recruited to join the journey to wealth. Men who were not afraid to lay a body down and put money before all else were the chosen ones. With business associates to launder the dirty drug money and the mayor's office as an overseer, they managed to move tons of kilos of cocaine annually.

Sam was the brains behind the whole operation—the headman in charge. The cocaine would arrive from overseas on boat before being dropped off at a secluded spot in the Delaware River, near the city of Camden, NJ. Some men working the operation were trained to scuba dive and would arrive at dawn on certain days to begin the long process of retrieving the cocaine from the dark, murky waters.

The drugs would then be transported to a stash house. Where they would be weighed, cut, and bagged by a different group of men. The drug processing would sometimes take days; the fellas took turns in two, 12-hour shifts, smoking on devils (weed laced with crack cocaine) throughout the night. The way the money was rolling in low-level drug pushers were balling. Almost drug kingpins themselves, they were raking in close to seven grand apiece per shift.

Fast-forward twelve years into this very lucrative business, Sam, the H.N.I.C., has been thinking of retiring to ravish the benefits of a wealthy life. Juice, a respected and feared drug lord in Puerto Rico,wants to expand his trade into the United States in hopes of living the American Dream, and what better way than through Sam's retirement. The Colombian cartel's creed is blood in, blood out. When word of Sam's retirement gets out, all hell breaks loose between his men and Juice's team of overseas killers.What will be the destiny of this multi-million-dollar empire? Will anyone be able to stop the bloodshed?

CHAPTER 1

Twelve years later, things hit a dramatic turn for this wealthy empire—pressure burst pipes, and fear built pressure.

"*Yo tambien* in the back?" the dealer shouted to the lookout stationed at the rear of the alleyway.

The dealer wanted to know if everything was okay since he had not heard the lookout's voice in over fifteen minutes. Each lookout held the responsibility of letting him know every few minutes that all was good.

"Yeah, everything's good back here," responded the young boy, who was more worried about the exotic weed he was blowing on than the police.

"Speak up! I can't hear you back there! *Yo tambien?*" shouted the dealer once again but to the front lookout this time.

"Everything's good up here," responded the lookout.

"That's why I hate using these little *motherfuckas* to look out for me while I'm working," Vic grumbled to his hustling partner, O-Dawg. "Police fuck around and rundown on us, and with these little rugrats watching our backs, we wouldn't even see it coming."

"I feel where you're coming from," said O-Dawg, "but the fiends are no better lookouts than the young guns. At least the youngguns don't be /nodding off from heroin or paranoid from smoking crack."

"Fuck that! The next time anybody messes up while looking out during my shift, I'm deducting twenty-five dollars from their pay. Fiend or younggun, I don't care!" replied Vic, letting his agitation get the best of him.

"Damn! Shit has been moving like hotcakes out here today," said O-Dawg in hopes of steering the conversation in a different direction. "I've done made over five grand in just a few hours."

"I see today's gonna be a good day!" Vic exclaimed as he lit a cigarette. "All this time I've known Sam, and to this day, I still don't know where the man gets his cocaine from. I guess that's a good thing. Whoever it may be must be a very wealthy man."

"Yeah, the shit's definitely some official raw. Crackheads rather buy powder from this operation and cook it up themselves than buy the shit already cooked up from any corner in the hood."

"Yo, how many?" asked Vic, turning his attention from his partner and focusing on the white male approaching.

"Let me get fifty twenty-dollar bags of powder cocaine," answered the customer as he pulled out a large wad of cash from his pocket and began counting the bills.

"This be that shit I be talking about right here—a thousand dollars in one sale!" Vic yelled excitedly as he served the white man his poison.

"Isn't that Sam walking this way?" asked O-Dawg.

"Yeah, I'm surprised to see him around. The only time he stops by is when there's a meeting."

"What up, boss?" both men asked at almost the same time.

"I have some important business I want to discuss with you fellas tonight," Sam replied without reciprocating a greeting. "I need everyone to meet me inside the basement at nine o'clock sharp, and I expect to see everyone in attendance."

He then turned and headed back in the direction he came from.

"I wonder what the hell he has to speak to us about," O-Dawg pondered outloud. "Shit has been running smoothly lately, and from what I know, no one been fucking up no money."

"Like you said, from what you know, no body has been fucking up money. But I guess the importance of this meeting will come to light in a few hours."

Both men were lost in their thoughts, wondering what this sudden meeting was about... O-Dawg recalled the last meeting—when the brains of one of his close associates ended up on the walls inside of the garage, because he ran his mouth about plans to take over the empire Sam had so carefully built.

***

It was five minutes before the start of the meeting, and all the men who belonged to the organization waited patiently for their boss to arrive. Some sat around on the plush sofa inhaling exotic herb, while others shot a game of pool while catching up on the hood's latest gossip. Will was the appointed chief in charge of overseeing the ins and outs of the operation. His home's basement was where they held meetings to discuss matters concerning the empire's status. It was also luxuriously customized with all the necessary accessories for these high-caliber men.

Two minutes after nine o'clock, the headman in charge made his awaited grand entrance, followed by a frail man in tow.

"Who the fuck is this country-looking clown," thought Ice, a long-time member of the operation, as he looked the unknown male up and down.

"Gentlemen, may I have your undivided attention?!"

The entire room fell silent upon hearing the authority in the headman's voice.

"I've gathered you all here tonight to discuss a very important matter," Sam continued. "As you all should be aware, we've been operating this business for over 12-years. I must say thank you for riding with me and sticking by my side throughout this long journey. With out all of you, I would not be the man I am today. However, all good things must come to an end, so tonight I am announcing that I will be officially retiring from the game."

Whispers began to circulate amongst the crowd.

"Hold on, fellas. Nothing is going to change. I will be stopping by to check on things, as I have been doing for over a decade, and as you know, I come unannounced. The meetings will continue when called on by the chain of command. Therefore, I would like to introduce my replacement and the new headman in charge—Juice."

The whispers grew harsher in tone as the crowd fell into discontent, and frowns spread across their faces. No one within the empire had ever laid eyes on this frail Latino man from Puerto Rico.

Juice was a well-respected drug lord and business-man in his country. Many men feared him, and his reputation superseded his character. The word on the street was he liked to decapitate his victims with a chainsaw, bury them alive, or torture them before setting them on fire. This man did not discriminate when it came to taking a life, and because of his frail looks, many men underestimated his power and thoroughness. For that, they paid dearly.

"Hold on a second, Sam," interrupted Ice. "No disrespect, but we've been holding you as well as this empire down since this shit was first put into effect more than 12-years ago. Correct me if I'm wrong, but wasn't I one of the first who helped you get this shit off the ground? How are you going to disrespect the whole crew by assigning this country-ass clown before any of us? It should be one of the original men who take over, not a man who doesn't know a goddamn thing about this operation!"

Chief Will brought Ice on during the early days when things had just gotten started. Both men had grown up together in the Eastside's housing projects; they sold drugs together on the corner when they were teenagers. Hot-tempered and feared, Ice jumped on anyone who disobeyed or disrespected his authority—he was known for it.

Sam understood how Ice felt, but he had no choice but to roll with the punches.

Juice pulled out the .357 Magnum he had secured under his waistbelt and approached Ice. With the gun suspended in the air, he shot the man point-blank in the face. Brain fragments splattered throughout the entire room. The loud noise from the powerful revolver made everyone's ears ring. The men stood with their mouths hanging open and eyes bulging, staring at the body of the person they once knew—half his face blown off.

No one dared to make a move on the frail man from Puerto Rico. The incident infuriated them even more since Sam forbade weapons in meetings. The men who wanted to speak up chose instead to keep their mouths shut and hope for the chance of retaliation in the future.

Seeing the disapproving look on the faces of his men, Sam finally spoke, breaking the silence.

"Gentlemen, as you all have witnessed with your own eyes, this man does not play games.

He is strictly about his business, with full intentions of playing for keeps. This is one of the many reasons I chose a man of his caliber.

"Now, gentlemen, remember to treat this man with the same respect as you do me," Sam continued. "The daily operations within this organization will not change in any way. Things will continue to operate as usual. Everyone will keep their same status, except for Ice, who is no longer with us. I always said his mouth would one day be the cause of his death,"Sam lamented as he faced Ice's body. "Rest in peace! I will personally make sure you have a proper burial. I have much love for you, but life must go on."

Sam was putting on a front for Juice. Deep down, he wished he could kill the man standing in front of him for the cold-blooded murder of his long-time friend, but he also knew he had to portray a ruthless image if he expected to earn Juice's respect.

"Juice will appoint the next capo to replace Ice. It is now his decision and no longer mine. Who ever he chooses, you are all to follow the normal routine. Remember, gentlemen, nothing has changed; the head and body remain the same."

Sam turned around and walked out of the basement, followed by the new headman.

***

"So, Juice...what do you think about the organization so far?" Sam asked.

"I've been observing this whole operation since my arrival here in the United States, and I have to admit I am impressed on the business operations end. I see why you are a very wealthy man. However, I disliked the man who underestimated me at the meeting. I hope you were not offended by the violence that occurred. My instincts react before I have time to control them."

"Shit happens. I understand how you must have felt at that moment. A man like yourself must never show signs of weakness under any circumstances. My boys will take care of the body; you have my word on it. The death of our friend Ice will in no way come back to haunt you. The fellas are as loyal as the hood that breeds them. So, what happened inside that basement stays within those confinements."

"I trust your words, Sam, but it is not you who I am worried about. We both know there is no trust or loyalty in this game. There is only respect and fear. A man would rather be feared than respected."

"I definitely agree with you."

"I will be working around these men on a consistent basis," continued Juice. "So, I will be rearranging things to fit my perspective. I will be bringing a few of my men from Puerto Rico to work within the organization. One of these men will be taking on the capo's position, while the others will be my eyes and ears within the operation."

"Juice, my friend, you are officially the new H.N.I.C. Do what you feel is best."

"Best believe I will do just that, but I want you to notify your men that I will be holding a meeting once my men arrive."

"Consider it done," responded Sam. "Just do me the favor of keeping things in one piece. I would hate for the palace that I've spent so many years building to crumble."

"I'll try my damn best to avoid such a tragedy," Juice replied before adding, "We're both businessmen, and money is our main priority; we also do not want to disappoint Juan."

CHAPTER 2

Sam was first introduced to Juice through his Colombian connect while vacationing with the Colombian drug lord, Juan, in Cancun, Mexico. What was supposed to have been a relaxed vacation turned out to be Sam's worst nightmare. When he arrived at the upscale restaurant lounge, he was greeted by the drug lord Juan with open arms.

"Sam, *amigo*! I'm glad you could make it! Please, follow me. I have a bottle of the most expensive Scotch on this side of this planet waiting for us. I would also like to introduce to you a very close associate of mine," Juan said and signaled to the reserved table. "*Amigo*! Have a seat, please!"

As they claimed their seats at the table, Sam noticed a frail man perched at the edge.

"Sam, this is a personal friend of mine I wanted to introduce to you," Juan continued while waving his hand towards the frail-looking man. "This man here is Juice, a very close friend and business partner. They call him the great king of Puerto Rico. In this country, he is respected as much as he is feared."

"Nice to meet you," said Sam before reaching over to shake the thin man's hand.

"Well, since we all now formally know each other, let's get down to business," interrupted Juan. "Both of you are great clientele to my cartel. So, to my understanding, Sam, you have been telling me about your plans to retire?"

"Yes, I have been thinking about it."

"I, myself, have been trying to avoid such conversation," replied Juan. "Truth is your departure will put a huge dent in my pocket. I am a man of business; I cannot allow this to happen."

Sam listened intently, wondering where this conversation was going. He had a bad vibe about this meeting and could feel the tension building.

"*Mi amigo*, when we initially crossed paths, I thoroughly explained to you that once the first deal was sealed, there was no turning back. It will crush my heart to have our long-time friendship end on bad terms, but since I am a man of understanding and business, I have a proposition that will suit all of our needs."

"And what might that be?"

"Well, you see, my friend Juice here would like to expand his empire into the United States. Your organization makes me millions of dollars annually, and, as I've just mentioned, I will not be a happy camper if I were to lose your business. So, *amigo*, the proposition is that you show Juice around your city and let him run your organization after your retirement."

"What! Are you crazy?"

"Can you let me finish, *amigo*? You will receive a nice, sizeable amount of cash at the end of each week for the hard work you put in organizing such a profitable trade. Nothing within your operation will change...only the headman in charge. Sam, consider this an illegal pension on an early retirement. You will be receiving payments even though you will no longer be running things.This is also the only way out without ruining our friendship.You catch the drift, don't you?"

"So, let me get this straight.You want me to let a man I know *nothing* about take over my organization?"

The question was rhetorical, but Sam still found himself expecting an explanation.

Juice sat at the end of the table listening to these two men with an expressionless look on his face. He knew Sam had no other alternative but to go along with Juan's proposition.

"*Mi amigo*, I understand you know nothing about this man. But I, on the other hand, know everything there is to know about him," continued the Colombian drug lord while waving his hand towards Juice. "I think he is the perfect candidate for such a position."

"I don't know about this," reputed Sam. "I would have to hold a meeting with the fellas and run this by them before making a decision. Understand that I have men who have been by my side since day one of this establishment. My chief of operations, who I have known for most of my entire life, knows all the ropes of the operation, and he is as loyal as they come. I think he would be the better candidate. I wanted to introduce him to you, but I know—"

"No!" Juan snapped, cutting Sam off. "I explained this to you when we first met... never mention anyone else's name while conducting business! You just offended me as if I were a low-level kingpin!"

Juan sighed deeply and said, "Look, Sam, you must understand that this is not a decision to be made by you. How can I put this? Oh, yes…this is an *order*. Disobey and suffer severe consequences!"

This man must think I'm some fool. If I wasn't out here alone, I would spit in his face! Sam thought as he clenched his fist.

"Did I get my point across, *amigo*?"

"Yes. I heard you loud and clear."

"Sam, if for some odd reason you have plans on running or dodging me, I suggest you don't try it, for I have people all over the United States as well as in many other surrounding countries. I just thought I'd bring this to your attention. As we speak, there are a few men watching over your house. One wrong move, and your wife and daughter will pay the price. So, if I were you, *mi amigo*, I wouldn't attempt anything funny."

How could this immigrant spic take it so far? Sam thought to himself furiously. *Really? Militant men watching over my family?*

Sam sat in silence.

"I've booked a flight for the both of you; it leaves tomorrow morning at nine o'clock," said the Colombian. "Now, if you'll excuse me, I have some fine Mexican women waiting for me back at the hotel suite. You fellas enjoy your night."

"I guess I'll be seeing you at the airport tomorrow morning," Juice teased before getting up from the chair and extending his hand towards Sam. "I hope there are no hard feelings between us. Understand that this was an opportunity I couldn't resist."

"There are no hard feelings."

***

Sam sat alone at the beach bar chugging shot after shot of Hennessey as the sun's beaming rays beat down on his pale skin. Having enough to drink, he got up from the barstool in search of his room. Stumbling inside of the hotel suite, he laid on his back across the waterbed and gazed up at the ceiling, unable to fall asleep. He thought about different ways to side step this threat. Knowing how well the Colombian drug lord was connected, he shook the thought off for fear of getting himself or his family murdered.

***

The following morning, Sam arrived at the airport thirtyfive minutes before his flight's departure. Juice sat patiently in the waiting lounge, browsing through the pages of the latest issue of the *DuPont Registry*car magazine. Seeing Sam making his way towards him, Juice stood up from the comfortable chair to greet him.

"Hello, my friend it's good to see you. For a minute there, I thought you might've had a change of heart and not show up."

"Do I have another choice?"

Ignoring the smart remark, Juice continued, "We have a long day ahead of us, so I hope you've come prepared."

Glancing down at the small carry-on bag in his hand, Sam stated, "Why should I have come prepared? Aren't we headed back to the United States?"

"Oh, no, my friend," Juice remarked. "Juan wants me to show you around my country as well as how I operate my business in my home state. Puerto Rico is such a beautiful place—"

His sentence was cut short by the voice on the loudspeaker: *"Attention, all customers. National Airline Flight 401 to San Juan, Puerto Rico, will be departing in ten minutes. All passengers who have yet to board the flight please make your way to gate fourteen. Thank you for flying National Airline."*

"That'll be us!" Juice said while handing Sam his ticket.

Sam could not believe what was happening. He needed time alone to think. A trip to Puerto Rico was the last thing he expected.

***

During the three-hour journey over the Atlantic, Juice tried to make small talk with his future partner, but Sam's thoughts were on his family and his current situation. He could not believe how such a good thing for decades had turned into his worst nightmare overnight. Hours later, he breathed a sigh of relief when he noticed the jumbo airliner preparing for its landing.

Exiting San Juan International Airport terminal, both men were greeted by the driver of a black Cadillac Escalade, which was illegally parked in a no-parking zone. Climbing inside, Juice reached for the bottle of Scotch before taking a seat. He poured two glasses of the expensive champagne.

"To a new business relationship. The sky is the limit," Juice said while raising the glass for a toast. "Sam, my friend, you seem a little tense and uncomfortable since our last conversation with Juan. You have no need to worry. I will run the empire just like you did. Your men won't even notice the difference."

Sam sipped his drink and gave Juice a disapproving look.

This asshole doesn't get it! It's about loyalty, you dumb fuck! He thought as he stared at Juice with a poker face. *How are my men going to look at me when they find out I've selected you as my successor instead of someone who helped me build my empire from scratch?*

The sound of Juice's cell phone ringing brought Sam back to the moment.

"Hello… Yes, yes, good work, my friend. I'll be there in a few minutes. I will also be bringing a friend of mine along."

Sam tried to eavesdrop but was only able to hear bits and pieces of the conversation.

The night before, Juice received a phone call from his chief of staff, notifying him of the capture of someone he had been looking for, for quite some time. Taking advantage of the opportunity, he planned to bring Sam along as a scare tactic.

"Sorry about the interruption, my friend, but understand that I am a man of quality. So, I must answer all calls," Juice said after he terminated the call. "Do you mind tagging along? I have an important situation that desperately needs my presence."

"You invited me when you mentioned to the other person on the other end that you were bringing a friend along," responded Sam. "So, I'm guessing it'll be rude for me to decline your offer."

***

Sam could see a huge red barn half a mile down a dirt road in the back of the secluded wooded area. As he eyed the old building from afar, his instincts told him it was their destination. The ride down the road was a bumpy one. The Escalade jerked from side to side as it made its way down the unpaved road. Coming into closer view of the place, Sam noticed men posted around the compound. They were dressed in militant gear and holding what appeared to be AK-47 assault rifles.

What the fuck is this? He thought nervously as his heart raced.

Noticing the worried look plastered on his face, Juice said, "My friend, there is no need to worry. This here is only for you to observe."

Climbing out of the SUV, all three men made their way towards the red wooden structure as they watched the armed guards part like the Red Sea. Upon entering the barn, Sam noticed more armed men stationed within the circumference of the barn. Focusing his attention towards the far-right corner, he could not believe his eyes. A man was chained down to a metal slab. He could hear the muffled screams as a couple of men poured what smelled like gasoline over the victim's body.

"Sam, my friend, I wish you didn't have to witness this cruel act of violence, but as you know, this is the fate of people who disobey me or disregard my orders. This man here thought he could test my *gangsta* by selling his product in my territory. After a few warnings, he obviously did not take heed, so he is the one who I will make an example out of," Juice said as he approached the victim. "Look at him regretting he went against my wishes, but it's too late. He must suffer the consequences."

One of Juice's men wheeled in a hospital gurney covered with razor-sharp operating utensils. Grabbing a surgical scalpel from the gurney, Juice began making small incisions into the man's upper body. Ignoring the man's muffled screams, he then began to pour a mixture of gasoline and rubbing alcohol over the victim's body. The helpless man shook violently as the liquid soaked the tiny incisions, sending excruciating pain throughout his entire body.

Picking up a pair of bolt cutters, Juice continued his assault by cutting off the victim's fingers one at a time. The thought of having blood ruin his seven-thousand-dollar Armani suit made him even more upset. He felt no remorse for the man shedding tears in front of him. Reaching into his pants pocket, he retrieved a book of matches. He ignited a matchstick and tossed it on top of the victim.

The stench of burning flesh made Sam's stomach turn, almost causing him to vomit. Fear was the only thing on his mind. Thoughts of what would happen to him or his family if he disobeyed the orders given by Juan haunted him as he eyed the burning body.

"Let's go, my friend," Juice said coolly, breaking Sam's trance-like state. "My work here is done. Time is of the essence, and we still have a lot to cover by day's end."

He could tell by the way Sam's face turned color that his scare tactic had worked.

***

Sam tried enjoying himself as Juice gave him a tour of the small island, but the events from the past week were still lingering in his mind along with the stench of death in his nostrils. Within a week, he had learned the ins and outs of Juice's operation and witnessed another brutal torture. It was now time for Sam to head back to the United States. Juice was nothing but a paranoid frantic who murdered for the pettiest reasons; Sam wanted to put as much distance between the two of them as possible. He needed to gather his thoughts, and being around such a psychopath was not amending his mental chaos. He decided that he had no other alternative but to go along with the Colombian drug lord's proposition.

"I know the fellas will be disappointed with me when I break the news to them, but I just can't bring myself to confess the truth. They won't understand, and it is in the best interest of my family to go along with what this Colombian prick wants," Sam pondered sadly.

He had to keep reminding himself that he was doing the right thing.

Why choose a sick bastard to run a multi-million-dollar organization? I see it all crumbling to pieces within a year or two.

CHAPTER 3

"Yo, dawg, what the fuck is wrong with Sam letting this clown take over the organization?" Vic exclaimed.

"I don't know, fam, but I ain't feeling this shit at all," responded Will. "I gotta have a serious one-on-one with Sam. I need to know what's the real deal behind this mess."

"I feel where you're coming from. You're the chief in charge of this operation, so you best handle this one way or another," O-Dawg said. "I'm sure we're not the only ones feeling this way."

After wrapping up the quick meeting with his two close associates, Will headed home to make the phone call he had dreaded making.

Ten voice messages later, Sam decided to return the urgent calls. As he sat there wondering what was so important for his chief of staff to blow up his phone, he unclipped the device from his waist and dialed the number.

"What's going on, Chief?" he spoke into the receiver.

"I know it might not be the time, but I need to speak to you concerning our last meeting." *I knew this shit was coming,* thought Sam. "Alright! When and where?"

"My house," replied Will. "Tonight at ten o'clock."

***

A knock at the front door brought Will back to the moment at hand. His mind was stuck on the basketball game playing on the 56-inch plasma television. After glancing at his diamond-encrusted wristwatch, he proceeded to get up from his comfortable La-Z-Boy chair. Approaching the front door, he cautiously looked through the peephole, making sure it was a familiar face on the other side. Satisfied, he immediately opened the door and welcomed Sam inside.

"Come in and take a seat. I was watching the 76'ers game. Do you want something to drink?"

"Nah, I'm good," replied Sam. "Let's cut the bullshit small talk and get to the point. What did you wanna talk about?"

"I mentioned earlier that I wanted to talk to you about our last meeting. So, I'm gonna make this conversation short," responded Will while taking a seat in his recliner. "We've known each other since junior high, maybe even a lot longer. As you know, I would never make a decision without first consulting you.Sam, none of guy's are feeling the fact that you chose a man we know nothing about—someone who damn sure did not help build this empire. We're the ones who built this thing from the ground up.I want to know why, Sam, and don't feed me the same bullshit you've told everyone else."

"The answer you're looking for is between me and the Columbian," Sam replied. "It is something I cannot disclose. Even if I did, you would not understand. Juice is an educated and well- connected man in the drug business, and I am positive he will do the job to its fullest and to the best of his ability. I apologize, Will, but it is what it is. If by any chance you happen to come across any problems, give me a call, and I will address Juice personally."

"Sam, we once shared a bond closer than brothers, butI can now see by your decision that bond no longer exists. It's fucked up you won't tell me what's really behind this sudden change. I guess you have your reasons, but just so you're aware, the fellas and I don't agree with your decision. We feel you should have come to us about the matter when it first came to mind, not after finalizing your decision.That was fucked up! I thought we were better than that."

"Everything done in the dark will eventually come to light," said Sam. "When that time does arrive, you will understand and hopefully see things from my perspective. No hard feelings I have always loved you and will always love you like a brother. Don't let this interference get the best of our friendship. One day, you will know the truth. Until then, continue to follow your gut."

He got up from the chair and let himself out.

Will lounged in the recliner, wondering what Sam meant by: *One day, you'll know the truth.*

CHAPTER 4

It was a big day for Juice. Early that morning, three of his best assassins arrived from Puerto Rico. This was the first phase of his plan. He knew it would not be long before the original men from the organization would be jumping at his command. The meeting was just about to start; everyone stopped what they were doing as Juice began his introduction.

"Gentlemen, I want to thank you all for attending this meeting on such short notice. I know you're all wondering what this meeting is about. These three men here behind me will be joining us in our road to riches,"Juice said, pointing at his men behind him. "These men are very close associates of mine from the Island. I have known them for many years and trust them with my life. Allow me to introduce them."

Juice turned and placed his palm on the first man's shoulder.

"This man here is Ruben; he will be the one taking on the capo's position. He is very talented in his profession. His English is far from perfect, but don't be fooled. He understands the language to perfection. This is Carlos here," he continued, this time pointing to the man standing in the middle. "He will be my eyes and ears to the operation, but only until I find a slot to assign him to. He will in no way interfere with your work.Consider him a watchdog."

Juice circled his palm around the arm of the last man in line and said, "Last but not least, this man is Matone—killer in English. His name speaks for itself. The only time you will ever see Matone is when I'm—"

"I have a statement to make," interrupted Justice, another veteran in the empire.

"Speak,"Juice demanded, annoyed by the interruption.

"We don't have a problem with your men hanging around. As long as they stay out of our way and let us continue to do things as we've been doing, there shouldn't be any problems."

"I hate to be repeating myself! Did I not just make it clear that my men will not get in the way of things? Are you hard of hearing?!"

"I was making a statement, not asking a question," responded Justice, upset that Juice had come at him in such a disrespectful manner.

Juice's first intention was to kill this man, but he knew if he wanted to earn the trust of the rest of the men in attendance, he had to keep his cool. Not wanting this meeting to go like the last one, he suppressed his instinctive urge to kill.

I have a nice surprise for this smart-mouth prick! Juice thought.

Brushing off the snarky remark made by Justice, he continued with the meeting.

"Alright, does anyone have any questions before I end this?"

Hearing no response from the crowd, Juice finalized the gathering.

"Well, my friends, I guess I'll be seeing you all soon. In the meantime, act like I'm not even around."

***

As the four men sat comfortably in Juice's Chevy Suburban, Juice addressed his three associates. Besides the boss man, everyone was twisting sweetly concocted blunts of weed and crack cocaine in their mouths. The late 80s and early 90s crack era had found its way to Puerto Rico, and these islanders were no exception to the gravitational pull of this potent drug.

"I can't believe that short bastard had the balls to interrupt me," Juice growled. "Matone, I want you to take care of that little prick immediately."

"No problem, boss. Consider it a closed casket funeral," Matone said with a chuckle.

"I want you to find out where he lives," added Juice. "The guys within this organization don't know a thing about any of you, so they won't be expecting a reaction so soon. Once you find out where he resides, plant a bomb underneath his vehicle. When I say I want him to disappear, I mean it literally! I want this done before the week is over."

"Done deal, sealed with my word," acknowledged Matone while inhaling the toxic fumes from the laced Philly blunt.

"Once he's out of the picture, Carlos, you will take on his position," continued Juice. "I meant it when I said there's a lot of money to be made within this operation. Give it some time, and I promise we will be the ones taking over this entire empire.These men do not know the power of the savages they done let into their kingdom. I have the owner in my back pocket right where I want him. He sees me as Satan's half-brother and has yet to witness the full capability of my madness."

Juice foresaw that the operation would be in his total control in a few months, and Juan would be the only supplier.

"These men here in the United States are weak! They lack guts and fear death. But don't go getting comfortable, for even the weakest will kill out of fear.So, treat this place along with its people as you would back at the Island."

***

Four days had passed since the last meeting took place. Juice had not made an appearance around the organization since then. His men, who abided by coded standards, were on trouper alert. Carlos, being the watchdog was up day and night, wired from smoking too many laced blunts. He constantly watched everyone's movement like a paranoid hawk. This stunt had the men feeling annoyed and uncomfortable. The tension was so thick that it was almost concrete.

Ruben, however, who held the capo's position, was running around barking orders and changing things to fit his perspective; he embodied the role of a fraudulent boss man. No one was feeling the way things were turning out, especially Chief Will, who was the only one allowed under Sam's rule to give such orders and make executive decisions.

Since Justice had not arrived for his shift this particular morning, an argument ensued between the chief and capo. Will knew that Justice being late was unusual; it was unlike him not to show up without first calling. Knowing that every minute gone by was money lost, Will repeatedly called his longtime friend's cell phone. He wanted to give Justice another half hour to arrive before putting in a replacement, but Ruben disagreed. He wanted to put Carlos on immediately. This sparked a heated confrontation that almost turned into a physical altercation between the two high-ranking members.

***

It was a bright sunny morning. As usual, Justice brushed his teeth while watching as his wife got the boys ready for school. After getting dressed, he made his way downstairs to pour himself a freshly brewed cup of coffee.

Placing the mug on the countertop, he decided to warm up the car while the coffee cooled down. Walking outside, he looked left and right out of habit, checking his surroundings as he approached the vehicle. He always kept his 9mm tucked under his waistbelt, ready for anything—except what was to come. The upcoming event was something no one would have anticipated.

Justice did not notice anything out of the ordinary, and his mind gave him the clear. As he climbed inside the vehicle, leaving the driver's door ajar, he inserted the key in the ignition and twisted it. The small compact car exploded with a thunderous boom. The powerful blast ignited into a massive ball of flames, sending the vehicle flying six feet into the air and shattering most of the house windows. The impact from the bomb was felt blocks away. Sirens illuminated the background as neighbors and people passed by, stopping to see if anyone was alive.

***

Everyone was surprised to see he had survived such a gruesome attack; over seventy percent of his body received third-degree burns. The explosion left the right side of his face entirely disfigured, while the left side completely untouched. With multiple broken bones added to his injury, it could be a few weeks before he would be released from the hospital. Doctors were amazed he survived the car bomb. What saved his life was the mere fact he had left the driver's door ajar. The powerful blast sent his body fifteen feet into the air and away from the vehicle. If he had shut the door, he would not have survived. Justice swore revenge on whoever was behind the attempt on his life. He had no idea who it was, but something in his subconscious kept telling him that Juice's hands were dirty.

The Feds were all over this case as this incident was considered to be an act of terrorism. The fellas steered clear of the hospital; they did not want their names associated with the bombing.

Get Well balloons and flowers flooded the small confinements of the Intensive Care Unit. Family members stopped by to pay their respects to the injured man. After two weeks of recovery and not a word from Juice or his men, his suspicions were clarified. Justice vowed to follow his gut feeling; he wholeheartedly believed Juice was the one behind the attempt on his life.

***

Will was at the hospital visiting his close associate. It did not matter to him that the Feds were watching and scrutinizing all visitors. Justice was like a brother. The risk didn't matter at a time like this was his brother in arms. He had his fake ID on him if they asked his name.

Today Justice decided he would speak his mind. He was not holding back any longer. None of they men from the team had stopped by to visit; Will was the first one. He was wrong about alot of people, but this time they had pushed his button.

As Will took a bite from his sandwich, Justice said, "Dawg, I've been doing a lot of thinking lately about what happened, and I know for a *fact* it was Juice who ordered the hit on my life."

"And what makes you think that?"

"It doesn't matter. I swear on my dead mother's grave when I step foot out of this hospital, Juice and his men are going to regret the day they chose to do business in the United States."

"Justice, when you get released, you need to just lay low and focus on healing. Juice already knows he didn't finish the job. So he and his men are gonna be on point, watching our every move. He is bringing in more of his men to work in the organization. I understand how you feel, but we have to go about it the smart way."

"I understand where you're coming from, but that *mothafucka* tried to take my life, and he will pay!"

"Slow your roll, cowboy. He will get his for sure, but only when the right opportunity presents itself.The only reason that comes to mind for the hit on your life is the day of the meeting when you came at him sideways. Ice also lost his life to that country-ass spic for similar reasons. That's double the torture he'll suffer!"

"Juice is a real grimy, sneaky dude," added Justice. "What goes around comes around."

23

CHAPTER 5

Juice was highly upset for the half-ass job Matone pulled. He was furious and could not hold back his anger.

"You stupid son of a bitch! I send you out on an important job, and you fuck it up!"

His pride was wounded. The mistake made him and his crew look like amateurs.

"You out of everybody should know that I'm *not* one for mistakes and that is one of the main reasons why I have lasted this long in the game! Now because of the rookie job you just pulled, I look like a half-fucking gangster to these pricks here in the United States!" he continued spazzing. "Next time I send you out on a mission, you don't leave the premises until you make sure everyone is *dead*! The next mistake will be your last mistake! Do you understand me?"

"You have my word it will not happen again, boss. I'll see to it that when he's released from the hospital, I finish what I started."

"Now that we have an understanding, go and find that apartment I've been asking you about. Manny and Lou will be here Friday morning. I want to make sure they're as comfortable as me when they arrive."

"Boss, there is something I wanted to bring to your attention," interrupted Ruben.

"What is it?" Juice snapped, still feeling agitated from Matone's faulty actions.

"On the day of the car bombing, me and Will got into a verbal dispute. I knew that Justice wasn't gonna make it to work that morning, but Will wanted to give it an hour before putting in a replacement. I wanted to put Carlos in as the replacement immediately.He disagreed with my decision, and that sparked a heated debate between the two of us. The situation is bothering me, and I would like to do something about it with your permission. Will is getting out of hand and needs to be put in his place."

"I'll take care of it," affirmed Juice. "I don't want things to get out of hand. A war would not be in our best interest right now. Our position within this empire must be concrete. Taking over this multi-million-dollar organization is our main concern, but it must be done with precision and on *my* terms. In the meantime, go apologize to him."

When he noticed the weird look Ruben gave him, he added, "It'll ease the tension a little between us all and make things easier. Be the bigger person and let him continue to think he is the chief. This is chess, not checkers, son."

***

Will was heated and frustrated at how things were turning out since Juice took over after Sam's retirement. He could not interpret how a man of Sam's caliber would let an uncaring individual take over an empire they had put so much effort into building. Needing to get a few things off his chest, he picked up the phone and began dialing.

After about the sixth ring, a frustrated voice answered. "Yes, Will, what is it?"

"Ever since the car bombing, you've been avoiding us."

Sam felt ashamed that he let down the man who had helped him climb from rags to riches. He had his hands tied behind his back; it was too late to turn back the hands of time.

"Sam, this whole thing with Juice and his entourage is really starting to get out of hand! He's playing in the major leagues now."

"What do you mean by that?" asked Sam, playing dumb.

Ignoring the question, Will continued to vent. "How much more leeway are we gonna give these guys before they kill more of our men? First, Ice lost his life, and now Justice gets blown the fuck up!"

"How do you know for sure it was Juice who ordered the hit on Justice?"

"Common fucking sense! When he introduced his companions to all of us in our last meeting, Justice spoke up just like Ice did. So, there's your reason why the hit was ordered. We can't keep allowing this fool to get away with this shit! We're looking like chumps in these men's eyes. Just give the word, and none of them will be breathing by tomorrow morning."

"Will, I understand how you must feel, but this is way out of your league. Juice is a very well-connected individual. Taking him out will start a war that we won't be able to win and that will put my family in harm's way. Maybe even *all* our families. It is a guarantee that by now, Juice knows where all of our families reside. I'm also damn sure he forwarded that information to his people back home."

"Fuck this!" Will shouted. "So, what you're saying is that you're just going to let this fool take over our shit? What we spent decades building! This is how we feed our families—our bread and butter!"

"Will, you don't understand! We are not in a position to take on his team or any of his connections. The people he has here with him are not my worries. I'm more concerned with how far his power reaches. Until we come up with a solution that will not incriminate us in any way, we let things be. In the meantime, I will voice your concerns to Juice."

"Look, Sam...he's bringing more of his men from the Island down this way.Common sense says he's up to no good. If we don't put a stop to this immediately, more of our men are gonna end up dead, and we're gonna end up without *any* means of income. I don't know about you, but I'm *not* gonna let that happen!"

"Like I mentioned before, I will have a talk with him."

"Answer me this question, why out of all people did you choose this man to run the operation?"

"I didn't answer it before, so what makes you think I will answer it now?" Sam taunted.

"Me and the fellas are starting to think you're getting soft on—"

Will did not get the chance to finish speaking before he heard the phone's dial tone in his ear. Slamming the phone down on its cradle, he shouted, "What the fuck is wrong with that man?"

After sitting down to gather himself, Will thought, *Sams getting all touchy about the subject as if he scared or hiding something. I don't know about him, but I might have to take matters into my own hands.*

***

Later that day, Sam confirmed his reservations at the *Elegante Nightclub*. It would be a one-on-one conversation with Juice in hopes of resolving the issues between both crews. As Sam entered the establishment, he did not realize he was being watched. Eyes traced his every move from the moment he left home until he arrived at the nightclub. Even though Sam was a weak link, Juice's better judgment told him to use caution. He advised his men to be on high alert, scattering them throughout the club's perimeters—both inside and outside. Learning not to trust anyone ever is what kept him alive and on top of his game.

Sam stepped inside the place looking like a million bucks. He shined bright on the outside, but internally, he was a nervous wreck. Noticing Juice waving his hand from the VIP section, he made his way to the back of the club.

This man has zero chance of survival in my country, Juice thought and chuckled while watching Sam make his way towards the table.

"Please, take a seat, my friend. Tell me, what's the reason for this meeting? Is there some type of problem your men can't handle?"

"It's not really a problem," responded Sam. "My men are dissatisfied with the way things are turning out in the organization."

"What do you mean dissatisfied?"

"My men don't like that your men are not respecting their status and pretty much doing as they please."

"Sam, do you not understand that I am now the head man in charge? My men are following orders. If your men do not agree with how I choose to run my business, they are free to walk. I have men who are anxious to fill any position in this operation. Now, if you'll excuse me, I have a business to run," Juice added before getting up from the table.

Sam sat stunned as he watched him make his exit.

It's best to let things be and let the man run the business whichever way he pleases. As long as my family is not put in harm's way, I wash my hands clean, he thought. *The guy's are just going to have to roll with the punches.*

Sam knew from first-hand experience that Juice was a cold-blooded, psychopathic killer, and he did not want to set the man off.

***

"The nerve of that fool to question my authority and the way I run things!" Juice yelled as he climbed into the backseat of the SUV. "The next time Sam meets with me for some stupid shit like that, I will give him a taste of reality. Now, did you two fools find an apartment for Manny and Lou? I know you haven't forgotten they will be here tomorrow."

"It's already taken care of, Boss…along with all of the necessities they will need," Matone assured him, hoping to gain back some brownie points.

"Great! I have to be back at the Island by tomorrow afternoon. My flight departs at nine a.m., so I will need one of you to pick them both up from the airport."

"No problem. What time do you want me to arrive?" volunteered Ruben.

"Their flight lands at four-thirty in the afternoon, so I advise you to be there a half-hour earlier. I do not know how long I will be gone. So, until my return, show them around and make them feel at home. Here's twenty-thousand dollars to be split between them both," added Juice while handing Ruben two bundles of cash. "Don't bring them around the organization until I give the word. I need them to stay as far as possible from the place."

CHAPTER 6

When released from the hospital, Justice received strict orders from the doctors to stay in bed and let his body rest. After three weeks under the care of the hospital's staff, most of the burns throughout his body healed. Aside from a few blisters in certain places, he was good to go.

Bed rest? These, mothafuckas must be crazy! I'm ready to go to war right now! I'm bringing nothing but havoc to everyone involved! He thought as his wife tried to help him inside the front passenger seat.

"Baby, I'm good. I can manage to get in the car on my own!"

Being the good wife she was, Judy ignored her husband's remark and made her way around the driver's side. Any other time, she would have checked him for the smart comment, but knowing what he had been through she decided to leave it alone. Arriving at the residence, Justice was the first out of the car and inside the house. His wife did not even have a chance to exit the driver's seat before the passenger door shut.

"What are you so in a hurry for?!" She yelled after him as he rushed up the stairs. He ignored her frantic voice and made his way to the closet in their bedroom that housed his arsenal of weapons.

"Where the hell do you think you're going with all those guns?!" Judy snapped upon entering the bedroom. "The doctor's specific order was to *rest*, not go out and start a damn war!"

Still ignoring his wife, Justice continued to stuff all the necessary weapons he felt he would need for this personal agenda. He zipped the duffle bag closed and tossed the 50-pound bag on the bed.

"Justice! Talk to me, damnit! Don't do this! I don't want anything to happen to you again!"

Her words fell on deaf ears as he proceeded to get dressed. After putting on a pair of black sweats, a black hoodie, black Timberland boots, and a bulletproof vest, Justice was ready for war.

At last, he looked up at Judy and said, "Look, stop asking fucking questions and listen for once in your life! Take the boys and head to your mom's house. Do not attempt to go anywhere until I call with directions on where to meet me!"

"Justice, baby, please don't—"

"Look at my damn face, Judy! Do you think for a second I'm gonna let these fools get away with this shit? Do as I say and wait for my call!"

Justice snatched the duffle bag from the bed and walked past his wife before taking the stairs two at a time, leaving Judy on the corner of the bed with her hands buried in her face, crying her heart out. She feared what the future held for her family or if her husband would return home.

***

Justice drove through the city streets like a maniac. Nothing could stop him from his self-destruction. Arriving at Will's house in record time, he found a spot and parked the Acura Coupe. He dialed the number to the only man he thought he could depend on.

"Hey, Will. It's me…Justice. I'm out front. Open the door."

"Dawg, when the fuck did they release you from the hospital?"

"I was released exactly thirty minutes ago. Now, hurry up and open the damn door! I don't want anyone to see me."

"Why are you wearing all black? You look like you're about to do some criminal shit," Will teased as he opened the front door.

When Justice kept a straight face Will felt the seriousness of the matter. Justice sidestepped him and took a seat on the couch.

"I'm ready to get at these fools. You riding with me or not?"

"I told you to fallback and wait till shit cools down."

"Fallback? My fucking face is disfigured, and you expect me to wait till shit cools down?"

"I understand how you feel. I spoke to Sam on some real shit the other day, and he wants us all to let shit be until we can come up with a solid plan. He claims Juice is a connected man. To betray him would be a death wish, and not just *ours* but our *entire* families',too."

Will went on explaining the rest of the conversation he had with Sam.

"I'm on your side one hundred percent! I want to get at these fools just as bad as you do, but I think it's best we fallback for now. You know, lay low. Keep everyone in the dark about your release from the hospital."

"Fuck Sam!" Justice shouted. "He's on some bitch shit letting these overseas *mothafuckas* run all over him and his empire! If Juice thinks he can just come to the U.S. and kill who he wants, he's got something murderous coming his way!

*** *** ***

Since the first day of business, it had become a ritual that changing stash houses daily was the best thing to do. The empire used this technique to confuse the Feds who were most likely surveilling the place; it was also a good way to throw off the malicious scent of potential robbers. Each day, one house was picked at random to sell the packaged drugs and another held the massive amounts of cocaine sold daily. Large duffle bags filled with cash would be taken out each night to an undisclosed location. Because of the empire's strategy, the Feds could never focus their attention on a single home when obtaining a search warrant.

Today was supposed to be Justice's day to hustle in the trap; he figured Carlos would be assigned as his replacement. From the information gathered, he knew which trap house they would be selling from. He also knew Ruben and Matone wouldn't be far away from their associate; the three stuck together like the Stooges. Juice was nowhere in sight, but Justice had a plan on how to get to the man of the hour. No one, except his men, knew Juice was in Puerto Rico taking care of business for the next few days.

Justice drove around, inhaling the exotic smoke from a sour, diesel-filled Dutch as he killed time. He had missed the mellow high since confined to a hospital bed, and he deeply craved the relaxation the herbal plant had to offer. As the high kicked in, he thought about his earlier conversation with Will and could not believe how his childhood friend had backed out on the murder scheme.

I've known this man most of my life, and this is how he shows his loyalty. We took an oath to ride or die, but when the beef got ugly, he was quick to turn his motherfuckin' back on me! If I can't trust him, who the fuck can I trust?!

Caught up in the madness, Justice did not realize it was starting to get dark out. He parked the small compact vehicle across the street from his target. Slowly climbing out of the car, he eyed his surroundings one last time before tucking the .50 Cal Desert Eagle underneath his waistbelt. Reaching back inside the car, he grabbed the 16-gauge, sawed-off shotgun before shutting the driver's door. As he made his way up the street, he thought about walking in through the alleyway where the fiends entered but quickly dismissed the thought. The front door seemed like the smartest choice.

The best place to hide is in plain sigh. He thought and smiled.

He was aware of the few innocent bystanders inside the house and knew one of the men might be a friend of his, but there was nothing or no one that could stop him from accomplishing what he had set out to do.

As he reached the front door, Justice quickly pulled the hoodie over his head and braced the butt of the shotgun on his hip for support. Cocking back the powerful weapon, he squeezed the trigger, letting out a thunderous boom. The force knocked the door right off its hinges and sent splintered wood across the living room.

Time was of the essence. He hurried inside, knowing his target would be in the kitchen—where they sold drugs from a back door.

The loud blast caught all three men inside off-guard. Duce was the first to react and took cover inside the kitchen cabinets, while Rolon went for the gun in the kitchen drawer. Carlos tried to unlock the deadbolts for the back door.

Justice entered the kitchen just in time to catch Carlos fumbling with the deadbolt's latch.

"I wouldn't do that if I were you," Justice said coolly.

He let out two rounds from the .50 caliber handgun, striking his victim on the buttocks. The powerful slugs immediately brought the man down to his knees, who was clutching his ass-cheeks and screaming from the pain.

"Shut the fuck—"

Justice's words were cut short as two loud pops rang out to his left. He had little time to react as the bullets struck him dead center in his chest. The force from the large-caliber weapon spun him around and knocked the wind out of him. If it were not for the Kevlar vest he had on, the bullet would have pierced his heart, but it lodged itself within the steel plate.

Rolon did not recognize the disfigured face, or else he would not have fired his weapon. Focusing his attention on the direction of the shots, Justice noticed they came from inside the laundry room. He made his way to the opening and repeatedly fired into the small confinement as he balanced the shotgun on his hip. Seconds later, he heard the loud thump and knew he struck his target.

When he opened the door, he noticed a body sprawled across the tiled floor. Upon taking a closer look at the dead man's face, he screamed, "Fuck!"

A tear ran down his cheeks as he made the sign of the cross with his fingers on the man's chest.

"Rest in peace, my brother Rolon! May our Higher Power be with you and grant you mercy. Until we meet again at the pearly white gates. I'm gonna miss you."

He sighed and exited the laundry room.

"Back to business," he said as he turned around and pointed the gun at Carlos.

Carlos remained silent.

"I want you to get Ruben over here ASAP! Call him and tell him you have an emergency and his presence is needed immediately. If you say anything other than what I just said, I won't hesitate to put a bullet in your *cabeza*," Justice said as he tapped his finger on his head.

Carlos lay on the floor with a massive hole in his buttock. The large wound was causing a large amount of blood loss. He could not feel his legs and knew he would die if he did not get help soon. Fearing for his life, he reached for the cell phone in his pocket and proceeded to dial his associate's number.

"I need to see you like right now!" he yelled into the receiver.

"Okay. Be there in five minutes," replied Ruben.

Carlos hoped his partner would notice the urgency in his voice and know something was up.

"He'll be here in ten minutes," he lied as he looked up at Justice. "Now, what is it you want?"

The disfigured face on the individual in front of him was almost unrecognizable, but even though he only met him once, he knew he was the man that Matone attempted to blow up. Justice's wounds—dispersed across half his face—made his face look surreal. Carlos knew Justice was out for revenge and tried his best to stall him.

"*I* ask the questions around here, not you," snapped Justice. "Now, where can I find your friend Matone or whatever the hell his name is?"

Carlos hesitated since he did not want to disclose that information. If Juice were to find out about his loose lips, he would surely be tortured in the most excruciating way known to mankind.

"Who the hell is Matone?!" he replied.

"Oh, you trying to play me?"

Justice let off two shots, striking the man in the shoulder.

Carlos fell on his back, screaming from the excruciating pain.

"Okay! Okay!"

At this point, he felt he had no other choice.

"He's at the Fairview apartment with Manny and Lou."

"Who the hell are Manny and Lou?"

Carlos explained as his lips quivered from fear.

"What's the address?" Justice demanded.

As Carlos spat the address, Justice typed in the location in his phone's GPS, but a knock was heard at the front door before he could finish.

"Don't say a fucking word. Keep quiet, or your brain will be all over the wall," Justice threatened.

Unlatching the deadbolt and security chain, he stepped behind the door to hide his figure.

After Ruben heard the door being unlocked, he turned the knob and stepped inside. The house was dark; the silence was ominous. He immediately got a gut feeling that something was not right. Not seeing nor hearing anyone around, his instincts told him to turn around and make a run for it, but before he got the chance to react, Justice came out from behind the door and placed the monstrous .50 caliber Hawk to the back of Ruben's head.

"Try some funny shit, and I'll put a hole, the size of an apple in your dome.Take five steps back, turn around, and face me."

After Ruben did as told, Justice remarked, "Good, fucking country boy. Now, lay face down on the floor next to your partner over there."

Ruben was upset with himself for not noticing the streaks of blood across the tile floor when he first entered the house. Glancing over at Carlos, he shook his head in disappointment.

"Hurry up! I don't have all damn day!" Justice yelled.

Ruben laid face down next to his partner. The piercing look he gave Carlos said a thousand unspoken words.

"You set me up, you fuck! How dare you go betray us?"

"He had no choice,"Justice interjected. "You spics come from the Island and think you can just blow shit up around here. I want the both of you to take a good look at me and remember this face when you're tossing in your graves! Now, where the hell can I find Juice?"

"Not in the United States," Ruben replied, smirking.

"Well, well, well. I'm disappointed he couldn't join our little party tonight, but he will eventually be joining you two at the devil's mansion."

Justice released two powerful slugs into the back of each victim's head—execution-style.

Knowing the cops could show up at any second, he wiped the blood off his face and exited the residence. Nearby neighbors observed the man with the disfigured face calmly climb into his car and speed away, engine roaring and tires screeching.

CHAPTER 7

Juice met with Juan at a hotel in Brasilia, the capital of Brazil. They both respected the mutual agreement not to talk business over the phone or on any communication device. Every time he contacted the Colombian, it was simply to share where they would be meeting to conduct business. Once he informed Juan how many kilos of cocaine he would need on the shipment, Juan would immediately ship the drugs to the United States. These business meetings would only take place every few months, depending on how fast Juice moved the weight. No one ever knew when Juice would be meeting with Juan; this information was kept strictly confidential. Juice tended to share when he would return to the Island, but he never revealed the second stop in his journey.

These two powerful men first met at a beach bar in the Caribbean Island of Jamaica. As they reveled in each other's company, they noticed their mutual fine taste in expensive scotch, which sparked their first conversation. From that day forward, the two influential businessmen formed a trustworthy friendship. Whenever one would go on vacation, the other would join for a week of gambling, champagne popping, and top-notch escorts.

At the time, Juice had a Panamanian drug connect to whom he was loyal. However, when the man ended up behind bars on a federal indictment for drug trafficking, tax evasion, and racketeering, Juice decided to give Juan a shot. The man was true to his word about having the purest cocaine in America. The coke was so raw that it had a pinkish hue. From the first business transaction, Juice never looked back, blowing up bigger than a New Year's blimp.

"How is business treating you in the States, *amigo*?" asked Juan as they settled at the bar inside the exquisite Brazilian resort.

A chilled bottle of *Dom Perignon* sat in an ice bucket between the two figures.

"I'm fine. Just trying to stay away from the snakes before they bite."

It did not cross Juice's mind that he happened to be the biggest snake to walk the face of the earth.

"As for business, everything is going accordingly," he continued. "The States are treating my comrades and me very well. Things could not have turned out any better. They welcomed us with arms *wide* open."

Juan noticed the sarcasm in his last comment and nodded.

"Should I say things are coming along with the organization?"

"Well, as with all trades, there were a few bumps along the way. But, nothing I can't handle."

"I knew Sam's men weren't gonna take lightly to a new boss, but I had faith in you. I'm sure a man of your caliber is able to keep everything under control. You know, *amigo*...after all these years of doing business with you, you never once attempted to cross me and you always stayed loyal."

"I do nothing but keep it real; betrayal doesn't run through my blood."

"That's why I hold you in high regards to the other cartel heads and have the utmost respect for you, *mi amigo*. You are a great business partner, so starting with this current shipment. I will lower the price for each kilo of cocaine to nine thousand dollars. Does this sound good enough for you?"

"It sounds fucking great!" Juice cheered. "I appreciate that. You always have been good to me. Not once have I regretted doing business with you."

"Speaking of business, let's get down to business. How many kilos of cocaine will you need on this trip?"

"Three hundred keys by the way these birds are flying west. It shouldn't be long before a new migration."

"Well, my friend, consider it a done deal," Juan said. "Give it a few days, and your shipment should arrive at the same time and place as the last."

"Should my payment be sent to the same Swiss account, or has the account destination changed?"

"The same account will do just fine. Believe me when I say, *amigo*, you will be one of the first to know if any future changes are to occur."

Both men shook hands and went their separate ways with a couple of fine Brazilian women by their sides.

***

The following morning, Juice awoke feeling exhausted from last night's sex orgy. Glancing at the Rolex watch on his wrist, he noticed it was almost time for his flight's departure. Jumping out of bed, he put on his jeans and approached the two sleeping beauties.

"Wake up, ladies! Thanks for the wonderful night, but you have to go," he said loudly as he lightly slapped each woman on their butt cheeks. "I have a long fucking day ahead of me."

***

The three-and-a-half-hour flight felt more like a ten-hour flight to Juice as he constantly shifted in the airplane's uncomfortable seat, bitching and moaning the whole time and driving the flight attendants crazy.

When the plane touched down in Puerto Rico hours later, Juice was relieved to be on solid ground; he hated flying. He maneuvered his way around the airport's terminal like a pro. He grabbed his bags from the convoy and proceeded to exit past the crowd.

The same black Mercedes SUV awaited him at the curb. He relaxed after climbing into the vehicle, wanting nothing more than to be inside his 3.4-million-dollar mansion. Yet, he had a few more important errands to run before basking in the luxury of his home.

He pushed the number three button on his phone, speed-dialing his chief of staff's phone number.

"Tony, is what we talked about the other day ready?"

"Yes, it is, boss. I also have someone you'll be very interested in seeing."

"Alright, I'll be arriving at your place in a few."

An hour later, the Mercedes SUV pulled up to the iron gates of an extravagant community located on the outskirts of Carolina P.R. The gate guard on duty automatically recognized the vehicle and its driver and waved them through. Watching as the Mercedes made the bend around the circular driveway the guard got on the radio and notified his boss of the guest's arrival. Tony immediately grabbed the two duffle bags full of cash and made his way outside through way of the double-oak doors.

"Those bags sure do look heavy!" Juice shouted out the window as the Mercedes pulled around to the front entrance.

"These things weigh like bodies. Tell the driver to pop the trunk so I can toss these bags in there." Once Tony had situated himself in the backseat next to Juice, he turned to him and said, "Everything is accounted for, and you're not a penny short."

"Great! Now, who is this person you think I would be so interested in seeing?"

"You remember the woman three years ago who turned informant with the Feds and snitched on Hector? We know that there has been no way of reaching her for the past few years because she was under the government's witness protection program. Well, it just happens she stopped by her mother's house for a visit last week."

"All of the money we've spent on surveillance at her mother's finally paid off. Where is she now?" asked Juice.

"She's at the barn…been there for over a week. I knew you would be coming around soon, so I held her captive."

"Tony, I appreciate your dedication to me. I promised Hector that I would take care of this for him no matter how long it took. That man received twenty-five to life without the possibility of parole because of that snitch bitch! During the trial, not once did my name come out of his mouth. Hector was a sincere, loyal man, and for that, this woman is going to pay dearly. She will suffer for every year that he has to spend behind walls. Take me to the barn!" Juice barked at the driver.

***

Inside the barn, Maria was chained to the back wall—naked as the day she was born into this cold world. The sight of her beautiful body made Juice's manhood throb from the extreme excitement.

As he approached the young lady, he asked a question, although he already knew the answer.

"*Cómo te llamas?*"

"Maria," she replied nervously.

She did not know why she was there or the reason for such harsh treatment. The only thing she could do was pray.

"Well, Maria, we've been searching for you for quite some time now. Because of your rat-face self, my good friend, Hector, has to suffer behind bars for the rest of his life. Honey, blame yourself for the pain you're about to endure. You're going to feel the wrath for every day he has to spend in that hell."

"Please don't hurt me!" cried Maria.

She knew exactly what and who Juice was talking about. It had been five years since her ex-boyfriend, Hector, was arrested. The sound of his name triggered goosebumps throughout her entire body. She began to quiver from the unknown.

"The Fe-fe-feds said if I didn't testify against him at trial, I wo-would be the one to receive twenty-fi-fi-five years to life," she stuttered from fear.

"Bitch, shut up!" Juice yelled and smacked her across the face. "No matter how you look at it, you're a fucking snitch! Unchain her and strap her belly down on the table!"

Maria kicked and screamed as she felt hands grabbing her. Her small physique was no match for the powerful hands that grappled her body. Overwhelmed by exhaustion, she gave in as her strength gave way, and the three men forcefully strapped her body to the cold metal slab. An old, rusted hospital gurney was brought out, hosting an array of different operating-room utensils on top. The dim lights reflected off the shiny razor-sharp objects.

Juice grabbed a police baton and rubbed some Vaseline on the long, black wooden stick, then rammed it into Maria's anal. She screamed at the top of her lungs as the driving force of the stick tore her insides apart. Bloody stool dripped down her thighs as she sobbed uncontrollably in pain.

Five minutes into the torture, sweat began pouring down Juice's forehead. Growing tired of the same technique, he pulled the bloody, shitty nightstick out from deep within its cave. Raising the baton, he swung down hard with all his might, striking Maria across her back. He repeatedly beat her with the rod numerous times throughout her entire body. Her screams of pain and horror were music to his ears.

"Untie her and turn her over!" he barked once again. "I want you to look me in the eyes and remember this face for the rest of your pretty life!"

Juice was red as a beet as he yelled into the young lady's dazed face. Placing the nightstick back on the gurney, he picked up the sharpened bolt cutters.

"You have such beautiful breasts, my love," he whispered into her ear and bent over to kiss each nipple.

He delicately placed the apparatus on her breast and cut off each nipple. Maria let out a blood-curdling scream as excruciating pain overwhelmed her body. She began going into shock as blood squirted from the quarter-size holes where her nipples once were. The red liquid splashed on Juice's face, which in some way excited him.

"Bitch, wake up," he shouted, striking her in the face with a closed fist.

Maria immediately awoke screaming in pain, her left eye shut from the hard punch. Ignoring her screams, he continued with his handy work, cutting off all ten of Maria's toes one at a time. The pain being too much to bear, her body went limp, and she drifted back into a state of unconsciousness.

***

After killing two of Juice's men, Justice drove in silence towards his next destination. He thought about what just took place and wondered if there was anyone else hiding in the house. If anyone happened to see him, he would be sure to silence them, before word spread like wild fire throughout the city and on every street corner.

"When I'm finished here tonight, best believe I'm leaving New Jersey for some time, but I will be back for Juice's soul," he muttered under his breath. "I will not sleep until I have that man's life in my hands."

Justice looked in the rearview mirror. The sight of the reflection made his blood boil. He parked the car across the street, turned off the headlights, and stared at the modest-looking apartment complex located near the back of a dead-end road. He would have to park the car out of sight and complete the journey on foot. He grabbed his Mac 11 submachine gun from inside the duffle bag. With the powerful machine gun in one hand and a shotgun in the other, he treaded toward his targets in confidence. Since it was late, the chances of getting the job done were higher. He caught his breath before knocking on apartment 4F. Using the same technique he used earlier, he placed the butt of the shotgun on his hip and waited for a voice from the other side of the door.

The three men inside the apartment sat comfortably on the couches while watching a movie. They were sipping Hennessy on the rocks and smoking laced Devil's weed. The weed and crack blend made them paranoid. All three men jumped in their seats and jerked their necks in the direction of the entrance upon hearing the knock on the door.

"Who the fuck is that," Manny asked without attempting to move.

"Nobody knows about this place except Ruben and Carlos," Matone said. "So, it must be Ruben since today is Carlos's day to hustle."

After another knock on the door, Matone yelled, "One of you clowns get up and open it!"

Lou sacrificed his comfortable position to open the door.

Justice could hear everything going on inside of the apartment. He braced the butt of the shotgun tight as Lou fumbled with the doorknob.

Here we go, Justice thought as the door began to open.

Cocking back the double-barrel shotgun, he let off two rounds from the monstrous weapon, sending the splintered front door and the man standing behind it flying halfway across the living room. The double blast from the powerful gun split Lou's body in two. Not wasting any time, he rushed inside and sprayed the entire confinement with bullets from the submachine gun.

Matone was the first to react. Jumping behind the sofa, he reached in his waist and retrieved the .9mm hand pistol. Returning fire, he struck the intruder in the right leg.

"Fuck!" shouted Justice as a hot burning sensation ran up his leg.

Focusing his attention on where the shots were being fired from, he turned his gun away from Manny's bullet-ridden body and pointed at the couch. When the shells inside of the clip finished, he reloaded by dropping the empty clip on the floor and slamming a full magazine in its place. Not hearing any movement or noise coming from behind the couch, he approached with caution. He noticed Matone sprawled out on the blood-stained carpet. Snapping out of this war-zone trance, Justice turned around and headed away from the crime scene as fast as possible.

Half-limping and half-jogging, he made his way to the car. Not able to move as fast as he liked due to the leg wound and the heavy artillery, he wiped the shotgun down with his T-shirt and tossed it in the bushes before moving on. Stopping one last time, he tore off his T-shirt and tied it around his wound to halt the blood flow.

Finally making it to the car, he climbed in just as the sound of sirens could be heard approaching. Justice cranked the car engine to life and raced through the apartment complex. Once he was at a safe distance, he picked up his cell phone and dialed his mother-in-law's number.

Hearing his wife's voice on the other line, he said, "Baby, it's me! Meet me at the Marriot Hotel in Center City, Philly. Don't tell anyone where you're going, not even your mother. I'll be there a few minutes after your arrival. I have to make a stop first to gather some things and some money. I'll call you when I'm downstairs."

Before she could get a word in, the dial tone was already humming in her ears.

CHAPTER 8

"Will, let me holla at you for a second," said Duce, one of the organization's underdogs.

"What's up?"

"Remember that shit that went down the other day at the house with Ruben and them?"

"Yeah, I remember. Why? What's up?"

"I was there. I saw the whole shit go down!"

"You were *what*? Keep talking."

"Me, Carlos, and Rolon were cooling in the kitchen waiting on some clientele when all of a sudden we heard aloud-ass blast. It sounded like a bomb! Rolon went inside the laundry room, and I hid my little ass inside one of the kitchen cabinets. The shit happened so fast that all I could think about was hiding. I heard two shots and knew Carlos had been hit by the way he was screaming. My thoughts were racing a mile a minute; I couldn't even make out what the intruder was saying. Then a couple more shots rang out. After the shooting stopped, I heard some talking going on. So, I cracked open the cabinet door and peeked out. For a moment, I couldn't figure out who was the man in all-black attire. When he turned my way, the sight of Justice's disfigured face hit me like a gutshot.

"I told him to fall the fuck back!" Will, yelled in surprise. "But this dumb motherfucker went ahead and took matters into his hands! Now he done started a war!"

"Hold on, let me finish," Duce continued. "Justice got Carlos to call Ruben. I don't know what the conversation was about, but Ruben showed up less than five minutes later. I closed the cabinet door for fear of getting caught. I saw it all, so why not murder me, as well? A few minutes later, I heard two more shots, and that's when I knew Justice killed them both. I let ten minutes of silence pass by before emerging from that cramped spot. As soon as I stepped out, I spotted Carlos and Ruben face down on the tile floor—a bullet hole to the back of their heads. Before the police could get there, I wiped my prints off everything and got the fuck up *outta* there."

"I had a feeling he was the one who pulled that crazy stunt," Will said, shaking his head in disappointment. "The man came to my house all suited up and ready for war—talking 'bout how he was ready to get back at Juice and his entourage for the hit on his life."

"Dawg, we might as well suit up for war ourselves," said Duce. "When Juice returns from Puerto Rico, he's gonna raise hell and go-on a killing spree. I'm protecting what's mine before he comes my way."

"I've gotta talk to Sam to see what he wants to do about this. Duce, this shit is gonna get ugly. Alot of bodies are gonna start dropping like flies. Now that it has gotten out of hand, Sam doesn't have a choice but to take these people to war."

"I say we murder his ass as soon as he returns from the Island," volunteered Duce.

Little did they both know that Juice had already heard the news. Matone had gotten hit pretty bad, but the vest he wore stopped the bullets from tearing through a vital organ.

"I'm going to see about this shit here. I'll keep you posted," finished Will before turning around and heading out the trap house.

***

An hour later, Sam was sitting on Will's couch catching a fit.

"You're the CFO of this operation. You are the chief in charge! How could you let this shit happen? Why didn't you put a stop to this?" Sam screamed like never before.

Drool dripped from the side of his mouth as he yelled at the top of his lungs.

"Didn't I tell you that our families' lives will be in danger if something like this were to happen? Why didn't you call to tell me Justice was released from the hospital? If you did, I would've put a stop to this madness myself!"

"Sam, I didn't think the man was dead serious. I told him to laylow for a while until we came up with a proper plan. I told him everything you said, as well. You know that man wouldn't even hurt a fly. That hit on his life must've really touched a spot."

"Will, haven't I taught you anything? A killer is lurking within us all; it just takes a certain experience to bring it out. Humble, innocent men like Justice are the ones we have to watch out for.

They are the worst and most dangerous men of all. Now, let me call Juice and try to solve this problem before shit gets crazy."

****

Immediately upon leaving Will's place, Sam had Juice on the phone.

"What's going on? This is Sa—"

"I know who the hell it is," interrupted Juice. "What the hell do you want?"

"We have a problem that has gotten out of control, and we need to talk about this immediately."

"I already know about the problem. I'm on the next flight back to the States. I will call you when I arrive. Let me tell you something, Sam. I am *not* happy with what happened out there."

"Juice, my men had nothing to do with—"

"That's enough of the bullshit, Sam! I'll talk to you when I get there," Juice yelled before hanging up.

"Fuck!" Sam shouted.

He knew he had to head home quickly to protect his loved ones. Deep within his heart, he felt Juice would eventually come for his entire family. His gut feeling told him to pack and run. If he stayed, it was guaranteed death.

***

Back in Puerto Rico, Juice frantically paced back and forth in his room. He decided to spend another day in the Island to keep Sam nervously waiting—a tactic he used quite often. One of his golden rules was: *Never let a man know your next move.*

"Tony, gather ten of the best assassins we have and meet me in the basement of my hardware store. Advise them to bring some extra clothes; they will be going on a trip with me for a few weeks."

"I'm on that now, boss man!"

An hour later, ten of Juice's best assassins were gathered inside of his hardware store.

"Gentlemen, listen very closely.Tomorrow morning, you all will be flying to the United

States. My guys there already have a place where you can crash. The job you will be assigned consists of eliminating over a dozen people's wives, kids, etcetera. You all know the drill. I will need you to stick close to me while keeping an eye on the organization. I have a feeling these guys are going to try something out of the ordinary. So, I expect you all to stay focused and on point from the time we land until I give the word. If you see anything out of character, you report it to me *immediately.* When we arrive in the States, each of you will receive an envelope containing specific information about an individual target. All of the necessary information will be inside."

The disrespect he felt made Juice ready for a full-fledged war. He wanted to wipe out all the men within the organization—from the low-level pushers to the big wolf himself. Making a move right away seemed tempting, but it would be a disaster to his and Juan's pockets if things went sour. He needed the organization and its power to influence the entire city eventually. Killing every man connected to the operation would definitely bring major heat on him and his team. It was something that needed to be done with precision and perfection but would take time. Reacting out of anger would only crumble his plans for a takeover.

His blood pressure continued to rise as the thought of confronting the men who disrespected him played in his mind. He knew Justice was responsible for the murders, but he felt the men of the organization knew about the ordeal before hand and might have even helped. The death of his comrades would not be in vain. He promised to hold everyone involved accountable.

***

At exactly 2:34p.m., the jumbo 747 jetliner touched ground at the Philadelphia International Airport. Juice and his ten men entourage exited the terminal and made their way towards the luggage carousel.

At his mansion, Sam had been waiting impatiently for Juice since their last call. His eyes were blood red from lack of sleep. He reeked of alcohol and looked like a crazed drunk man whose nerves were shot. An AR-15 assault rifle rested on a shoulder strap, and a Kevlar vest hugged his chest. He had convinced his wife to take their daughter on a two-week boat cruise to the Bahamas. He could not face telling his family the truth about his current situation. So, a vacation was the best way to keep them out of harm's way.

The cell phone's vibration caught him off guard, and he knocked over the fifth of cognac. Sam nervously fumbled for the phone; he did not recognize the number but answered anyway,

"Who am I speaking to?"

"Good afternoon to you, my friend."

Recognizing the voice, Sam quickly toned down his arrogance.

"Juice, I've been waiting for your call since yesterday. I didn't recognize the phone number, so pardon me if I sounded a little arrogant."

"No need to apologize, Sam. Meet me at the Elegante Lounge in half an hour. Come alone."

"Okay, I'll be there."

After ending their brief conversation, Sam thought about what Juice had said. Even though the man sounded calm, he knew Juice was outraged about what had happened. Coming to the meeting alone was out of the question. Scrolling through his call log, he dialed Will, who answered on the third ring. Sam did not even give Will the chance to greet him before he began blabbering.

"I just received a call from Juice. He just got back and wants me to meet him alone at the Elegante Lounge in half-hour. I know what this man is capable of, so I want you to gather up whatever men are free and tell them to meet me in your basement in fifteen minutes.

***

Sam arrived at the basement looking like he had not slept in days. The bags under his eyes aged him twenty years. He felt awkward walking into the small confinement, feeling for the first time that he was no longer the man in charge. Thirteen men in total were lounging around the customized basement. He looked every man in the eye and wondered which ones were the snakes among the crowd.

"Gentlemen, we're going to the Elegante Lounge tonight for a meeting with Juice. He is very pissed at what took place. Matone survived the assassination attempt and told him everything. I don't trust this man one bit, so I want you all to join me at this meeting."

As Sam gave the announcement, he felt a dry lump in his throat. He had a funny gut feeling about this meeting.

"I want you all to follow me from a distance. *No one* is to follow me inside," he continued. "I already have four men from Philadelphia stationed inside the lounge. My cell will be on speaker throughout the entire meeting; the team will know what's going on at all times, and everyone will act on Chief Will's orders. Anyone have questions?"

Silence filled the air; only deep breaths could be heard as every man felt the negative energy circulating in the room. There was a mole inside his crew, and Sam was determined to find out just who it was.

***

Juice sat patiently at the VIP table, sipping on a foreign scotch on the rocks. His men were spread throughout inside and outside the lounge. The snake he had inside Sam's crew notified him of his arrival and the small army in tow. Juice knew there were thirteen heavily-armed militant men surrounding the building. He had six well-trained assassins in every corner of the lounge and four snipers on rooftops. Each scope-mounted .223 rifle was capable of taking out three souls seconds apart. These men would be dead before they realized what hit them. Juice watched as his opponent entered the lounge, his body language emanating fear.

"With thirteen men on his side…and the man is still a pussy," he whispered into his associate's ear.

Sam spotted Juice sitting at a far-end table towards the back of the lounge. Making his way through the thick crowd, he approached the table with his right hand extended.

Giving him a hand back, Juice said, "Thank you for showing up, my friend. Have a seat. Excuse us, Junior. We have some important things to talk about."

The man sitting on the stool next to Juice quickly got up from his seat and made his way to another table.

"Sam, my friend, I see you did not take heed to what I said about coming alone."

"What do you mean?"

"Do I look stupid?" Juice asked while gritting his teeth. "I know about the thirteen men you have posted all around this place. If I want to, I could have them all dead within seconds. I am not upset with you about this, Sam. I brought you here tonight to tell you that I know you and your men had nothing to do with the murders of my men, but I do feel you are all somewhat responsible for not keeping a close eye on Justice. I will miss my men dearly, but life must go on. I blame Matone for their deaths. If he had done the job of eliminating Justice well, my men would be alive today."

When Sam nodded without responding, Juice continued. "Sam, for future reference, do not underestimate my power or insult my intelligence. I know your *every* move. I even know about your wife and daughter's little cruise to the Bahamas."

Sam's heart sank at the mention of his family. He could not swallow Juice's audacity and cruelness.

"By underestimating me, you are questioning Juan's power and authority as well as mine. He would be disappointed if he were to hear otherwise. Now, Sam, I've been meaning to ask you, how do you launder your money?"

"I have a business associate who I happen to know very well. For the right price, he will launder as much money as you need through legitimate enterprises. I've been doing business with the man since day one of the empire's ground-breaking. I will bring it to his attention and see if he would agree to meet with you. I will contact you as soon as I get an answer."

"I have a lot of cash sitting around. I will be anxiously waiting on that call," said Juice as he extended his hand for a farewell shake.

"I apologize for the inconvenience."

"No need to apologize, Sam. Just make sure it doesn't happen again."

***

Junior was a well-known business mogel in the city; he had political connections and close contacts with the police. Laundering money was no problem for this man. He and Sam grew up in the same projects and had been childhood friends ever since. They were also well acquainted with the city's mayor and contributed large sums of money to his political campaign. These powerful and influential figures had the capacity and connections to help the mayor win every election, and the mayor, in return, helped Sam's and other associates, construction companies win city contracts. The mayor also gave Sam inside information regarding investigations within his organization, all for a small kickback. With connections inside the mayor's office, the operation became untouchable.

"Junior, what it do, baby?" Sam asked as he entered the shop.

"Oh shit! If it ain't my man, Two Cans Sam," joked Junior. "What brings you around here?"

"I need a favor!"

"What kind of favor? You know I only do certain favors."

"I need some money washed. Well, not me. Let's say a good friend of mine. He's willing to pay top dollar."

"Taking your word for it! Tell your good friend to stop by my store tomorrow morning at nine o'clock.What's his name? I might know him or of him."

"Juice. He's from Puerto Rico. I met him through my Colombian connect.This man is one *crazy* son of a bitch!"

"Nah, name doesn't ring a bell."

CHAPTER 9

"Matone, I want you and Tito to find Justice and *finish* what you started. If it wasn't for your half-ass job, Ruben, Carlos, and the other guys would still be alive today.This time, make sure you do the job correctly or else don't bother coming back," Juice threatened him.

Matone felt a little guilty and somewhat responsible for the deaths of his comrades. All of the problems started when he made the stupid decision of not putting enough explosives in the car. This time around, he would make sure to finish the job.

After a week of surveilling the houses of both Justice and his mother, Matone gave in and reported back to his boss with the bad news.

"Boss, I've been keeping an eye on his house, his mother's house, *and* his mother-in-law's house for almost a week, but to no avail. I think he might've skipped town on us."

"Don't you worry. I will find a way to get to him," said Juice.

Later that day, Juice met with Duce for a private conversation. He was using his trump card on the matter and did not care what it would cost him.

"My friend, I need a huge favor from you, and I am willing to pay you twenty-five grand for your services."

The sound of that much money caught Duce's full attention. He did not like Juice, but he could do a lot with that amount of money.

"Why me?"

"Are you willing to do the job? A yes or no will suffice, or will I have to find someone else?" Juice asked slyly, feeling irritated by the question.

"I'm listening."

Juice was not worried. If Duce did not accept this offer, somebody else would.

"I am offering this money for the life of your comrade Justice. He has caused me hella problems."

"I don't know about this, Juice. I would have to sleep on the decision. Give me a couple of days, and I will get back to you with an answer."

"Alright, my friend. Here's my phone number. Give me a ring when you've made up your mind, but if someone else takes me up on the offer, I won't hesitate."

As Duce walked away, he thought, *This man is crazy, offering me twenty-five grand to take the life of my own friend. Damn, though…that amount of money is tempting. If I don't take him up on the offer, someone else will. But how will I be able to look Justice in the eyes before pulling the trigger?*

Arriving at Will's house, Duce entered through the basement door to find him watching the 76'ers game on the television.

"Get up and let me whoop your ass in a game of pool. There's only a minute left in the quarter before halftime."

"I'll play but for fifty dollars a ball," responded Will as he got up from the recliner.

"Say no more. Rack 'em up!"

"Money on the wood, make a game go good," sang Will, placing a fifty-dollar bill on top of the pool table as he racked up the balls.

"Yo, could you believe Juice offered me twenty-five G's to off Justice? The man has a bounty on my boy's head. Best believe it won't be long before someone snatches up the offer."

"It wouldn't surprise me if he has a bounty on one of *our* heads," Will mocked. "So, what was your answer to the twenty-five-thousand-dollar question?"

"What the fuck do you think was my answer? Justice is my peoples… I will never do no shit like that!"

Duce's exaggerated and offended tone only revealed to Will that he was lying.

***

A few days after putting the bounty on Justice, word spread like a virus throughout the entire city. Everyone within the organization was suspicious of one another. As the days passed, each man kept his distance—waiting for the moment one would go against the grain.

***

"This man is working my last nerve. What the fuck does he want now? If he wanted me dead, I would've been dead by now!" Will reminded himself.

The men sat around the basement impatiently waiting for their boss's arrival. Juice entered the basement, followed by Matone and a team of ten highly trained assassins. The first person he laid eyes on was Duce; he had a surprise for the young gunner, which would surely bait him along with every other member of the organization.

There was total silence as every eyeball in the room followed Juice's every move. The tension in the air grew thicker by the second between both rivals as each man stood shoulder to shoulder.

"Gentlemen, I'm going to make this meeting brief, so let me get straight to the point," Juice began, breaking the silence. "First, by now, I'm certain you all know about the bounty on Justice. No one has taken me up on the offer, so I'm raising the price to fifty-thousand."

The sound of such a large sum of money made every man in attendance do a double-take.

"There are going to be a lot of changes taking place within this operation," he continued. "I'm going to start by replacing Ruben and Carlos. I am also announcing the termination of Vic, O-Dawg, and Duce. You guys have made more than enough money within this empire throughout the years. It is now our turn to eat the fruit and enjoy the lifestyle of the rich and famous.These orders will take effect immediately."

"Hold on, Juice. No disrespect, but what have we done to lose our positions?" asked O-Dawg.

"Nothing. You guys have done nothing. I feel it is now time to move on. You guys aren't the only ones to lose your job. There will be more changes taking place in the near future. So, I'm giving everyone a heads-up. Get your shit together!"

O-Dawg got up from his chair and stormed out of the basement.

"Fuck it! I'm gonna do *me* and open shop in the projects," he whispered to himself as he made the way towards his vehicle. "These dudes are soft. I can't believe they're letting this clown walk all over them. If they let him get away with it, pretty soon, none of them will have a job. There will only be non-English speaking *mothafuckas* hustling in the organization."

The more O-Dawg dwelled on the situation, the more it ate at him. Justice was his family, so he knew this was the real reason behind his termination.

"If any of you feel the same way as your partner, feel free to walk out now. I don't want to hear any complaining or whining." When no one spoke up, Juice continued, "In the meantime, you fellas keep doing what you've been doing. I appreciate your labor and hope to keep things in good terms amongst us all."

As he exited the basement, Duce quickly got up from his chair and followed him out. Being suddenly jobless, he had no choice but to take Juice up on the offer. His gut feeling told him the meeting was setup from the beginning to bait someone into taking the offer.

"*Jefe*, can we talk?"

"Make it quick. I'm on a schedule."

"Remember what we spoke about a week ago concerning the bounty? Well, I want to take you up on the fifty-thousand offer."

"I knew you would come around," Juice replied with a huge smirk. "I'll give it a couple of days before the rest of your comrades come around, as well. Duce, I'm going to tell you something very serious. Once you take this offer, there is no turning back. If you cross me, you will suffer severe consequences."

"Don't worry. I will get you what you ask for. Just give me some time to find him."

Juice nodded, and after climbing into the SUV, he poured himself a drink. He wanted to notify Sam about what took place at the meeting before anyone went to him crying about losing their job. He also wanted to know what was taking Sam's friend so long to call him about the money laundering.

"Speak to me, Juice," answered Sam.

"I wanted to update you on the meeting I had with the fellas. Just so you know, it didn't end well."

"Don't tell me you killed another one of my men."

"Now, why would I do that?" Juice answered sarcastically. "I fired O-Dawg, Vic, and Duce. I also assigned two of my men to take over my fallen soldiers' positions. So, in total, five of my men were put into a position of power."

"Juice, like I've said before, it is now your operation. Do as you please. When my men come to me, I will explain this to them."

"Well, now that we have an understanding, I would like to know what is taking your friend so long to contact me?"

"I will be giving him another call immediately after we hang up."

"Please do.This dirty laundry is starting to pile up. There is so much that it's starting to have a funny odor," spoke Juice in code.

"Meet me at the Elegante Lounge tonight at nine o'clock," said Sam. "I'll make sure our special friend joins us for drinks."

***

The Feds had an eye on Juice, who now seemed to be the one making decisions and running things. They also had been keeping a close tail on Sam and noticed he had not been hanging around his operation lately. They had his phones tapped and a GPS tracking device on all of his luxury vehicles. The tracking device on his car gave them a front-row seat to all the meetings with Juice.

Juice was no dummy; he knew about such things, along with all the games played by the alphabet boyz. They found tracking devices on the vehicles on two separate occasions, so every morning, he would have someone from his crew sweep all of the vehicles for such devices.

***

"Sam tells me that you need massive amounts of dirty laundry washed," Junior said. "I usually don't do business with people who I don't know, but since you're a friend of Sam, you're a friend of mine."

"It's good to know I'm well-spoken of and liked in the States," responded Juice before taking a sip from his drink. "I have 10.4 million dollars that needs to be washed. Would you be able to handle that for me?"

"That's a lot of *dinero*, my friend. It would not be an easy task, and it might take some time, but it's definitely achievable. My charges for that amount of money will be ten percent—half upfront and the other half upon completion."

"That's a high percentage. Yet, I'm a man of business, and I know how risky the trade is. Taking all this into consideration, I say we have a deal. I will call you tomorrow morning with the location on where to pick up the money. Here is the Swiss bank account number you will be transferring the funds to once you're done the laundry."

As Junior got up, he said, "Great! Hope to be doing more business with you."

The Feds sat inside their unmarked vehicle, snapping pictures at the three men from the time they arrived at the lounge until the end of their meeting. Since they were already investigating Sam and Juice, they wondered who the third party might be.

***

Tonight was to be Sam's last night in New Jersey. In a few hours, he would be heading to his private mansion in Daytona Beach, Florida. Only a handful of people knew about this location, and none of them were from the organization. It's the place where he would go at times to get away from all the drama, relax, and ease his mind. The massive mansion was located a mile deep within the woods. If one were to look for it, it would take quite some time to find the place.

For years, the land stayed abandoned until Sam acquired it and built a mansion on it. It was the most expensive piece of real estate in Daytona Beach. He was once offered $48 million for the property by a wealthy Arab businessman drenched in petroleum money. If he could have foreseen the future, he would have definitely taken the Middle Eastern up on his offer.

Sam knew the moment Juice found out he skipped town, the man would turn on the fire. Juice still needed Sam as a pawn to finalize his take over plan. Without him, the plan was impossible. The influence Sam held over the entire city was what Juice needed, which is why he had men watching his every move.

Six heavily armed men in three separate teams had been surrounding Sam's residence for weeks now. These men followed his wife and daughter everywhere they went—work, shopping, and even school.

Tonight, Sam planned on skipping town. He invited everyone over from the organization for a celebration. A few days ago, he mentioned to everyone about celebrating an anniversary party for him and his wife's seventeen years of marriage together—the perfect opportunity to divert the surveillance team's attention away from his family. With the huge crowd in attendance, it would be impossible to keep an eye on everybody in the vicinity. Each man on guard held a two-way radio with an earpiece connection to contact any other guard. Each one also carried an AR-15 assault rifle with a 50-shot banana clip for emergency purposes. Luxury vehicles lined the street as kingpins and drug lords roamed the property in their six-thousand-dollar suits.

The only person Sam trusted telling his plans to was, Will. He needed help in getting out of there safe and undetected. He did not share this with anyone until about two hours into the party. Their luggage was packed and stacked in the back compartment of the Cadillac Escalade parked on the other side of the property. Sam's family were to run through the woods toward the dirt road, which ran parallel to their property for a few blocks and where the SUV would be parked—doors open and keys in the ignition. The only thing left to do was get his family safely to the vehicle without being spotted by any of the assassins on duty. This was where Will would come into play; he was to create a diversion by starting a fight between two of the guys from the organization.Of course, they, too, would know all about the escape plan. This diversion would give Sam and his family the chance to make a run for it.

***

"Hey, Jose, do you hear that?"

"Hear what?"

"That loud ruckus coming from the house," replied Marco.

Both men had been on overnight patrol and were restless from the long night. The party had died down in the past few hours, so there weren't many people left.

Cuffing his right ear with his hand in an attempt to amplify the noise his partner talked about, Jose remarked, "Yeah, man, I hear it. What is it?"

"Dummy, I don't know! Let's go and find out what the fuck is going on in there!"

The two men were the only guards on duty protecting the back area. Without their presence, the back property would be unguarded. Aware of this, Sam used the opportunity to rush his family out of the house. He knew he only had minutes—if not seconds—to make it to the other side of the property.

Sam ran as fast as he could through the bushes. His wife was holding his hand, and their daughter was holding her mother's hand. It was a half-mile run to the truck's location. The run was exhausting.When his daughter's legs gave in, Sam scooped her up and carried her for the rest of the journey. If it were not for the flashlight he was carrying, they would have lost their way.

When they reached the truck, a huge burden lifted from everyone's shoulders. They all released a sigh of relief. After buckling up, Sam started the SUV—ready to drive away to their new life in Florida and leave the past behind.

As he drove through the night, the thoughts that clouded his mind felt more like a dream to him. He wondered when it all started to crumble and why he never saw it coming. The power and respect he once embodied had vanished into thin air and in such a short time. Sam felt the life begin to drain out of him; he no longer felt like the powerful man he once was. Pain and sorrow flooded his heart while torment and stress flooded his brain.

CHAPTER 10

Two months had gone by since Sam's departure, and no one had heard a word from him since. Despite Juice's fury at Sam's disappearance, things had calmed down within the organization. So, Juice decided to send five of his ten assassins back to Puerto Rico. He kept his word and fired four more of the original members, replacing them with his soldiers. He was adamant in finding Sam, even if it took tapping into every last one of his resources. The man's whereabouts would eventually come to light.

***

Juice felt played each time but continuously tried to win the attention of Gloria, the young lady who worked as a salesperson at a local cell phone store. Every time he laid his game down, she would ignore the short, bald man. He offered to give her the world wrapped in a bow and even brought her flowers from time to time. The flowers would just get returned, and his game would always be rejected. On this day, the young lady grew fed up, gaining the courage to confront the older gentleman finally.

"Look, I've been trying to be nice, but it seems like you can't get it through your little-ass pea head! How many times do I have to tell you? I am married! Now, leave me the hell alone!"

"Do you know who I am?"

"No. Does it look like I give two fucks? I'm gonna have to ask you to please leave the store before I call the police!"

Hearing the word "police" brought Juice back to his senses. He turned around and exited the store.

"Bossman, when are you going to give up trying to fuck that young girl?" Tio asked him as he entered the SUV. "That bitch acts as if her pussy is gold."

"Shut the fuck up! I don't want to hear it right now!" Juice snapped.

Juice began to boil inside as Gloria's words echoed in his mind. He could not get over the way Gloria had spoken to him; he had his mind set on what he wanted to do to that little bitch. During the ride through the city, not a single word was spoken.

***

As he lazed on his recliner, Juice glanced at his Rolex and realized there were thirty minutes left until the store closed. He grabbed his keys from the coffee table by his side, ready to embark on his next wicked adventure alone.

On the way towards his destination, he could not shake the images from his mind—a naked and inviting Gloria. His heart pumped an extra beat per second as the eagerness of vengeance flowed through his veins. His palms were sweaty, and his hands were shaking. None of these symptoms came from being nervous or scared. It was the way he always felt when executing an act of vengeance.

He parked a block away from the cell phone store and exited the car to go wait out of view for her around the corner. From this standpoint, he had a clear view of the storefront. As he tapped his foot on the ground impatiently, waiting for Gloria to close the shop, he noticed her shutting the outer gate and locking it with a key. Gripping the Swiss knife in his hand, he sauntered toward her while humming a dreary tune.

Gloria placed her keys in her purse and continued across the street towards the bus stop. She hated having to take public transportation during this time of night. She could see the bus stop in her view, but what she did not see was the man creeping behind the corner. She crossed the street without paying attention to the lurking shadow. Juice popped out like a jack-in-the-box, catching the young lady by surprise. Terrified, Gloria let out a screech, immediately dropping her purse and turning around to run. Juice reacted quickly, extending his arm and yanking her hair.

"Bitch, shut the fuck up unless you wanna die right here! I won't hurt you as long as you do as I say," he lied, hoping the young woman would temporarily calm down.

He picked up her purse and dragged her to his vehicle as she tugged and pulled.

"If you kept your mouth shut this morning, you wouldn't be in this situation. Now, get inside," he ordered, forcing her into the car.

"Where are you taking me?!" cried Gloria. "Please, don't hurt me! I apologize for what I said!"

She could not control her sporadic sobs that exploded like water springs. She fought hard, kicking and screaming in hopes of attracting someone's attention. Thoughts of her child growing up motherless flooded her thoughts, which gave her the strength to fight even harder.

"Get inside the fucking car!" Juice yelled. "This is your final warning!"

He struck Gloria in the face and forcefully shoved her into his vehicle.

***

Arriving at his place of residence, Juice pulled the vehicle into the garage. With the knife still in his left hand, he used his right hand to yank open the back passenger door and grabbed the frightened woman by her hair, aggressively pulling her out of the car. Gloria pleaded for her life; she hysterically kicked, scratched, and screamed with every ounce of strength she could muster, but was no match for a man.

"Get comfortable and make yourself at home," said Juice as they entered the house through the garage door, which led into a modern kitchen with stainless-steel appliances.

Gloria was afraid yet could not help but notice her luxurious surroundings. She would have never imagined such an old creepy psychopath living such a lavish life. Judging by his looks, one would never believe he had such expensive and elegant taste.

"Please let me leave, and I'll forget this ever happened. I won't mention it to anyone," she pleaded.

"Didn't I tell you a while ago to shut the fuck up? Since you can't seem to do that, I have something that will shut you right up."

Juice went back into the garage to retrieve a roll of duct tape. Once her kidnapper was out of sight, Gloria ran to the front door. Her dreams of getting away quickly shattered as she desperately fumbled with the deadbolt. Without a key, there was no way to unlatch the lock. With her adrenaline pumping, she still harbored an ounce of hope to escape. She hurried to the back door, praying it was open as she reached for the doorknob.

When Juice entered the living room, he noticed his captive missing. There was no way out of the house; both doors were locked, and every window was equipped with black iron bars. So, escape was not an option.

Gloria felt like crying as she tugged on the sturdy doorknob.

"The only way out is through me, young lady," Juice teased.

She almost peed herself upon hearing the chill in his voice.

"I will scream if you don't set me free!"

"No one will hear you, honey. But just so you know, screaming turns me on," he said while approaching her.

He tore a piece of duct tape from the roll and placed it over her mouth. The crazed look in his eyes made Gloria want to run for her life as she kicked and screamed in self-defense. Her resistance made Juice furious and aroused him at the same time. Feeling the scratch on his face, he wiped at the blood, reached for the gun on his waist, and cocked it.

"Bitch, if you don't calm down, I will shoot you," he shouted, bringing the butt of the pistol down hard on Gloria's face.

The impact instantly split her upper lip and broke her jaw, knocking her unconscious. For a second, Juice thought he killed the girl. Picking up her wrist and feeling a pulse, he continued to put the tape over her mouth. He so badly wanted a piece of this young girl and did not feel like waiting until she awoke from her stupor. Thoughts of having intercourse with the unconscious body flooded his mind, but he quickly shook the thoughts away because it would not be fun without witnessing her face contort in agony. Making his way over to the sink, Juice filled a cup with water and then tossed the cold liquid on Gloria's face. When she did not wake up, he smacked her repeatedly.

Coming back to her senses, she felt the excruciating pain from the broken jaw. She wished she could wake up to discover it was a bad dream. Gloria could not believe this was happening; all she could hope was to make it out alive. She thought about her mother, little sister, and baby brother. How would they survive without her? Her mother was diagnosed with Alzheimer's disease, which was worsening every day, and her sister was autistic. Gloria was willing to do everything possible to make it out of this ordeal and back to her family.

Juice was ready to get the party started. His hands and legs were shaking from excitement, and his manhood throbbed. Retrieving the razor-sharp Swiss army knife from his pants pocket, he got down to business—first cutting her shirt and bra. The sharp instrument sliced through the material like a hot knife through butter. Her brown, perky nipples were hardened from fear as goosebumps spread over her entire body. Juice wiped the drool from the side of his mouth as he continued to sexually assault her. Next, he cut off her jeans and underwear. He could not contain his excitement as he stared at her neatly waxed vagina and its purple, pinkish lips.

Gloria was numb. She silently told herself: *This is just a dream. This is just a dream. This is just a dream.* She coldly stared at her assailant with tearful eyes as drool dripped from the monster's mouth. The box cutter was inside of her bag. If she could somehow get to her purse, which was in the car, she would surely cut his jugular. The only thing she could do was lay motionless as she stared at the shiny sharp instrument. She feared that at any moment, the blade would enter her flesh. She prayed for him to spare her life.

Fully aroused, Juice stripped off his clothes until he was bare-ass naked and began feeling on Gloria's body parts.

"I haven't had a pretty young thing like you in quite a long time. I'm gonna enjoy every minute of this."

He felt no remorse or shame for the act he was committing. The sordidness of the events excited him furthermore that he could not contain his joy. It was not the first time he had sexually assaulted a young woman at knife or gunpoint. Whenever he would not get his way with a female, this was his way of taking what he wanted.

"I bet you taste so sweet," he said as he got down on his knees.

He spread her legs apart and bent his head towards her vagina, licking and nibbling on her clitoris. The salty-sweet taste was one he surely missed. He thought about running upstairs to get the Viagra but could not contain his patience. Grabbing hold of his penis, he hastily tried entering her. Her vagina walls were super-tight; Juice was having a hard time thrusting his manhood inside. There was no way he was not getting any of this pussy. Gripping his penis once again, he forced himself inside the soft muscle.

Gloria let out a scream. She had heard from friends that having sex for the first time was a painful experience, but she never imagined it would hurt this much. She could not believe she had just lost her virginity to a total stranger—to a vulgar man who brutalized her and robbed her of a beautiful first act of love.

Her insides were very warm, almost hot. Juice let out a loud, animal-like moan. He stopped and looked down to find blood trickling down his leg.

"Bitch, why didn't you tell me you were on your menstrual cycle?" he yelled, putting the knife to her throat. "Answer me!"

Gloria tried her best to speak but the duck tape would not let her. Only muffled sounds were heard. Juice realized she was trying to say something and quickly cut the tape from her mouth.

"I'M A VIRGIN!"

Juice thought about what he just heard and wondered if it were true. He did not smell any blood when he ate her pussy, and he had a lot of trouble entering her. The thought excited him even more because he never had a virgin pussy. Moving the knife from her throat, he quickly mounted her once again—not holding back his excitement this time. He pounded the poor girl for less than two minutes before ejaculating inside her. His limp rod could not go on any longer; however, he continued stroking it until he had released every drop of his semen.

What took only minutes felt like an eternity to the tormented girl. She could not believe she had been raped and violated in the worst way possible. Never before had she felt so trifling and dirty. She swore if she made it out of this situation alive, she would search high, low, hell, and Earth for this man until she had his dick in her hands.

"Mmm, that was the best pussy ever! Has anyone ever told you how good your pussy is?

Oops, I forgot. You were a virgin," Juice joked. "Tonight's gonna be a Tony the Tiger night as I enjoy every minute with you. You will forever be engraved in my mind. I don't ever want this night to end."

He grabbed Gloria by the hair and helped her up, half dragging her up the stairs towards his bedroom. Juice shoved the beautiful young female on the mattress face first. Then he walked to the armoire and opened the top drawer, removing the bottle of Viagra. Popping two in his mouth, he swallowed the little blue pills without water.

Gloria glanced over at Juice and noticed him taking some medication. Not once did it cross her mind that it was a hormone enhancement. She would soon find out what that medication was capable of; what she would endure for the next few hours would be the most horrific, brutal time of her life.

With the knife still in hand, Juice began approaching the bed. The effects of the Viagra were starting to kick in. Seeing the crazed look in his eyes, Gloria leaped from the bed and attempted to run out of the bedroom. She did not know what kind of drugs he had taken, but she had a feeling this was not going to be good.

"Where do you think you're going?" Juice asked.

Before Gloria could make it out of the door, he yanked her by the hair and threw her back on the bed.

"Lay your ass back down and turn on your stomach! I'm not finished with you yet. If anything, I'm just getting started!" he added, pointing the sharp blade in a threatening manner.

His Jekyll and Hyde personality was in full swing. The gentleman-like characteristics were gone, and the demon within had been unleashed. When angry, he shocked himself at the violence he was capable of inflicting. It would take hours for him to come to his senses. Many men were terrified of him and would try their damn best not to upset him for fear of being dismantled.

Gloria noticed Juice rubbing lubricant on his penis and automatically knew what was to be the outcome. His cock was rock hard.

"Come here," he said, reaching over to remove the tape from her mouth.

Gloria inched back further towards the headboard, trying to escape this creep's touch.

Yanking the tape from her mouth, he tossed the sticky material on the floor and positioned himself on all fours on top of the bed.

"Bitch, I said come here!"

Wrapping his hand around her hair, Juice shoved her face into the mattress, grabbed her waist, and quickly slid his penis inside her from behind. After a few strokes, he quickly pulled out and fiercely forced his rod into her anal. He'd purposely taken the tape off her mouth so he could hear her screams. The loud shrieking noise was like music to his ears, which made him even more aroused as he continued to ram her faster and harder. Fart noises escaped her anal as he pulled out and rammed his penis inside repeatedly. The pain was unbearable; Gloria cried and pleaded for him to stop, but to no avail. The more she pleaded, the harder and faster he would pound. She tried getting away, but every time, he would punch her in the ribs, knocking her air out.

The pain and pressure were too much. Without realizing it, Gloria released a stream of watery diarrhea. The brown, smelly substance dripped through her inner thighs and onto Juice's manhood. Enjoying the great sensation of a virgin's anal, he did not notice until the foul stench reached his nostrils.

"What the fuck! Bitch, did you just shit on yourself?"

Glancing down at his rock-hard penis, the sight of the brown substance made him so angry that his veins bulged from his forehead.

"You nasty hoe!" he barked as he climbed out of bed and made his way over to the closet.

Opening the door, he removed a wire hanger from the clothes rack. This time, he would purposely make sure she would go on herself.

"So, you wanna shit on me, huh?"

Clenching his fist tightly around the hanger, he approached the bed.

"You could have avoided all this if you played nice from the beginning. Now that you've pissed me off, I wanna kill you! You stupid bitch!" he snapped as he began to repeatedly whip her across the back with the metal object.

Gloria cried and screamed as the thin wire cut through her skin. Each lashing left a trail of blood as it tore her flesh. The more she screamed, the harder he beat her. She tried her best to get away but found herself on the floor instead. She now wished he would hurry up and kill her. Exhausted from the exercise but still filled with rage, Juice picked up the knife from where he had set it on the nightstand. The sight of the sharp blade sent Gloria into panic mode. She knew this moment was coming. Closing her eyes tightly, she silently began to pray.

Juice felt a surge of adrenaline flow through his body. The thought of killing excited him like an Apex animal that hadn't had a meal in days. Without the slightest hint of remorse, he approached his victim. Raising the knife, he brought the sharp instrument down on her chest. The blade entered her flesh and stopped at her breastbone. He removed the blade and continued to stab the limp almost-corpse viciously. Blood gushed out of Gloria's mouth as she struggled to grasp her last breath. Juice lost count of how many times he had stabbed her. Winded from the brutal exercise, he stopped for a few seconds before forcefully shoving the entire width of the blade into her vagina—twisting and turning the long, sharp object.

Juice knew the woman was dead; however, his adrenaline was still at its fullest. Bringing the knife up to her neck, he slowly slashed her throat and did not stop until he reached the opposite ear. He was enjoying every second of this barbarous act. In total, there were seventy-five stab wounds throughout his victim's body. Drained from the attack, he sat down in the recliner. Juice stared at the butchered body and smiled as he admired his handiwork. His facial expression immediately changed when he noticed the expensive white plush carpet drenched in blood. Twenty grand in the trash.

"Stupid *bitch*! Why did you have to piss me off? I was enjoying myself. I could have fucked you all night long," he yelled at Gloria's disfigured body.

He glanced down at his rock-hard penis; it would be hours before the Viagra would start to wear off. Getting up from the recliner, he retrieved a T-shirt. Using the piece of clothing, he wiped the brown smelly substance from his manhood and legs. Walking past the corpse, he headed for the shower but not before making a phone call.

"Matone, it's me. I need your assistance. I have some garbage at my place that needs to be disposed of right away. Drop whatever it is you're doing and make your way over here, pronto! The door will be unlocked, so let your-self in."

He clicked the end button, tossed the cell phone on the dresser, and hurried to the bathroom. The stench was becoming unbearable and making him nauseous.

***

After his fresh shower, Juice walked into the living quarters and sat on the oversized sectional couch. A few feet away lay the mutilated corpse of Gloria Sanchez. It did not faze him one bit that a dead body lay in his circumference. He rolled the body up in the expensive blood-soaked rug and dragged the fabric down the stairs.

"I hope Matone hurries the hell up," he said to himself as he surfed through the television channels.

Juice must have spoken the man into existence because, just then, the front door swung open.

"Bossman, where are you?" Matone shouted as he walked into the vast, luxurious foyer.

"I'm in the living room watching TV!"

"Oh shit!" Matone screamed as he entered the room. "What the fuck happened here?" he asked while staring at the red rug in the middle of the living room. "Is that a body in there?"

Juice side-stepped the question, knowing Matone already knew the answer.

"What took place is irrelevant. I need for you to dispose of the body immediately. Take her down to the basement and make her disappear. I'll be sitting here watching the baseball game until you're done."

With the rug slung over his shoulder, Matone took it to the basement, set it on the cold concrete, and began to unroll the fabric. He jumped back at the sight of the body. He was not expecting the young, beautiful female from the cellular phone store to be the victim. She was such a sweetheart towards him every time he went to pay his phone bill. He pictured her bright smile the last time he entered the business and could hear her soft voice.

Shaking off the temperamental thoughts, he concentrated on the grisly task at hand. After slowly slithering the rug from underneath the girl's body, he cut the duct tape from her wrists and ankles. Picking up the corpse one last time, he placed the carcass on a metal table. This had never happened before. Gloria was the first person Juice had ever killed or dismembered that Matone felt sympathy towards.

Even the toughest have feelings, Matone thought as he shook the feeling away.

He reluctantly reached under the table and removed the rain poncho, rubber gloves, and pair of safety goggles. Putting on the apparel, he then made his way over to the corner of the basement and grabbed the chainsaw. As he pulled on the throttle cord, the chainsaw sputtered, and the blades came to life. He had a love/hate relationship for this part of the job but had become accustomed to such violence. He had mastered the craft at a very young age. His uncle, who was like a father, always made him observe whenever he would torture a man. Uncle Kane was a vicious man and gave Matone his nickname at the age of thirteen. It was Matone's thirteenth birthday when his uncle first murdered a man in front of him and made young Matone cut the man's tongue and toes off with a bolt cutter.

"You're a born killer just like your father," his ***uncle*** used to say.

With the chainsaw blaring, Matone approached the corpse and began to saw into the legs. For some reason, he found it to be much easier to start from the bottom up. By the time he would reach the neck, he would be numb from feelings. Most of the blood had already drained from the body, so he did not have to worry about cleaning up a huge mess. However, every square inch of the basement was covered in plastic up to the ceiling. The less he thought about it, the faster he would finish. He did not see himself as a serial killer or a monster. He was institutionalized into believing he was just doing a job he was very good at doing.

***

As Juice poured himself a drink from the refrigerator, he was surprised to see Matone enter the kitchen through the basement door. Glancing down at the trash bags, he was amazed to see the man finished the task so fast.

"Put the bags in my truck; we're going to bury them. I'll be out in a minute. Let me get dressed."

Matone walked out of the house and placed the three bags in the truck's cab. As he climbed into the truck's passenger side, he placed Gloria's head between his legs on the floorboard.

Twenty minutes later, Juice exited the house shaking his head. He really did not want to do what he was about to do, but he was left with no other choice. It would definitely be a huge loss to him, but his freedom came first. Making his way over to the garage, he punched in the code to the keypad and watched as the door slowly ascended. Walking over to the far-left corner, he grabbed the five-gallon tank of gasoline from the top shelf. Then he made his way to the family room and poured half the container's contents on top of the Versace cashmere sofas. Satisfied with the amount of liquid spewed on the fabric, he retraced his steps back outside, leaving a trail of flammable fluid along the way.

Digging inside of his pant pockets, he retrieved the old-school flick lighter, which he'd had for many years. Flipping open the top half, he flicked the igniter and stared in awe as the fire came to life. Bending over, he placed the flame to the gasoline and watched as the trail of flames raced towards the house. Within seconds, the entire lower section of the house was ablaze. He had no idea the fire would spread so rapidly and was startled as the enormous balls of flames shattered and escaped through the downstairs windows.

Sitting in the passenger seat with his eyes wide in astonishment, Matone watched the trail of flames race towards the multi-million-dollar estate.

"This dude really has lost his damn mind. He could have hired someone to clean this shit up, but he torches the place instead," he muttered.

CHAPTER 11

His plans were starting to take shape. It had only been a few days since the drug operation opened in the housing projects, and business was booming. It was his turn to eat, and the only thing stopping him was a bullet with murder. Sitting in the driver's seat of his SUV, O-Dawg pulled on a blunt of Blueberry Skunk as he observed the block. Teenage boys ran back and forth from the stash, pushing dimes and twenties of the potent heroin and crack cocaine. The line of addicts waiting to buy the poison looked like the line at a social service building handing out food stamps. It was only the fourth day of operating, and already he was raking profit margins in the tens of thousands range.

"If I knew there was this much money in these projects, I would've left the empire a long time ago."

There was a huge black cloud hanging over the organization since Juice's arrival. O-Dawg could not believe how drastically things had changed.

"That man is going to be the downfall of that empire while I just sit back and watch it crumble to pieces," he said to himself as he blew out a cloud of smoke.

His thoughts drifted off to his cousin Justice as he drove around inhaling the exotic smoke and coughing from the strong fumes entering his lungs.

"I'm not mad at you for what you did. Shit, I would've done the same thing if I were in your shoes, but you should've come to me like I told you. Together, we could have done a lot more damage," he spoke to the air as if Justice was listening.

He thought hard about where Justice could be hiding and could only think of a few places. Puerto Rico was out of the question; Juice held too much power and influence in that territory. Most of the fellas knew about his family in Florida, so Justice knew better than to head there. Auntie Juanita's sunny Florida beachfront home was the place they would always stop by for a bite to eat whenever visiting the Sunshine State. Her cooking was not to be reckoned with; she once won Best Caribbean Chef in Puerto Rico when she was only twenty years old.

"Okay, think! Think! He has to be somewhere.Come on! Think harder."

O-Dawg knew his cousin had to be some-place in the country. He was upset that Justice did not contact him. After a few minutes, it finally dawned on him.

"I bet he's in Chiraq."

Chicago was both their fathers' hometown and stomping grounds. They hadn't been back there since kids and rarely spoke to the sperm donors. O-Dawg wondered if Justice even knew where his father lived or how to contact him. Chicago was a long way from New Jersey, but there was no better place to hide. He thought about making a phone call to one of his relatives but remembered he did not have anyone's contact information. He stored it in the back of his subconscious mind to visit his uncle for the phone number the next day.

O-Dawg pulled into the parking lot of Junior's Auto Parts, hoping the pre-ordered rims had been delivered. He was tempted to show off his new BMW 745 Series. The metallic, wine-colored paint job and 24-inch Giovanna luxury rims were a sight out of this world. He pictured the envious stares that would come his way, but malicious looks were the least of his worries. His mind was set on money and avenging the death of his confidants.

"Is Junior here today?" he asked one of the guys at the shop.

"He's in the office.Who should I say is asking for him?"

"Tell him O-Dawg."

Two minutes later, the fat burly man walked out of his office.

"O-Dawg, what the fuck is going on? Ain't see *you* in quite some time. How's the family?"

"The family is great. Everything is great. I stopped by to check if my car is ready. I know an OG like myself is worthy of a discount? I spent close to five grand on the rims and tires I pre-ordered."

"If you already paid for them, how am I gonna give you a discount? I know you ain't expecting me to give you some of your money back?"

"I was thinking maybe some dark tint for the windows on the house?"

O-Dawg was trying his best to get something for nothing. He didn't admit that the teller had given him a twenty percent discount for the purchase.

"Why wouldn't I? We've known each other since childhood! I'll also have one of the guys detail the car if you have time."

"It's all good. Tint is just fine."

"Which one belongs to you?" asked Junior as he waved at all the cars being serviced in the garage.

"The burgundy one over there."

"You must be doing big things driving a seventy-thousand-dollar car. I was wondering who that car belonged to. The organization must be treating you exceptionally well."

"I'm doing my own thing. I'm staying as far away from the empire as possible. Shit ain't the same ever since that schizoid Juice took over. I wouldn't give it long before that place crumbles. He already murdered a few good men and tried to kill Justice by planting a bomb in his car. I don't know who the fuck he thinks he is, but this is not Puerto Rico. Karma will eventually bite him in the ass before he realizes what hit him."

Junior took in what was being said and wondered if he had made the right decision laundering the drug proceeds for Juice. He did not know much about the man except what Sam had mentioned in their first meeting. He had taken Sam at his word, but O-Dawg was making the man sound like a maniac, and now he was starting to regret the deal. He should have followed his gut instinct and did his homework beforehand. He heard a few circulating rumors around the hood and across the bridge in Philadelphia but nothing major. People often tend to speak out their asses or out of anger, but what O-Dawg spoke of did not sound like bullshit.

I have to give this a thorough overview, Junior thought, then said to O-Dawg, "Well, I gotta get going, but I'll advise the salesclerk about the complimentary tint."

Junior quickly rushed out of the auto store and climbed into his truck. The tires screeched as he accelerated the car. He now knew Sam was not keeping it one hundred about Juice. Reaching for his phone, he called the only man he knew would tell him the truth.

"Will, I need to holla at you about a very important issue. Meet me at the dealership in fifteen minutes! I'm heading that way now."

***

Junior paced back and forth insides his dealership's office as he impatiently waited for Will to arrive. He hoped Sam had not put him or his businesses in jeopardy; he did not need any unnecessary heat. He could only pray O-Dawg was fibbing out of anger.

"I came as fast as I could," said Will as he entered through the doubleoak doors of the luxurious office.

"I'll get straight to the reason for why I invited you here. Someone told me some hideous things about a man I am now in business with, thanks to your boss. I need to know what you know about this man and what kind of person he is."

Will immediately knew who Junior was speaking of. There was only one man who Sam would introduce to the powerful business mogul.

"I'm pretty sure you're talking about Juice."

"As a favor to Sam, I am now engaged in a money-laundering deal with this fool. I need to know what kind of person I'm dealing with and what kind of situation I've gotten myself into."

"You're not in a very good predicament, to say the least. The man is deranged. He will go to extreme measures to get his point across, and he's not afraid to use explosives. Keep this between us Sam would be on fire if he were to find out I told you this."

***

Justice propped his feet up on the ottoman as he prepared to watch ESPN. The newly-acquired apartment he dwelled in was located deep within the suburbs of Chicago, Illinois. His father wondered why he would move back to Chicago after all these years. Justice arrived with nothing but the clothes on his back. The only explanation he had given his aunt was that he needed a change of scenery and decided to relocate. One look at his disfigured face, and she knew the story was much deeper than that.

Whenever she bombarded him with questions, he would say, "Auntie, the less you know, the safer you will be."

It took some pleading, but he convinced her to keep his arrival and whereabouts a secret. In no way did he want his father or aunt involved in his problems; after a few weeks, he moved out. His wife insisted on tagging along with their daughter. Hell would freeze over before she would let him leave without her. *Till death do us part* was her motto in times of distress.

The sudden knock on the front door immediately brought Justice to his feet. His wife was working at her new job, and the kids were in school. Not expecting company, he was curious as to who this person was at the door. Reaching between the recliner cushion, he grabbed the hammerless .357 Dirty Harry Magnum revolver. Quietly tiptoeing to the front door, he looked through the peephole. A sense of relief rushed through his body when he noticed his cousin on the other side. Tucking the revolver in his waist, he unlatched the deadbolt and opened the door. Seeing the teenager crying, he immediately tried calming the hysterical girl.

"Nay-Nay! Calm down! Why are you crying? What's wrong?"

"This man slapped me in the face while I was waiting in line."

The thought of a grown man putting his hands on a kid made Justice furious, especially if the kid was his family member.

"I was at the Chinese take-out, and this man cut in front of me," she continued explaining. "So, I said something to him about it. Next thing you know, he turned around and *smacked* me."

Without saying a word, Justice quickly grabbed his jacket from the coat rack, snatched his little cousin's hand, and stormed out of the apartment.

"Show me who the fuck he is," he told her.

He only lived a few minutes away, so he hoped the man was still at the take-out place waiting for his food.

"The nerve of this *mothafucka*...putting his hands on a woman. A young girl at that!"

Justice drove like a crazed maniac towards the Chinese restaurant. After recklessly parking the car next to the fire hydrant, he hastily entered the restaurant.

"Which one was it?" Justice asked as he callously stared at the few patrons still inside the business.

Two men noticed his monstrous revolver and ran out of the place.

"It was him right there, Uncle Jus," Nay-Nay responded, pointing her finger at an overweight man.

Justice approached the man and yelled, "You like putting your hands on girls? Try putting your hands on a man!"

"Uncle Jus, he's not worth it! Just smack him like he did me," she tearfully pleaded.

"Nah, fuck that," replied Justice, letting off three rounds from the muscular .357 revolver.

The impact from the powerful weapon made the large man stumble back, knocking him down to the floor. Blood spewed out his mouth as he clutched the large holes in his chest to stop the blood from rushing out. Justice quickly grabbed Nay-Nay by the arm and headed out of the restaurant.

"There's *no* way I'm going back to prison," he mumbled nervously, still gripping his gun tightly.

Sirens could be heard approaching in the distance as he swiftly climbed in the running vehicle. He stepped on the gas pedal and weaved in and out of traffic, trying to make it home without any accidents. After a few blocks, he glanced at the rearview mirror and noticed two patrol cars closing in.

"Fuck!"

He didn't know if he had outstanding warrants for the murders in New Jersey, but he wasn't pulling over to find out.

"Put your seatbelt on, Nay-Nay. We going on a wild ride," he said, pushing the accelerator and turning the ordeal into a high-speed chase.

He was looking for an escape route. Taking the sharp turn around a bend, Justice tossed the gun out of the window and watched as it bounced off the pavement a few times before falling in a stormdrain.

Up ahead, the traffic light was about to turn red. Thinking he could make it across the two lanes of traffic, Justice slammed on the gas pedal and gripped tightly to the steering wheel. It happened in seconds—the compact Honda T-boned the passenger side of the SUV. The woman in the truck did not have enough time to react as the collision spun her vehicle, wrapping it around a utility pole. Her body was ejected from the SUV upon impact, sending her petite frame flying twenty feet in the air before landing on the hood of a parked car.

"Don't fucking move! Put your hands where I can see them," shouted one of the police officers that were approaching the mangled wreckage.

Justice sat dazed and confused in the driver's seat. The intense pain from multiple broken bones sent needle-like aches throughout his entire body. He could not feel his legs and begged his Higher Power not to come out of this incident paralyzed. Nay-Nay sat in the passenger seat unconscious. He was grateful for telling her to put her seatbelt on before the chase started, or else she would have been ejected from the vehicle. Justice tried reaching for his gun but remembered he had tossed it; the excruciating pain was unparalleled. If his shoulder had not been dislocated in the crash, he wished to have shot it out with the police.

It felt like an eternity, but within seconds of the accident, hands were grabbing at him through the open window. He cursed and yelled as he was yanked from the vehicle and slammed on the pavement. Justice could no longer take the pain as it became unbearable.

The police officers punched and kicked him until he passed out. Then they placed his unconscious body on the gurney and transported him to the hospital. Even though he was out cold, the police handcuffed his left foot and left wrist to the metal railing.

"Just making sure he doesn't go anywhere," said the sergeant. "He's facing some serious charges and will run if given the slightest chance."

The EMT technician continued staring at the officer, dumbfounded. "The man is in a comatose state. Running is the furthest thing on his mind."

All parties involved were seriously injured. Justice and Nay-Nay were transported by ambulance to the nearest hospital. The female in the SUV sustained severe head injuries and had to be airlifted by helicopter to Philadelphia's Einstein Medical Center. Since Justice's injuries were not life-threatening, he was released from the hospital after several hours and transported to the city jail with bail set at $350,000—bond.

The charges were endless—attempted murder, attempted murder of a law enforcement officer, aggravated assault by auto, possession of a firearm, endangering the welfare of a child. Justice knew if he did not post bail within twenty-four hours, his fingerprints would come back, and the homicide warrant out of New Jersey would show up on the search.

Nay-Nay was kept in the hospital for a couple of days under observation. The doctors wanted to keep a close eye on the juvenile because of the severity of her head injury. Neurosurgeons wanted to make sure there was no brain hemorrhaging or swelling. Before being discharged from the medical center, she would undergo a thorough examination.

Detectives fiercely interviewed the minor without a guardian's consent. The plainclothes officers knew they were violating the law by questioning the teenager without the presence of her parents. However, because the victim in the SUV happened to be a lawyer, they took whatever shortcuts necessary to close the case. Nay-Nay had never been under so much pressure and eventually confessed the truth to the detectives. She told the officers how she tried to stop her uncle from committing the crime. After a few hours of intense questioning, the detectives decided not to charge the juvenile with any of the criminal activities committed and called her mother to arrange for the minor to be picked up.

CHAPTER 12

Fat-Chop was one of the original men from the empire who grew up with the rest of the big guns in the organization. He made hundreds of thousands of dollars within this foundation. Years later, he decided to do his own thing in the heroin trade. It was time to be a leader; he was done being a pawn in someone else's game.

His block was located within a few hundred yards of the empire. Even though Chop went his own way a long time ago, he was still very close to some of his allies and would meet up with the guys from time to time for a drink. Growing up in the same neighborhood and attending the same schools, they all held a brother-like bond—one's problem was everyone's problem.

Fat-Chop had been beefing with Kenny lately. For the past two years, Kenny held the block down while Chop served his prison stint. During Fat-Chop's incarceration, he heard from a few sources that Kenny was putting his own workers and drugs on the block. He couldn't care less about Chop's money and didn't give two fucks about his clientele. Kenny even fired everyone and appointed his own team to move his work instead and in broad clear view, he took over the block.

When Fat-Chop was released from prison, his first chess move was to rid Kenny from the block permanently. Kenny had grown in popularity and was not trying to hear it. He wanted his cut for holding down the fort while Chop was gone, which was fifty-fifty on out. The block would not have survived without Kenny's guidance, and Chop would not have come home to $250,000 in a shoebox. Both men disregarded each other's request to take their drugs elsewhere and, for the past month, had been competing against one another—each trying to outdo the other and sell the highest quantity and best quality heroin.

Kenny's connections were based out of New York, while those of Fat-Chop were based in New Jersey. However, Chop had close ties with the organization, so the heroin was more potent coming out of Colombia. The New York China white was no match for the Colombian black tar.

From sun-up to sun-down, fiends stopped by in the hundreds to try the potent heroin. This made Kenny upset since he was not seeing any money. Tired and on the verge of being broke, he decided to step it up a notch. One way or another, he was going to make sure Fat-Chop and his black tar disappeared.

Kenny sat in the driver's seat of his car waiting for his rival to arrive. He noticed fiends scattering like roaches to purchase the black tar. This agitated him and made him even angrier. He only had $500 in his pockets and half a tank of gas. As he deeply inhaled from the blunt, he thought about all the money he had been missing out on. He quickly needed to get back on his grind, and his mind was set on the only way of making that happen. When he saw the Escalade pull up, Kenny cocked a round into the chamber of the .40 caliber. Switching the safety button to the off position, he stepped out of the car and slowly shut the driver's door.

Fat-Chop climbed out of the SUV, grinning without a care in the world. Not paying attention to his surroundings, he failed to notice the figure across the street creeping up behind the vehicles.

"Chop! Watch your back!" one of the workers yelled suddenly.

Turning around to see what all the commotion was about, he caught a glimpse of his enemy.

"What up now, fool? You should've left when I gave you the chance," said Kenny, raising his weapon and firing four rapid rounds.

Chop reacted in the nick of time, ducking for cover behind an old, rusted pick-up truck. He wasn't slick enough, however, to evade the bullet that struck his left leg. With the adrenaline recharging him with strength, he got up from behind the vehicle and ran while using the parked cars as a shield.

Kenny fired the automatic pistol until the magazine was empty.*Click, click, click.*When he was out of ammunition, he reloaded his gun and sprinted towards the vehicle where he last saw his target. Fat-Chop was gone—the blood on the concrete was the only sign that he was there.

"Where the fuck did he go?" Kenny thought as he eyed his surroundings.

The fat man was faster than one imagined and escaped with only minor injuries. Kenny's concern was now to make it out of there safely without any bullets flying his way. He hurried back to his car and raced towards the Besty Ross Bridge.

"Fuck!" he yelled. "I should've planned this shit smarter!"

Fat-Chop was heated at the stunt Kenny just pulled.

"I can't believe this *mothafucka* tried to kill me! I swear on my mother's grave that when I catch him, I'm gonna end him! He's a dead man walking!"

A little shaken up from the incident, the realization of coming close to losing his life hit Fat-Chop hard. If it weren't for one of the dealers yelling to give him a heads up, he would be on his way to the morgue. His leg throbbed from the bullet wound, but he was grateful it entered and exited his left calf on its own.

Grabbing a shirt from the dresser, he wrapped the V-neck tightly around the injury and began to plot his next move for vengeance. Pushing the speed dial button for the only man who he trusted besides his cousin, he waited for the person on the other end to answer.

"Riddles, meet me at the boulevard in ten minutes and bring the Choppa!"Fat-Chop instructed.

"I'll be there in five minutes!" the man replied.

There was no need for questions. Word of Kenny's failed attempt on Fat-Chop's life had already circulated throughout the entire east side of town. Riddles tried to call Chop as soon as he heard the news, but the fat man wouldn't answer his phone. After disconnecting the call, he immediately headed upstairs to his bedroom, flipped his mattress, and retrieved the AK-47. He was a long-time member of the empire—one of the first original thoroughbreds Sam recruited. Only a few people within the empire who were his "ride or die,"and fat boy was definitely one of them.

Exiting the house, he climbed into the Range Rover and sped off, racing towards the boulevard. Minutes later, he pulled his truck over into the Exxon Mobile gas station next to Fat-Chop's Yukon Denali XL.

"What it do?"

"Did you bring the Choppa?"

Without responding, Riddles raised the assault rifle, showing off the large caliber, and nodded his head. The 50-round banana clip was sure to sweep any block.

"So, is this shit about Kenny true?" Riddles asked.

"Can you believe he tried to murder me right on the block?"

"Say word!"

Riddles was not at all startled by the news. The two had been beefing for over a month.

"I'm surprised you two didn't try to kill each other sooner."

"Somebody gotta die, and it ain't gonna be me," replied Fat-Chop. "I know where he rests his head in Philly, and I'm out to get his neck. He's gonna wish he killed me when he had the chance. Let's take your truck 'cause I'm pretty sure he'll be expecting me."

During the long ride over the Besty Ross Bridge, both men sat in silence as they finally entered the ghettos of North Philadelphia known as *Badlands Killadelphia*. It was one of the worst—if not *the* worst—cities in the state of Pennsylvania. Latino—mostly Puerto Ricans—occupied a majority of the territory. This ghetto held a fearsome reputation of having one of the country's highest murder rates per capita.

"Stop right here! This is the house!" shouted Fat-Chop.

Riddles immediately pulled the vehicle over in front of the red brick row home.

"Are you sure this is the spot? Let's not go shooting up the wrong crib."

***

Kenny and his uncle were in the upstairs bedroom bagging up the half kilo of crack cocaine and heroin from the night before. As Kenny scooped the dope from a plate with a small golden spoon and put the potent powder into wax bags, his uncle chopped the half pie into twenty and forty-dollar pieces and put the crack rocks into pink heat-sealed plastic baggies. Kenny had been rambling on for hours about that morning's incident. His mind was not on the money or the prize but on putting an end to this beef. Hearing his nephew talk about Fat-Chop all morning started to annoy Uncle Phil. He lost his count a few times and had to start over every time.

This new generation is lost in this game, Uncle Phil thought to himself, than turned to address his nephew. "Look, when you do something, you do it right the *first* time. That way, you don't have to worry about watching your back and dwelling on it like the shit you pulled this morning. You young guns got the game fucked up. You all do shit without thinking…in broad daylight! You don't even check to see if kids are playing outside!"

Suddenly, a hail of gunfire erupted like fireworks on the 4th of July. Both men dropped what they were doing and immediately dove for cover. The 7.62mm projectiles tore through everything in their path, shattering windows and shredding walls.

Kenny could not comprehend where the gunfire was coming from until he realized it was coming from outside. When the gunfire paused, he immediately sprang into action, flipping over the mattress and grabbing the Mossberg shotgun. Uncle Phil's reaction was about ten seconds ahead of his nephew's. Without delay, he crawled to the closet and retrieved the AR-15 assault rifle. Kenny joined his uncle against opposite sides of the wall and cautiously inched towards the bedroom window. Peeking through the blinds, he noticed Fat-Chop and the guy he knew as Riddles reloading their weapons.

"Who the fuck is that?" Phil asked while peeking through the shattered window.

"That's Fat-Chop and one of his cousins. How the fuck did he find out where I was?"

Uncle Phil knew this was a life or death situation; his life depended on how fast he reacted. Cocking a round into the chamber, he aimed the AR-15 and relentlessly fired a spray of bullets, catching both men by surprise. Kenny quickly joined in on the shooting spree, repeatedly firing the powerful shotgun. The thunderous boom echoed and set off car alarms for numerous blocks. Not prepared for such retaliation, Fat-Chop and Riddles scurried behind the SUV. Riddles opened fire with the AK-47, hoping to give them time to escape.

"Get in the whip," Riddles yelled as he quickly climbed into the driver's seat.

Fat-Chop nervously fumbled with the door handle before jumping into the rear passenger seat. Tires screamed like an opera singer as bullets ricocheted and pierced the lightweight SUV.

"I'm hit, dawg! I'm hit," cried Chop, clutching his abdomen.

"I'm hit in the leg," replied Riddles as he swerved in and out of traffic. "Where are you hit?"

"My stomach..."

Riddles, turned around to get a glimpse at his partner and was shocked by all the blood. Chop's once white T-shirt was now beet red.

"Oh shit! We gotta get you to the hospital!"

As Riddles struggled to find a nearby hospital, panic began to take over his train of thought.

"Where the fuck is this hospital?!" he shouted in frustration.

"I don't know, but if I don't get to a hospital soon, I'm gonna die."

"You're not gonna fucking die!"

"Tell my girl and kids I love them and will be keeping an eye on them from above," added Fat-Chop as his body went limp.

The only nearby hospital that came to Riddles mind was Temple University Hospital, located about 7 miles from their location. It did not take him long to make up his mind. Flooring the gas pedal, he reached his destination in less than ten minutes.

Pulling up to the emergency entrance, he quickly climbed out of the Range Rover and began shouting, "Get a fucking doctor over here!"

***

"Hey, Auntie Lola, it's Omar. Have you seen or heard from Justice lately?"

Out of respect for his aunt, O-Dawg always used his government name.

Lola thought about not telling her nephew of Justice's whereabouts, but she was left with no other alternative after the stunt he pulled that morning.

"Omar, what a coincidence! I was thinking about you today. To tell you the truth, your cousin done went and got himself in some serious trouble. He almost got my daughter killed with his crazy 1ass! He asked me to call you about posting his bail and mentioned something about needing to get out before his fingerprints came back. I swear to the Almighty above if he wasn't my nephew, I would've killed him myself! He better thank God I'm a saved Christian. How *dare* he put my daughter in such danger?"

"What's his bail?"

"Three hundred and fifty thousand cash bond! He's lucky the man he shot didn't die, or he would never see the light of day."

"Auntie, call around in your area for the cheapest bail bondsman. I'm on the next flight with the money. If he contacts you, tell him I'm on my way to post his bail. Sit tight."

"He's already called the house five times since this morning. I'm sure he'll be phoning again very soon," replied an agitated Lola.

"Okay, Auntie. I'll see you in a bit. God bless."

There was not much time left before Justice's fingerprints came back from the FBI. O-Dawg had to rush to Chicago if he expected to make it before the deadline.

"You were supposed to fall back and laylow. Instead, you get yourself locked up," O-Dawg said to himself as he opened the door to his walk-in closet.

Pushing the expensive designer clothes to the side, he punched in the digital combination to the heavy-duty wall safe. Staring at the never-ending bundles of cash, he removed $100,000 from his life savings. He thought about paying the entire $350,000 bail but knew he would just be throwing money away, and the Feds would be all over him. In no way was Justice showing up to court, and the courts would eventually revoke his bail. Since departing from the empire, O-Dawg was profiting forty to sixty grand weekly. Placing the stacks of bills inside a black Gucci bag, he headed downstairs and exited the house. He had one important stop to make before heading to the airport.

***

Arriving at the projects, O-Dawg pulled up to the block and rolled down the driver's window.

"Moses, come here real quick," he said, waving the young lieutenant over. "I have to take care of some business and will be gone for a few days. I want you to hold shit down till I get back. If you come across any trouble, call this number."

"O-D, you know I stay holding the block down regardless," replied the lieutenant, abbreviating his boss's name. "I have a gang of killers behind me if beef decides to make a pit stop!"

O-Dawg was amused by the young man's braveness—one of a handful of youngins he trusted blindly. It was something about the young lieutenant that reminded him of himself as a teenager. On multiple occasions, he proved he was definitely about putting in work. There was no reason for bossman to question the young gunner.

"Say less," O-Dawg said before pulling away from the curb.

***

The thirteen-hour journey had exhausted O-Dawg. Entering the state of Illinois, he continued to follow the GPS coordinates to his final destination. It had been over twenty years since leaving Chicago, but the surroundings seemed all too familiar. The abandoned houses, forgotten projects, and littered streets reminded him of New Jersey. This city was once the epicenter of the auto industry but was now a hollow shell of its shadow. Violence and depression roamed the streets.

Arriving at Aunt Lola's, O-Dawg was grateful she had all the necessary information to post Justice's bail. She had already spoken to the bondsman and filled out all the required paperwork. The only thing standing between Justice and freedom was a team of Ben Franklins.

"Auntie, you take the money to the bondsman since you're a property owner, have a six-figure paying job, and have been a taxpayer all of your life. The Feds won't come knocking on your door. Me, on the other hand…they would kick mine down if I were to sign for the bail."

As he handed Lola a white Salvatore Ferragamo designer bag containing the money, he added, "There's an extra ten grand inside for your services, Auntie. I'm exhausted. I'm gonna make love to the couch while you handle the bail situation. If for any reason you need me, give me a call."

"You go ahead and rest. I'll head over to the bail bonds office to sign his freedom papers."

"Take a pillow, Auntie. It'll be a few hours before they release him."

"It's okay. I'll run to the Chinese takeout place and grab us something to munch on before heading to the county jail. Are the inmates still released out back through the large gate?"

"I'm not sure how they do it up here, Auntie, but the bondsman should be able to tell you."

***

"Javier Hernandez, roll up! You've made bail," the freckle-faced corrections officer shouted into the cellblock.

It was recreation time, and every inmate was out on the tier enjoying the privilege. Justice was sitting by the back television—eyes glued to the sports channel. With every soul speaking at the same time, he did not hear his name called.

"Jersey, police calling you up front...said you posted bail."

All the inmates referred to Justice as Jersey since he was from out of town.

"What?! Stop playing!"

For a second, he thought his cellmate was joking until he heard his name called a second time.

"Hernandez, pack your shit!"

Justice quickly got up from the table, almost running to the front gate.

"I'm Javier Hernandez."

"Pack your bags; you made bail. Make sure to bring your linen, pillow, mattress, and ID with you. If you're missing any of the items I just mentioned, the county jail will issue you a bill for the cost of those items."

Justice could care less about a bill; he was ecstatic someone posted his bail. Time was of the essence, and his nerves had no chill. Turning around, he ran up the stairs and hurriedly stuffed his belongings inside the state-issued laundry bag. On the way back down, he skipped the steps two at a time, almost tripping off the last step. His heart raced a mile a minute as he made his way to the front gate, hoping his fingerprints would hold off for another hour until his release. A few hours ago, he was starting to doubt if he would ever see the light of day again.

Who posted my bail? He wondered while being escorted to the Processing and Release Division.

He thought about his cousin but quickly shot that theory down. Whoever posted the bail had to know he was on the run. It was a large sum of money being forfeited. He could only think of two people who would be willing to throw that amount of money away. The thought of Sam or Juice posting his bail and waiting on his release outside sent a cold chill throughout his entire body.

After going through the standard pat-down procedure, Justice was ordered to place his linens in a large gray container. He took in his surroundings in search of any U.S. Marshalls. Freedom wasn't official until the sixteen-foot barbed-wire gates opened, and he walked out.

"Excuse me, I would like to know who posted my bail?" he asked the officer processing his paperwork.

Glancing down at the forms in front of her and then back up at the inmate, the officer replied, "Looks like Lucky Bail Bonds posted your bail."

Justice thought Lucky Bail Bonds was some kind of joke. In his mind, the officers were playing him, and he was actually being transferred to New Jersey for multiple counts of first-degree murder. His face turned beet red from the feeling of being disparaged.

"Look here! I'm a grown-ass man! Treat me with respect."

The officers in the room looked at one another dumbfounded. They didn't understand the reason for his sudden outburst.

"You asked me a question, and I gave you the answer," responded the female officer. "If I were the judge of your case, I would let your ass rot in prison for the reckless shit you pulled. Lucky for you, state law requires a person a right to bail."

I best keep my mouth shut, he thought as he signed his release papers.

His heart raced with anticipation. After scribbling his signature on each piece of paper, he handed the forms back to the correction officer.

I can smell freedom.

"Mr. Hernandez, go inside cell three and get dressed. The belongings you had at the time of your arrest are in a plastic bag on the bench. You have ten minutes, or you'll have to wait until I finish processing the next inmate."

Justice hurried into the cell and began changing. He wanted out of the plantation before the homicide detainer popped up. After putting on his Timberland boots, he searched the plastic bag for his wallet. Locating the leather object, he looked inside to find it empty.

"Where the fuck is my money?!" he shouted.

The loud profanity got everyone's attention in the processing area.

"Sir, another outburst and you will not be going home today," said the sergeant in charge. "If you read Section Two in the rulebook given to you upon admission, it explains we are not responsible for your personal belongings. You also would have noticed where it mentioned a five-dollar charge to your account for each day you spend at the Carlton Ritz Prison Industry. This means any money on your personal will be confiscated to settle the debt. The rules, regulations, and expectations were explained to you when you first arrived at this facility. If you were paying attention, we wouldn't be having this conversation."

Justice ignored the smart remarks; he figured if he wanted to walk out of jail a free man, he best keep his mouth shut. There wasn't a second chance; all it took was the click of a mouse, and he would be spending the rest of his life behind bars. When the Department of Corrections realized they released a wanted murderer, a lot of officials were going to end up without a job. By then, Justice hoped to be as far away as possible from the jail and the state of Illinois.

"Hernandez, make your way over here and have a seat!" said the female correction officer, her tone firm. "Your paperwork is ready."

Situating himself in the chair, he grabbed the pen from on top of the desk and asked, "Where do I sign my autograph?"

***

The loud, mechanical, cranky sound of the bars sliding open was like music to his ears.

"These *mofos* are really letting me go," he mumbled in disbelief.

His heart raced more and more rapidly the closer he got to freedom.

"I say this to every inmate who walks out these revolving doors. Don't let the knob hit you in the ass. Now enjoy your newfound independence, and hopefully, I never see your ugly face in here again.Close, Sally Port," the officer added.

Justice encountered his aunt Lola waiting outside the facility for him. The look on her face spoke a million words—her eyes emanated pure hatred. There was a good reason for the evil look and cold stare.

"Hey, Auntie. How—"

Smack, smack, smack, smack. Each blow struck its target with brute force, turning both cheeks red and puffy. Justice grabbed her hands, holding her wrists tightly.

"Auntie, I'm sorry!"

"That's for putting my daughter in harm's way and almost killing her! I give thanks to the Almighty for protecting her.Your mother taught you better than that! What the hell were you thinking?"

"My bad, Auntie! I got caught up in the moment and let rage get the best of me. The man put his hands on my little cousin, and I reacted with what I know best—violence! I had no intentions of getting in a high-speed chase or a car accident. Will you forgive me?"

Lola understood where her nephew was coming from; if her daughter had instead come home to her with the news, she would have reacted with violence, too.

"The Lord says to forgive," she acknowledged. "I guess temperament is a trait of the family."

Embracing her nephew, she hugged him tightly and said, "Let's go.Your wife and kids are home waiting on you, but first, we have to stop at my place. There's someone who wants to see you."

"Who?"

"You'll find out when we get there."

"By the way, who posted my bail? You don't have that kind of money, and I doubt you put up your house as collateral."

"Boy, even if I had that kind of money, I would not have bailed your ass out. I haven't seen your little rascal butt in almost twenty years. Then you appear out of nowhere and almost kill my little angel. You're lucky I signed the bail papers! Anyway, this person traveled a long distance to bring the money for your bail. I just took the Benjamins to the bail agency and signed the paperwork."

***

When they arrived at his aunt's house, he made Lola circle the block a couple of times before parking and exiting the car. It was a habit he developed a long time ago. As they say, *better safe than sorry.*

"I don't see anybody," he said upon entering the house.

"Look in the living room.He should be asleep on the couch," Lola told him.

Justice walked into the living quarters but did not see anyone on the couch. Confused, he thought his aunt was playing him for a fool. He did not realize the presence of the figure standing behind him until he felt a hand grab his shoulder. This caught him off guard and automatically sent him into defense mode.

"Who the fuck—" Justice gasped as he took a good look at the tattoos on the huge hand. "Oh shit! What it do, O?"

O-Dawg hugged his cousin tightly and teased, "You owe me a hundred grand and a vacation."

"I owe you my life! If you didn't post my bail when you did, the homicide warrant from New Jersey would have eventually shown up, and I would be spending the rest of my life behind bars. So, who else put money up for my bail? Or did you borrow some of it from one of the fellas?"

"Fuck is you worrying about where the money came from? You're out of jail and not sitting in a filthy cell and rotting for the rest of your life!"

When he noticed Lola eavesdropping on their conversation, he said, "Let's step outside where we can talk."

Walking over to the patio, he slid the glass door open and stepped outside. Justice followed suit and slid the door shut behind him.

"I left the empire and set up shop in the projects across the street. I'm moving four kilos of heroin every week on the block and another twenty keys on the side. If I continue this winning streak, I will be rich within a year. I'm not gonna get ahead of myself, but I *am* generating a lot more money now than during my years in the organization. Oh, and by the way, Juice and his boys are looking for something crazy. One would think you killed his mother. They are turning over every rock possible. There's even a fifty-grand bounty on your head! This man has connections all over the world, so you and your family best keep it moving because it won't be long before he finds out you're laying low in Chicago, and you definitely *don't* wanna bring any drama to aunt's crib."

Handing Justice the remainder of the money he brought along, O-Dawg said, "I know it's only fifty-five grand and won't last forever, but call me in a week, and I'll have some more money for you. The law won't let me wire more than nine thousand without scrutinizing, so just meet me at 30th Street Amtrak Station in Philly, and I'll hand you the cash. I'll even drive to New York, but I'm not coming all the way the fuck out here again. I think Texas would be a good place to hide out since it's close to the Mexican border. So, if the pressure starts to build, all you have to do is jump the wall."

Justice was in no mood for jokes; his life was on the line from all directions—law enforcement and Juice.

"I'm your eyes and ears back home. If I hear anything, you'll be the first to know."

"Thanks for coming through as always."

"We family. That's what we do! On that note, next time, holla at me before you go doing some Superman shit. You wouldn't be hiding or going through all of this right now if we took care of it together. It would've been done properly, and none of them fools would be alive as we speak."

"How did he find out I was the one who killed his men?"

"Matone survived the attack, but even if he hadn't, you did that shit in broad daylight. Everyone out on the block saw you leaving the crime scene."

Justice decided to change the subject; it was starting to get touchy.

"I know you keep a stash of Granddaddy on deck.My lungs are screaming for some purple."

CHAPTER 13

"Boss, word on the street is Pete's running his mouth and saying the wrong things to the wrong people. Shit like how he's gotten away with murder a few dozen times and how he's been putting in work for you for over a decade and has more than thirty bodies under his belt. I guess he's trying to make himself out to be some sort of hero or some shit," explained Matone. "I was gonna kill him myself but wanted to run it by you first."

"Thanks, but this one is personal. I have the perfect solution for his problem."

This information hit home. Juice had known Pete since childhood; he attended his wedding and even played a part in his daughter's christening.

Pete was one of ten assassins from Puerto Rico sanctioned to the United States and one of the few allowed to stay. When the firing of the original guys first took place, he was chosen as a replacement, even though he was still on the payroll as a hitman. He had never been to the U.S. The atmosphere and Americano lifestyle were something he quickly became accustomed to. Money came faster than any hit he had ever committed, which in turn went to his head. This disturbed Juice, for he had known the man for many years and never faced problems with him. He always took care of his assignments and had yet to make a mistake on the job. He was known as a loner in Puerto Rico. So for Pete to be out in the open and running his mouth was a hard pill for Juice to swallow.

"Let's pay our friend a visit. He knew the rules to this game and the consequences for breaking them when he first came on board."

Matone knew exactly what his boss meant; he had heard the saying before plenty of times. Murdering Pete would definitely hit close to home—both were friends since grade school and even played with Matchbox cars together in the sandbox. The fact that Juice was willing to kill one of his own assassins terrified Matone. It was only a matter of time before a price tag would be put on his head. He knew too much and had already been warned that the next time he fucked up a job, it would cost him his life. All it took was a slight slip-up, and his body would be chopped to pieces. This had him walking on pins and needles; he did every job with the utmost precision.

As they drove towards the residence, flashbacks of good old memories shared with his friend flooded his thoughts. Matone could not shake the ill feeling from the pit of his stomach. When it came to murder, he knew Juice did not discriminate, but he had never taken the life before of such a close confidant. He was starting to wish he had kept his mouth shut.

Arriving at the complex, he took a deep breath before parking the black Lincoln Continental in front of apartment 1202-D.

"Wait right here," said Juice, climbing out of the backseat.

He believed all respected men of his caliber should be chauffeured around in an expensive, luxury sedan.

Pete was about to head to the grocery store when he noticed the black sedan on the monitor.

Who's this? He thought, reaching for the .40 caliber on the coffee table and cocking a round into the chamber. He stared dumbfounded at the multiple camera screens when he saw his boss climbing out of the sedan.

"What the fuck is *he* doing here?"

He set the gun back down on top of the coffee table and quickly approached the front door.

Juice was about a second from knocking on the door when it opened. The apartment was pitch-black; he could not see a damn thing besides the little peanut head that popped out from behind the door.

"Pete, my friend, how is the wife and kid?"

The unannounced visit made Pete feel uneasy; all kinds of crazy things ran through his mind. If the head man in charge was standing at his door, it must be something serious and of importance.

"What's up, boss? I was just on my way out."

He could not let Juice sense his nervousness, or he would take that as a sign of weakness.

"What brings you to *mi casa*?"

The fake smirk on Pete'sface upset Juice. It took every ounce of patience in him not to shoot the man at the entrance of his house.

"Aren't you going to invite me inside?" Juice asked impatiently.

Pete froze. He didn't know whether to invite his boss in or find a way to take the conversation outside elsewhere.

With witnesses around, he might think twice about trying anything, he thought.

He took a step backward and said, "I was just stepping out to grab some milk for my daughter, but hey, why not? I always have time for my boss! Come inside."

"Why the hell are you in the dark?" Juice asked, carefully inching his way towards the family room.

"My eyes are sensitive to light," responded Pete. "Have a seat. Let me take your jacket."

Juice did not seem impressed by the generosity and was disturbed by the skittish behavior. He was aware that Pete knew the reason for his sudden appearance but was just trying to play along as if things were normal. Not wanting to spoil the act, he played along.

"Pete, I'm having a birthday party at the mansion in Puerto Rico this coming weekend and wanted to know if you and the wife wanted to come. I want to enjoy this special day with my family and friends."

"I forgot it was your birthday this week. Sorry, bossman. I guess I've been moving too fast."

Pete stopped for a second and pondered whether it was really Juice's birthday. He didn't remember it falling around this time the previous year but went along with it anyway.

"That's right! You'll be turning the big five-oh!" Pete said, trying to make the situation lighter.

"Of course, I'll be at your birthday party! I wouldn't miss it for the world."

"Make sure to bring the little one. Alisa will enjoy playing with my daughters. Speaking of Alisa, where's the family?"

"They're at Lori's mother's house."

The mere mention of his family sent a cold chill down Pete's spine.

Quickly changing the subject, he continued, "This is the first time in all of the years we've known each other that you invite me to your party."

"I've always celebrated my birthday in the privacy of my home. In previous years, only a selected few were invited to enjoy this special day with me, but this year is different," Juice expressed. "I'm only getting older. So, I decided I'll make this one an open-door party for all my friends. You know, half a century of life on this planet opens you up to try new experiences," he continued, a skilled manipulator. "One day, you're here, and the next, you're gone. We live to die and die to live."

This gibberish was starting to blow Pete's high. The mixed signals were making him paranoid.

"I feel where you're coming from, bossman. Maybe when I reach your age, I'll feel the same way."

Not once did it cross his mind that maybe the party was a fabrication.

"Saturday it is."

"Make sure to show up, my friend. Don't disappoint me," responded Juice before getting up from the couch and walking towards the front door. "I'll see you there."

As Juice turned to the door, he thought, *Dumb fuck, if you weren't too busy clouding your brain with all kinds of drugs and pills, you would remember that a few years ago, we celebrated my 47th birthday at the strip club. You would also remember my birthday is during the summer, not winter.*

***

The weekend came around, and Pete was still going hard. It had been over two days since he got some sleep. The weed laced with crack had him speeding and running his mouth like some big macho with a point to prove. Most of the guys were inside Will's basement shooting pool and watching the LA Lakers play the Philadelphia 76ers.Others hung out on the patio inhaling some Loud.

"Y'all know its Juice's birthday Saturday, right?" he interrupted. "Are any of you bringing your kids? No disrespect, but you know how Juice's birthday bashes be…"

Everyone looked at one another in bewilderment. No one had heard a thing about Juice having a birthday party, and if Pete was the only one to know about such an event, they wanted no part of what was really about to occur.

"We'll be in Puerto Rico, but we damn sure ain't bringing kids along," said Matone, the only body in the room who knew what was going on. "Now, sit your high-ass down and watch the basketball game!"

His tactic worked. Pete sat down and immediately became engrossed in the game.

Everyone's intuition told them Pete's death certificate had been signed, sealed, and approved by Juice. If he were willing to kill someone he's known since his childhood, he would not make the slightest hesitation to murder anyone in his circle. Matone could read everyone's facial expression and sensed they knew this would be the last time they would see Pete alive. He felt like they were all on the same page or had some kind of understanding in not answering Pete directly. No one wanted to be in his shoes. Even though the majority of the men in attendance barely knew the islander from Puerto Rico, they all felt some kind of sympathy towards their comrade.

Pete was so high that he did not pickup on everyone's vibe. Since he ran his mouth so damn much, he was used to being ignored. To him, it was like any other day when they would all gather to watch sports or shoot a game of pool in the basement. For the first time, he felt all eyes on him, but when he tried staring back, each one would turn his face. Maybe it was the cocaine, but right now, his mind was playing tricks on him. An uneasy feeling started to settle in as he began to come down from his high.

Jose noticed Pete's perplexed body language and passed him the blunt.

"Here, take a few puffs."

Pete eyed the entire room and noticed the many stares his way. The man wasn't even dead, yet to them, it already felt like he was.

***

"Matone, I need for you to watch over the empire while I'm at the Island taking care of that fool Pete," Juice said.

"Can you believe his diarrhea mouth mentioned the birthday party the other night," responded Matone. "I had to interrupt him by saying we already knew about the party. I'm glad no one responded to the party remark," he continued. "At that moment, I could read all of their thoughts. They looked confused as hell!"

"I should've sent his ass back to the Island with the rest of the assassins. I guess the saying is true—a person's true character will eventually come to light."

***

Expensive luxury vehicles lined the pavement outside the ten-acre mansion. *Happy Birthday* balloons and decorations were tied to individual trees and bushes. Pete parked the rented Jaguar in a space next to the rest of the foreign cars.

"Looks like the party already started," he whispered to his wife as they both exited the vehicle.

He watched as his wife unbuckled their two-year-old daughter. He did not want to bring his daughter on this trip, but he did so out of respect for his boss. That funny feeling he felt in the US came back, running through his body as he and his family made their way towards the mansion's oak double doors. They heard no music playing, and most of the lights inside the house were off. Immediately, Pete started having second thoughts about coming this far. His gut told him to turn back around and leave, but his logic said that Juice would not try anything in front of his family.

"Babe, do you think this is the type of birthday party we should be bringing our daughter to?" asked a concerned Lori, who also felt a funny vibe about them being there.

"Everything will be fine, baby. Juice said there will be plenty of kids for Alissa to play with. He has two daughters of his own, so she'll be entertained. We'll have a good time. I promise."

Feeling safe in the presence of her husband, Lori shook the uneasy feeling away and prepared herself for a good night.

"Wow, this place is magnificent! I've never seen anything like it. It reminds me of a house from the television show *MTV Cribs*."

Juice had been staring at his phone's screen for quite some time now. He immediately knew who the caller was but let it ring a few times anyways. He had been watching the family since they first arrived at the estate. After the fifth ring, he answered.

"Pete, my friend, glad you and the family could make it. Someone will be out front to escort you and the family inside."

There was a spooky setting about the way the place looked. Pete's heart started to beat faster as he fought the tricks his mind played on him. The squeaking sounds of the oak doors opening snapped him out of his trance.

"Pete, *amigo*, longtime no see. How have you been?"asked Ralph, who knew the family very well. "And this must be the new addition to the family."

If there were an Oscar for best actor, Ralph would have won it hands down. His body language and behavior made Pete feel somewhat at ease.

"Follow me inside.The party's taking place in the back at the pool house."

I'm panicking for no reason, thought Pete as he stepped inside, followed by his family.

Pete turned to Ralph and said, "We've been doing great. The United States of America is a wonderful place to raise a family. You should try moving there someday. Doesn't have to be permanent. You can stay with us for a few months to see if you like it."

"I'm doing just fine here in Puerto Rico, *hermano*. It's all I have known my entire life. Plus, America is too fast-paced for me. The Caribbean lifestyle suits me fine."

Pete glanced over at his wife and noticed she looked frightened.

"Why isn't there any music playing?" he asked Ralph, who did not respond.

The deeper they traveled into the mansion, the more things seemed to be out of place.

"Where the hell is everyone?"

Deciding to finally follow his gut instinct, Pete stopped in his tracks, grabbed his wife by one arm, and started moving in the direction of the front entrance.

"Fuck this party. Let's go!"

Ralph knew if he let them leave, Juice would kill him. He witnessed first hand on numerous occasions the punishment violators received when plans did not go accordingly. He hated to be in this predicament, but he had a job to do, and he did not want a part in any of his boss's violence. Without hesitation, he raised the .45 caliber and fired at Pete's leg.

"Sorry, Pete, I can't let you leave."

Lori let out an ear-piercing scream as she watched her husband drop to the floor while clutching his leg. Pete's mind was sucked into a whirlpool of negative thoughts. He knew it was a set-up; he had been involved in many assassinations to recognize this was a hit on his life. His only desire at this point was that Juice spared his family.

"Get up," Ralph ordered, aiming the gun. "I tried to make this as comfortable as possible for you, Pete. Next shot will be a death sentence!"

Pete clutched the wound on his leg. The pain was excruciating, but he blocked the feeling from his mind. His family's life was at stake. He reached for the .380 caliber in his waist. He intended to put a bullet to the back of Ralph's dome, but his hopes were short-lived when he heard footsteps approaching. He would have to hold out on this one. He could not risk his wife or daughter getting shot in the process of him playing hero.

"Everything okay?" asked Felipe. "We heard the shot and thought—"

"I have everything under control!" snapped Ralph. "Let's go! I don't have all fucking day!"

He hated to bring this side of him out but he could not disappoint his boss.

***

Entering the dimly-lit quarters, the many dark figures surrounding the entire room were the first thing to catch Pete's attention. He could not make out the faces but knew who some of the men were behind the bulky physiques and ski masks. Not long ago, he was standing amongst these men.

Every dog has its day, he thought, sad that his day had come in the company of his family.

Pete's heart sank to the pit of his stomach as they were ushered to the middle of the room, facing the man who held their lives in his hands.

"*Atencion!*"

Pete held the hands of his wife and daughter tightly. His eyes shifted towards the voice he so deeply despised. His eyes cringed as the lights were turned to their brightest capacity.

"Surprise!" sang Juice. "Welcome to your death party!"

Juice laughed at his own humor as Pete's family stared at him dryly.

Pete could not believe this was actually happening in front of his family.

"What the fuck is this?!" he barked. "Is this some sort of sick joke?"

In no way was he going out like a coward in front of his loved ones. If he was going to die in their presence, he was going out with honor.

"How long have we known each other, Peter? I would have never thought of you being a rat!"

Pete stood there with a *WTF* look on his face. He knew where this was going and wanted to say something but was more focused on trying to formulate a plan to escape.

"You're wearing a stupid look on your face like you have no clue what I'm talking about! Running your mouth about my business and how much I pay you to silence my enemies is the same as going to the police with the information. I trust no one! Especially fools who run their mouth so damn much!"

"Where are you getting this information? I would never break the code of honor! I've been with you since day one and have never said or done anything I wasn't supposed to."

Juice had already made up his mind that the man was going to die. Someone else might have believed his words, but his many years of experience and wisdom in the game led him to follow his gut instinct.

"A man will do or say anything to save himself from dying in front of his *familia*, but not even God Himself can save you from death," Juice said as he eyed every assassin in the room. "You all know what to do!"

If I'm gonna die, this motherfucker is dying with me, Pete thought.

Pete quickly retrieved the small .380 caliber pistol from his waist and aimed the gun directly at Juice's head.

"Let my family go! This shit is between you and me!"

Before Juice could get a word out, all seventeen men stationed throughout the confinements reacted simultaneously and drew their weapons. Pete glanced around the room and noticed most of the guns were pointed in the direction of his family. It was a no-win situation. Dropping the pistol, he turned towards his wife and daughter and hugged them both tightly. His tears began to fall uncontrollably as the thought of never seeing them again became overwhelming.

"I love you both. I'm so sorry. Please forgive me."

Loco-Loco had to literally pry the family apart.

"We can do this the easy way or the hard way. It wouldn't be wise to choose the hard way in the presence of your loved ones. Now would it?"

Deep within, Pete wanted to believe that after his death, Juice would free his family. He knew just how ruthless and cold-blooded Juice could be but hoped he would not take it to the level of a coward and murder an innocent female and her child.

"You go up the stairs first, and I'll follow behind," said Loco-Loco. "Keep your hands raised where I can see them. If you try some funny shit, I won't hesitate to put a bullet *en tu cabeza.*"

Entering the third floor's master suite, Pete turned to look back and saw his wife and daughter following him into the room. His heart skipped a beat as he observed his surroundings and noticed every assassin had also made their way into the suite. Juice was in the far-left corner sitting in his throne-like chair. His attention shifted towards his two-year-old daughter, who screamed, kicked, and scratched at her assailants as they separated her from her mother. The mere thought of his only child being hurt crushed his heart. The true realization of his family also being in grave danger finally sank in. Not only was he going to die, but his family was going to witness his death—and then be killed.

Before the psychological abuse turned into physical torture, Pete sprang into action. Quickly retrieving the four-inch hunting knife from his right pocket, he lunged at his daughter's assailant. No one noticed the small shiny object in his hand until he was about to reach the man. However, he was whacked over the head with the butt of a rifle, knocking him unconscious.

***

Pete awoke from his slumber with the realization it wasn't a dream. Several trails of dried blood covered the left side of his face, and his head throbbed from a tremendous headache. He tried to get up, but his hands and feet were duct-taped to a chair. A small strip of tape also covered his mouth. Examining the room, his eyes immediately focused on the king-sized bed. His wife Lori lay naked, her hands and feet tied to each bedpost as more than a handful of men stood drooling over her beauty. His eyes opened in bewilderment; he could not entertain the thought of what was about to take place. Searching for his daughter, he spotted Alisa on the balcony with Juice holding her hand—her tear-stained face staring at her helpless father.

Releasing a cloud of smoke from the expensive Cuban cigar, Juice looked at the pessimistic figure in front of him.

"Welcome back, *amigo*. For a second there, I thought we lost you. That would have spoiled our entire night. Peter, don't sit there looking pathetic. You knew the rules of engagement when you first joined my organization."

Approaching the bed with the little girl by his side, Juice stared at the beautiful creature in his midst. Her flawless body was an instant turn-on. He wanted to badly climb on the bed and immediately penetrate her, dispensing every drop of semen deep within her walls.

"Lori, you're such a beautiful woman. Every time I lay my eyes on you, blood rushes through my manhood, giving me the hardest erection I have ever felt."

Making a bold move, he reached for her breasts and softly pinched each nipple. Lori flinched and cringed at his touch. Tears fell from her eyes as he groped her body. She told herself that if she made it through this ordeal, she would never forgive her husband. He should have known better than to put his family in danger under these circumstances. Looking at Pete, she noticed the flood of tears streaming down his cheeks. She did not want to cause anymore drama with this crazy lunatic, but she didn't want to lie there and let this pervert continue to touch her. Her husband had told her stories about this man, and she now wondered if they were going to become part of his sick plot.

"You sick bastard! How dare you?" she yelled, spitting in his face.

Lori was not afraid. Even if it took her last breath, she was going to depart this life with dignity. Pete shook his head. He wished she had not done that. If his family had any chance of surviving, she just blew it.

Juice wiped the spit from his face and licked his fingers. He thought about putting duct tape over her mouth but decided against it. He wanted Pete to hear the terrifying screams from his wife that were to come.

"Now, why did you do that?" Juice asked teasingly as he reached inside his back pocket to retrieve the small army knife he always carried, placing the sharp blade against her throat and pressing it hard enough to make a small incision.

"Now, if you try anything else, I will slice your fucking throat! Do we have an understanding?"

Lori knew the man in front of her was serious and would keep true to his words. She shook her head in agreement and kept her mouth shut. All she could do was pray. She could feel the many eyes on her and the lust that filled the room. She closed her eyes tight, trying to shutout her surroundings.

Lord, oh Lord, let this all be a dream, she silently prayed.

Her beauty aroused every man in the room except for her husband, who was traumatized by the sight of her laid out like a feast. She was a supermodel with just the right amount of weight in all the right places. These hungry wolves each wanted to go first, but like in every pack, the alpha male outranked every member.

Lori's entire body trembled from fear of the unknown. She did not know what to expect next; all she could do was pray silently. She could hear her baby crying and yelling for her. Never before had she imagined something like this playing out in her life; this was something she only witnessed in movies. Seconds felt like hours; time lost its value in these confinements. Her entire mood changed; her body contorted in aversion as she felt what she knew to be a tongue between her legs. She immediately opened her eyes in bewilderment to find Juice giving her oral sex. She could not believe this was happening. The trauma brought flashbacks of her childhood and how her father sexually assaulted her for many years. She no longer saw this stranger but the face of her father.

"You have a very fine pussy, my darling," said Juice, wiping the fluids from the corner of his mouth.

He could not wait to feel her insides. His penis throbbed as he hurriedly unbuckled his jeans, dropped them to his ankles, and quickly climbed on top, but he was immediately met with resistance. Lori could not bear to go through the trauma of yet another brutal rape.

"Don't make this harder than it has to be!" he yelled and put the blade to her throat.

She felt she had no other choice but to let the creep do as he pleased. What she did not realize was the pack of hungry wolves was patiently waiting to do the same. Lori closed her eyes tightly and tried her best to blockout the entire ordeal. The only sounds echoing throughout the room were grunts and moans coming from Juice.

Two minutes later, Juice released his semen, not caring about leaving any DNA traces. He had no intentions on letting the family live. Climbing off the bed, he buckled his jeans and got himself together.

"This, by far, is the best pussy I ever had," Juice shouted as he looked at every man in the room.

Noticing the lust in all of their eyes, he added, "Gentlemen, she's all yours for the taking. The K-Y Jelly is in the bathroom if she begins to dry up."

Loco-Loco, head of security, was the first to spring into action, muscling his way to the front of the line. The last time he had a piece of ass was six months ago in a similar situation. Not many women approached him due to his ugly looks, so he took full advantage whenever an opportunity presented itself. Two minutes later, he was pulling his pants back up and making his way to the back of the line for another shot. Each man took a turn according to their status.

Pete had his eyes closed throughout the entire ordeal. The only thing he could hear were the cries coming from his wife and daughter. At times, he would peak to find a different man on top of his wife. He tried his best to cut through the tape that had him bound to the chair, but to no avail. He swore if by any chance he lived to see another day, he would torture and kill every single man involved.

"You did this to your wife, you disgraceful fool!" Juice screamed into Pete's face. "I've done nothing but treat you with respect. I honored you for your good craftsmanship, and this is how you repay me?! You should have known better than to bite the hand that feeds you!"

Despite his love for bloodshed, Juice hated torturing and killing the men who worked for him, but one had to make an example. In this game, a person of his caliber could in no way show any signs of weakness whatsoever.

"Fellas, that's enough!" Juice said bored with hearing the woman's cries.

If the men continued with their sexual desires on Lori, the poor woman wouldn't be able to walk or might even pass out, which she had already done a few times.

"Tie her to a chair," he ordered. "I want her to witness the hurt and pain her husband brought upon his family. Jose, bring me the little girl."

Following instructions, Jose brought the little girl over to his boss. No one knew what his plan was with the infant. Juice picked the crying child up and carried her towards the open balcony. Everyone watched in bewilderment, wondering what the psychotic man was going to do next. This was something Juice had never done before. Since the mother and father were both going to die, he figured why not the child, too. Ignoring Lori's screams and Pete's muffled noises, he raised the small child in the air and threw her feather-light body from the third floor. The young child'sshrieks kept diminishing until they turned into a loud thud and absolute silence.

No one could believe the atrocity that Juice had just committed. Everyone knew the man was crazy, but no one thought he was capable of doing anything like this.

When Lori saw her only child murdered, she could no longer take the hurt and agony and passed out. Pete's chair tipped over, and as he lay on the floor, he banged his head repetitively on the hardwood flooring. He knew this was all his fault. If it weren't for his big mouth, none of this would have happened.

It was now time for Juice to finish what he had set out to do; the job was taking longer than he expected. He was lucky to have been able to pull some strings the day before and get the heavy machinery needed for the job. The Bobcat bulldozer was rented to him by a close associate who was a big shot in the construction business. Juice himself had operated the heavy machinery and dug a massive hole behind his mansion.

Pete and Lori were taken to the field; Lori was carried by one of the assassins, and Pete walked on foot. Juice thought she had seen and endured enough, so he decided to put her out of her misery while she still was unconscious. Approaching the naked figure, he made sure Pete was watching before delivering three bullets to the back of her head.

Pete's ankles were no longer bound since he had to walk to the field. Seeing the window of opportunity, he rushed at Juice at full speed. He was a few feet away from reaching his goal before the blast of fifty or more bullets stopped him short. Both bullet-riddled bodies were then placed in the grave in a crucifixion position. Throughout the acres of the property, there were at least a hundred bodies buried in this manner. This was one of Juice's many private cemeteries.

CHAPTER 14

Andy was heated at the news of the death of his cousin Fat-Chop. The man walked around constantly with a TEC-9 semi-automatic gun tucked in his waistline. Every day for the past two weeks since his cousin's death, he went over to the house in Philly where the shooting took place. He was hoping to catch Kenny slipping, but slip he did not. By this time, everyone knew who the murder suspect was since his face was televised all over the news.

Andy wasn't the only person in search of Kenny; everyone wanted a piece of him. The DA's office had issued a warrant for his arrest for the murder of Charlie Sanchez—known in the streets as Fat-Chop. The police and U.S. Marshals were on a hunting spree for this armed and dangerous suspect.

Kenny was no fool; once he saw that the SUV had sped away with its occupants still alive, he knew the police would be hounding him and kicking down every door of all his addresses. He was angry with himself for a job poorly done. His face was plastered all over Pennsylvania, New Jersey, Delaware, New York, and Maryland tri-state news channels.

The same day the shooting took place, Kenny got on his grind. He would not sleep until he had enough money to live comfortably, and he reached his destination. He stayed awake until the sun came up—robbing drug dealers, corner bodegas, and anything else that crossed his path.

That very same night, he caught the next train to Houston, Texas. There, after a few weeks of playing tourist, he got plugged in with one of Houston's biggest drug dealers/gang bangers. His name was G-Money—a name that definitely spoke for itself. This man had the whole south side of Houston on lock; he supplied every dealer in that area, some from out of state, and even some hustlers from the north and west sides. Almost a hundred percent of the drug money that flowed through that area belonged solely to him.

Four weeks into his arrival, Kenny was already on his grind, raking in anywhere from ten to fifteen grand on a good week. With his connection between New York and the Dominican Republic, he had the entire state of Texas chasing after that China White heroin. He could wholesale the product and move it faster, but it was better if he bagged and sold the product out on the streets to triple his profit margin. He had begun to gather up some haters around the area since he was an out-of-towner making massive cash in their hood. With G-Money on his team, he felt his worries weren't worth losing sleep over.

***

After the anger subsided, Andy got on full mode and took over Fat-Chop's operation but kept the same team players that his cousin had on the squad. The block was still doing its numbers despite there being no product out on the block for a couple of weeks. Andy was the only man who knew all of Fat-Chop's business and resources. He made it his responsibility to follow through with his cousin's trade. After speaking with the connect, he was stamped as hood-certified and given permission to take over the drug connection. The Peruvians had no problem coming to a conclusion. They even agreed to keep the prices for the kilos the same as long as things stayed the same as when Fat-Chop ran the operation.

A proper burial was given to Fat-Chop, which put Andy somewhat at ease. As the days went by and the money started flowing in like a leaking faucet, he shoved his cousin farther away in the back of his mind. Every week, he would visit the cemetery where Fat-Chop was buried and put fresh flowers next to the tombstone. Andy also never forgot to pour out a little liquor for every fallen soldier. He dreaded these visits since they always made him shed a few tears, especially when he started to reminisce about the good ol' days. There was a thirty-thousand-dollar bounty on Kenny's head, and Andy was willing to pay even more if he were captured and brought to him alive.

Money was spent faster than it was coming in. Andy kept a lawyer on retainer and also sent him gift cards to exquisite restaurants on many occasions. It was a sure way for the attorney to keep the judges and prosecutors in his favor. Due to his MDMA habit, most nights were a blur to him, which meant massive amounts of unaccounted-for money and unnecessary spending. The pills were making him paranoid, and he stocked up on artillery like war was coming. This lifestyle had finally started to take a toll on him. Money brought problems, and problems brought more problems. Becoming depressed, Andy began to dabble in his own product. Everyone knew the number one rule: *Never get high on your own supply*. Letting the monkey get the best of him became his downfall.

Not having any money left in the stash, he approached the only person he knew would help.

"Juice, I'm kinda short on my next re-up. With bailing out my workers and paying for their attorney fees, my money's kinda funny, and I'm not tryna step to the Peruvians like that. That'll look bad for business, and I can't let that happen. These guys are my bread and butter— my food on the table," he lamented with a sorry-ass look on his face.

Juice was always trying to find ways to scheme, so he looked at this as an investment. Once he reeled in Andy, the man would forever be indebted to him.

"I will front you the money needed, but there will be a twenty-percent interest rate for every week it takes you to reimburse me."

Andy had no other alternative—his drug addiction getting the best of him physically and mentally. He quickly jumped on the offer without giving it a second thought, but it was something he would later regret.

"Alright, we have a deal!"

A handshake sealed the deal. Deep down, Andy knew better than to break that deal with Juice, but at this point, the drugs were doing the thinking and talking for him. All he wanted was to have that re-up money so he could make money, party, and get high.

Juice didn't yet notice that Andy was getting high on his own supply; there were no early signs of the drug addiction's deterioration of the body. All he saw were dollar signs because he knew he would get his money no matter what.

***

So far, Andy was staying true to his word and reimbursing the twenty-percent interest rate. He still maintained the same lifestyle, but if it weren't for Juice's helping hand, his daily seven-hundred-dollar a day heroin and coke habit would have left him broke and in debt—eventually becoming the death of him. He was now at the point where he could no longer feel the effects of the poison in his body. The drugs were attacking his immune system, and his body and facial features were starting to show signs of deterioration. Up close, one could easily tell he was using some sort of heavy narcotic. He would always wear a long sleeve shirt to cover the track marks on his arms.

Almost four months had gone by since the deal with Juice, and again, Andy was short on payment. He had been paying the debt but would always come up short. Within this short period, he was already $250,000 in the hole. Each time, he promised Juice that he would have his money ready the next time around. Andy knew making false promises would only last for so long, so he drove around with a loaded Glock on his waistband. At night, he would try his best not to fall asleep, shooting cocaine through his veins, hoping not to get caught slipping.

Juice wasn't really worried about the money; if Andy had kept it real from the beginning, Juice wouldn't be feeling the way he was now. He knew Andy was getting high; one only had to look at his face and the tremendous weight loss to figure he was using something. Growing tired of the same old story, Juice felt he wasn't ever going to see his money. So, he decided to order the hit on Andy. He knew the perfect candidate for the job. Since Duce had taken half the money upfront on the Justice job but still failed to locate the man, Juice knew he would have no problem in doing this job at no charge.

After contacting Duce and explaining what he needed to be done, Juice hoped it would not take him long to do the job. Since Andy and Duce had known each other for quite some time, it shouldn't take long at all. He would be able to get close to the man but had to make sure he did not show any signs of betrayal. The two men were from this city, and Duce hung around all the guys from this city.Therefore, he would be able to get close to any of them. He did not care for Andy but had much respect and love towards his cousin Fat-Chop. If he was willing to kill Justice, who was a close friend, why not kill Andy?

Duce knew he was out of hand by going against the grain, but he needed the money and wanted to get away from all the madness anyway. It wouldn't be the first time he took someone's life.

When the perfect opportunity presented itself, he spotted Andy standing alone on the block; he pulled up alongside him in the stolen Buick.

"What up, dawg? What are you up to?"

"Tryna get this paper," responded Andy. "I couldn't find someone this morning to bang these packs out to the fiends, so I had to stand out here on my own."

"I feel you on that, but, check it. I was on my way to go to Fat-Chop's burial site to pay him some respect. You wanna ride with me over there?"

"Shit, why wouldn't I wanna pay my cousin some respect?" answered Andy.

On the ride over towards the cemetery, both men reminisced about the good and bad times they shared with Fat-Chop. Duce hated to have to do this, but if he did not complete the job, it would surely be his name and picture in the obituary.

As they arrived at the graveyard, the sun was just starting to set. Duce had to be careful driving since the tombstones were only a few inches away from the pavement.

"Do you remember how to get to where his stone is?" Duce asked, playing dumb.

Andy would've picked up on the funny vibe if he weren't so high; he would've questioned why Duce was even paying his respects, when he never even showed up to the funeral.

After both men climbed out of the car, Duce followed as Andy led the way towards the stone.

Your own people will deceive you. That's something I learned when I first got in the game, thought Duce as he swatted the mosquitoes away from his face.

Andy approached a large 17th-century statue of a Roman knight holding a beheaded head in his hand. Duce had to hand it to Andy—the man had good taste and must've paid a fortune for the statue.

Bending down on his knees, Andy closed his eyes and assumed a prayer position. He silently said a prayer, knowing one day they would both reunite someplace, somewhere, somehow.

He believed it in his heart.

Duce stood behind Andy with his head also bowed, reciting a prayer of a completely different intention: *Forgive me for what I'm about to do to your cousin, but you know money rules all evil. You, out of everybody, should know this because you experienced it first hand. Look where it got you!*

Duce was arguing with himself—one side of him wanted to do it while the other side opposed the idea. It was like a constant battle going on inside his brain. Duce poured out some Hennessy from the bottle he had been sipping on; he was feeling a little tipsy.

"Rest in peace, homie. You might be gone but never forgotten," said Andy as the brown substance splashed on the ground.

"You alright, dawg?" asked Duce.

"Yeah, I'm good. It's just that every time I come out here, I start feeling all emotional and shit. Me and him were real tight."

"I feel you. You already know me and Chop go back since diaper days," added Duce. "Let's go to Philly and grab some Wet. Tonight's a night to feel zoned."

Telling Andy that they were going to get some PCP was all part of the act. Andy just didn't yet know it.

"It's whatever, homie. I could go for some Wet at a time like this."

It was the wrong decision for Andy to be making. The heroin had his mind so clouded he could not think straight, even at a time that concerned his well-being. He was just anxious to pull over so he could get his fix in a service station's restroom.

On their way towards Philadelphia, Duce made as much talk as possible. He didn't want Andy to pick up on anything or even have the slightest idea of his plan. He could see the anxiety in Andy—the man's legs were shaking as if he were freezing.

Duce knew about the drug habit, so he pulled over at the first gas station he saw once they were over the Benjamin Franklin Bridge. This gave him time to think his plan over and play out the entire event in his head. Andy must have been in a rush; the man got out of the car and almost ran to the restroom. Duce also climbed out of the car and went inside the store to purchase some blunts. When he returned to the car, Andy had yet to come back from the restroom. He was now regretting having pulled over. Not wanting to attract any attention, he parked the car in a spot by the convenience store. Ten minutes went by before Andy finally returned.

Duce was heated. If it were the right place, he would've taken the man's life then and there.

Andy looked and felt much better now that he had his fix. He could see the anger in Duce's eyes as he made his way towards the car.

"My bad I took so long," he sheepishly said as he climbed into the passenger's seat.

"You lucky I ain't leave your ass to walk," Duce joked. "What? You got diarrhea?!"

"Yeah, something like that."

Duce still looked angry as he drove away from the parking spot. After stopping at a couple of drug corners and buying what they were looking for, he pulled into a secluded area and parked the 1998 Buick Regal next to a tree.

Andy wasn't used to smoking Wet, so he inhaled deeply on the embalmed cigarette. It was like smoking a blunt, but this method was supposed to be a more potent way of inhaling the drug. When he finished, he passed it back to Duce, who, in return, passed him a rolled PCP blunt mixed with weed. As the session got on its way, the walk down memory lane also started.

"I remember me and Fat-Chop used to go around running trains on all these hoes. We were only about fifteen at the time and already fucking like champs," reminisced Duce. "One time, we were both fucking this same chick. I was hitting it from the back doggystyle, while Chop stood in front of her getting head. Right when I was about to cum, I started to beat faster and harder. I pounded her so hard she choked on Fat-Chop's dick and puked all over him. I will never forget that night. I had the ball of my life. He was so mad that he left her walking out in the boonies. The girl didn't even know where she was at."

Andy broke out in laughter as he pictured the scene in his mind. One second, his attitude was cool, and the next, it dramatically changed.

"I swear on everything I love, I will find Kenny, and when I do, he will suffer for every second me and my family had to suffer! The painful moments we had to endure—the sleepless nights, the sad memories."

It went on until Duce snapped at Andy, bringing him back to his senses.

"You just high as fuck! Calm your ass down! Here, drink this," he ordered, giving Andy some cold water. "I'll be right back. I'm gonna take a leak."

Andy sat in the passenger seat on cloud nine. His surroundings were blurry to him, and he did not know where he was. The PCP had him stuck. The car no longer felt like a vehicle—it now felt like an airplane. He saw himself in an airliner on its way to some other dimension. While in this trance-like state, he barely noticed the figure approaching the window on his side.

Duce walked up to the passenger window and noticed Andy was super high, spaced out in another world. He knew better than to continue to inhale the potent drug. So, after about the fourth pull, he stopped inhaling the toxic fume and just let the blunt burn before passing it back to Andy every time. If he hadn't done this, he, too, would be in the same mental state.

Duce pulled out the 45. Caliber, semi-automatic handgun and tapped the passenger side window; its thick, heavy barrel almost cracked the window. Andy slowly turned his head towards the noise. His vision was so blurred from the drug that he did not see the weapon aimed right at his face. The last thing he saw was a bright flash of light as the bullets went right through the window, shattering the glass and striking Andy in the face. Bones and brain fragments splattered all over the dashboard and windshield. Duce quickly set the stolen car on fire and left the crime scene in a hurry, flagging down a taxi two blocks away.

CHAPTER 15

Between the block and wholesale, O-Dawg was now raking in anywhere between $90,000 and $120,000 weekly profit. He also decided to get into the crack cocaine business and put the product for sale on his block. Day and night, fiends rushed the block to buy the most potent heroin and crack cocaine in the city. Non-stop, bodies moved in and out of the strip looking like zombies hungry for a hit or fix.

"Cop and go," shouted the young hustlers throughout the entire day.

The cars that pulled up to buy were served the drugs through the window like a drive-thru. The block lieutenant didn't want to attract the attention of any detectives or vice squads. The block was controlled and run like a business; hanging around the block or stopping to speak with someone was prohibited. It was constant moving in and out.

A lookout was stationed at the end of each side of the block. One hustler would serve the customers who pulled up in a car, while the second hustler would serve the customers who approached on foot. Things were organized in a solid structure, yet the constant traffic was bound to attract the attention of the authorities.

Once the cops picked a spot to fuck with, they would be on it like flies on shit, shaking down all the workers and at times stealing their money and stashes. O-Dawg knew this, but these were consequences every drug dealer had to deal with. When the serious cash started coming in, he stopped hanging around the block and would now only show his face occasionally. He had runners he paid to make sure things stayed running smooth and his money was always correct.

Usually, like today, he just drove by. Looking down the entire block, O-Dawg's heart skipped a beat. When he noticed there wasn't a soul standing out there making him money, he immediately slammed on the brakes. The strip looked like a ghost town. Leaving the car parked in the middle of the street, he climbed out and retrieved his cell phone from his waistband to dial his lieutenant's number.

"Yo, Nate! What the fuck is going on?!"

Before he could continue ranting, Nate cut in, "O-Dawg, the block got raided this morning. They locked up Lil Moses with thirteen packs of heroin and Ray-Ray with seven packs of coke. I tried calling you a few times but kept getting your voicemail."

"Do you know how much their bail is?"

O-Dawg was true to his workers and would not let them spend a day in jail if he could prevent it. He was making massive amounts of cash, so a few thousand dollars wasn't much to him.

"Lil Moses's bail was set at fifty thousand—cash or bond," replied Nate. "I spoke to the bail bondsman, and he said five thousand will do the job, with no installment payments. As for Ray-Ray, he's a juvenile. So, he'll be home the next day if a guardian picks him up."

"Say no more. I'm on my way with the money," responded O-Dawg. "Where are you right now?"

"I'm at the crib."

"Give me a few, and I'll swing by."

Five grand was play money to O-Dawg. Since he always carried that amount of cash with him and didn't have to stop anywhere to get the money, he headed straight to Nate's place.

Pulling up in front of Nate's apartment, O-Dawg honked the horn a few times before his lieutenant exited the residence wearing nothing but his boxers. Reaching in his pocket, he took out $6,000 and handed it to Nate.

"Bail him out and give him the extra G-note. Tell Lil Moses if he needs anything when he comes out, not to hesitate to give me a call, and I'll take care of it.After you finish running that errand, open shop back up. Things should be cool by then."

***

Two weeks had gone by, and the police were still shaking down O-Dawg's workers frequently. This had him furious every time he had to keep coming up with bail money—which really wasn't anything. However, the constant presence of the authorities had the fiends scared to buy his product for fear of getting arrested and thrown into the county jail. So, the slow profit margin was starting to put a dent in his pockets. As he sat on the recliner chair in his living room quarters, he thought of a potential solution to his problem.

His phone vibrated from an incoming call that displayed an out-of-state area code.

"Who's this?"

"It's Justice! What's good? I took heed to what you said about leaving Chicago, and here I am at the 30th Street train station in Philly. My train to Texas departs in an hour; I just figured I'd let you know. I remember you said to call you once I got here."

"You've made the right decision, cuz. I'm proud of you," said O-Dawg. "Stay right where you are. I'll be there in a few. I'll call this same number when I get to the front."

O-Dawg quickly made his way up the stairs and into his bedroom. Walking to the far corner, he kneeled and peeled back the carpet, revealing a large floor safe. Punching in the digital combination, he opened the small vault door and removed $150,000 from his stash. Stuffing the bundles of cash into a small Gucci bag, he then made his way down the stairs, through the garage, and into his vehicle.

As he made the way over the bridge, he wondered when he would see Justice again. He hoped they wouldn't meet again under the same—or worse—circumstances as the last. Maybe next time, there won't be a bail. He prayed whatever Justice had planned for the future was solid and would keep him out of harm's way. As he arrived at the train station, he spotted Justice approaching his passenger side window.

"Are you gonna let me in or what? I promise not to rob you!" Justice joked.

Unlocking the door, O-Dawg waited until Justice was fully seated in the passenger seat and said, "How the hell did you know this was my car?"

"Man, I recognized your big-ass head as soon as you turned the corner. If you had your windows rolled down, your ears would've been sticking out both sides of the car."

"That's gotta be the oldest and lamest joke I've ever heard," O-Dawg said but laughed hysterically as he pulled away from the station. "Here, light this up," he added while handing over a Sour Diesel-filled blunt.

"So, how's everything with you in the city?" asked Justice.

"Everything is everything. You know what this game be about. The block has been on fire for the past few weeks now. I'm feeling the decrease in profit, but the police still can't stop my hustle."

"Every time they lock one up, there's a replacement waiting for his turn in the game. It's a non-stop cycle!" Justice cheered.

"You're right, but the bail money is hurting my pockets. Can't forget these faggot-ass lawyers, too. They're starting to dig a huge hole in my pockets. Shit, every time I turn around, money falls out of my pockets. Speaking of money, here's a little something to keep you out of trouble for a bit."

He handed Justice the Gucci bag full of cash. Justice did not know the amount of money inside but could tell it was no small change from the weight.

"Good looking, bro. I appreciate it a lot."

"Don't you want to know how much is in there?"

"It's probably about a hundred grand, right?"

"Try one fifty! Add ten more bands if you count the money I spent on the designer bag."

"I was only fifty grand shy," replied Justice as both men broke out into laughter.

"So what about the case in Chicago? What are you gonna do about that? Skip bail?"

"Listen, I already have four bodies I'm on the run for. I'm not risking the chance of going to court in Chicago and getting bagged for the bodies in Jersey."

"I'll be checking up on you," said O-Dawg. "Don't be surprised if I call you from the airport in Texas so you can pick me up. Shit, I could use a vacation," he added.

"I'll be looking forward to that call. Best believe by the time you come there for that vacation, I'll be right, and you won't have to worry about a thing while you're there with me."

They had an hour left before Justice's train departed, and the third blunt was almost done burning. Taking the last two drags from the roach, O-Dawg rolled down the window and tossed the finger stinger out.

"Don't hesitate to give me a ring if you need something. I don't give a fuck what it is, I got you," he said as he made the right turn onto 30th Street, illegally parking the car in front of the train station. "Where's your bags?"

"What you see is what I got," answered Justice. "I wasn't beat to be carrying bags around. I'll get up with you. Good looking on the money."

"Don't ever thank me for no blood money. You're family. I love you, cuz. Keep your head up in Texas."

Driving away from the train station, O-Dawg felt a little stressed over the situation. He did not want anything to happen to his cousin. It would crush his heart to see Justice in any tragedy. He would have to send his aunt money to cover any extra charges for the bail bond's men, since Justice has officially skipped bail. He definitely did not want her to lose her house; she had centuries of sweat put into that place. He knew if Justice had made that phone call to him on the day he caught those bodies, he would be on the run right along with his cousin, and they would both be in the same situation. He did not care for Juice or his men but was glad things played out the way they did. His cousin was on the run, but at least the man was alive.

The heat from O-Dawg's block was starting to rub off on the empire. Since both drug trades were across the street from one another, police arrested anyone they suspected of buying or selling drugs within that perimeter. Although federal investigators kept a close eye on the empire, they hid their presence well—never arresting anyone or involving the city police.

***

Both parties felt a dip in profits because of the heavy police presence all day and night. This had Juice very upset because he did not know about the crack and heroin trade across the street, going on right under his nose—not until the heavy police presence came underway. His lieutenant's investigation had led him to the drug set across the street. Finding out the name of the block owner, he brought the information to his boss's attention. The news made Juice even more upset. He felt that O-Dawg had disrespected him by opening shop right across the street from the empire. He desperately wanted to speak with O-Dawg to make a conclusion for this critical situation. After a couple of failed attempts to contact the man, he finally caught up with him on the phone.

"This is Juice. You probably already know the reason why I am calling you. I would like for us to hold a meeting in person so we may fix our little problem."

O-Dawg replied, "Look, if there is anything you need to speak to me about, do so while you have the chance. I don't have any interest in talking to you, let alone meeting up with you in person."

"Well, if you insist, I'll get right to the point of the matter. Your little trade across the street has been bringing a lot of heat to my spot. I'm seeing a large decrease in my profit margins because of this. I don't know who gave you permission to open shop across the street, but this stops today! I suggest you take your little corner elsewhere, and we will still stand on good terms. If you don't listen, I will use force in a very destructive and dangerous way! It's your call."

O-Dawg wanted to interrupt Juice badly but kept his cool and let him finish what he had to say. If Juice thought he was like the other men, he would soon find out wrong.

"Let me explain something to you! Your threats don't mean shit to me! I would have more respect for you if you approached me differently or used a different perspective, but since you didn't...fuck you!" snapped O-Dawg before hanging up.

Hearing those disrespectful words and the nerve of O-Dawg hanging up the phone in his face made the veins bulge out on Juice's neck and forehead. It was the first time someone had ever spoken to him in such a manner.

"I'm going to kill that son-of-a-bitch along with every living thing he loves!" shouted Juice.

He took this beef between the two of them personally.

O-Dawg knew that in this game, beef of this nature would one day come his way. So, he had prepared himself ahead of time for this moment. Stocking up on his gun collection, he told all of his workers to buy any and all guns the fiends came by to sell or bargain for drugs. Within a few days, he acquired all kinds of artillery, from bulletproof vests to machine guns and assault rifles.He even had some grenades and C-4 explosives in his stock room in a storage garage within the suburbs.

Since O-Dawg was once involved in the organization, he knew a lot about their insights and manpower. He was ready for war and would make sure he made the first move. He knew their weakest and strongest points. So, attacking from the top and working his way down to the bottom was the best way to do things and critically hurt them. You cut the head off, and the organism will suffer.

Juice did not expect O-Dawg to retaliate first, so he gave him the benefit of the doubt. He decided to wait a week and see if his threat had any effect. In the meantime, his lieutenant would be keeping a close eye on the block.

O-Dawg wasn't playing. He gathered up his soldiers and met with them immediately, explaining the block's situation and the circumstances. These young boys were loyal to him and looked up to him as an idol. They were loose cannons and would do whatever it took to satisfy their boss. O-Dawg knew this, which was one of the main reasons he treated them as men while schooling them on the game of life.

After explaining the situation and breaking down the entire scenario and plan, he added, "These men that we're dealing with are trained professionals and experts at what they do. A lot of blood will be shed; some might even be our own. So, I want all of you to be prepared for what's to come. I will respect it if anyone backs out now."

When no one took a step back, he continued, "This is some real serious shit we're about to get deep into. Are y'all ready to catch bodies?"

"Fuck yeah!" shouted the crew in unison.

"Dawg, you know we're with you a hundred percent," said Lil Moses. "Fuck all those organization clowns! They don't put fear in our hearts!"

"Them clowns bleed just like us. So, whenever you're ready, we are," Nate chimed in.

"Alright, meet me back here in forty-five minutes and have a stolen mini-van with you. I'm gonna hit the storage and grab some guns," said O-Dawg.

"You don't gotta go anywhere. We got all the guns you need," said Dwayne, another crew member. "Let's get this shit poppin' right now!"

O-Dawg laughed at the young man's remark. "Shorty, it's more complicated than that. Haven't you heard anything I said? I have machine guns, some grenades, and explosives I want y'all to use."

O-Dawg walked out of the apartment and climbed into his truck. In record time, he made it to the storage place. Since it was starting to get dark out, he backed the SUV into the garage and loaded it with as many weapons and ammunition as possible. Almost forgetting about the Kevlar Vest, he made sure to put all seven of them in the back compartment before closing the door.

Making his way back to the projects, he parked the truck in the same spot as earlier and patiently waited for his crew to arrive. Fifteen minutes later, the young boys pulled up in a stolen black caravan. Their discipline and braveness put a smile on his face.

O-Dawg stepped out of his truck as the crew, dressed in all black, did the same. He then made his way to the back of the SUV and popped open the compartment door. He motioned for the crew to come over and help unload the truck.

"Here, put these on," he said while handing them each a bulletproof vest.

"Damn, these vests are heavy," Dwayne said in surprise.

"Yeah, and they can save your life, as well," replied O-Dawg as he also handed them all assault rifles.

"Oh shit! The only time I ever saw one of these was in the movies!" sang Bucky.

After showing the crew how to hold and use the large-caliber rifle, O-Dawg put two of the grenades in his pockets. The C-4 explosives would come in handy some other time—but not this time.

"Alright, now that we're lock and loaded, are y'all ready to bust ya guns?"

Even though the young boys had heart, they had never before dealt with such serious beef.

O-Dawg hoped they would prove themselves worthy and handle things well.

O-Dawg climbed in the driver's seat of the stolen mini-van as his crew followed suit, climbing inside through the sliding door. Once they were all situated, he went over the plan one last time. He wanted to make sure they were all on the same page. When he finished, he had to laugh to himself; the sight of the small figures wearing the vests was unbearably funny.

The small mini-van was jam-packed to its capacity. Being second in charge, Nate sat in the passenger seat. The rest of the crew were spread throughout—five in the back and two in the front. In total, there were seven guys. The side sliding door was left ajar for easy access purposes. This time of day was perfect because cars were bumper to bumper on the main streets. So, it would be difficult for the police to get through, which gave them more than enough time to do the job while maintaining a means of escape without worry.

O-Dawg turned left into the alleyway. All eyes were on the black caravan with the tinted windows.

The front lookout noticed it was O-Dawg and yelled, "*Está bien!*"

The lookout was not aware of the beef between the two bosses and was not told to be on alert for any retaliation.

After hearing from the front lookout that all was good, the men that were hustling let out a sigh of relief upon seeing the black mini-van coming their way. What they did not notice was the drama that was about to unfold right before their eyes. "Everyone put on your ski-mask." O-Dawg said.

The caravan came to a sudden halt about fifteen feet from where most of the fellas were gathered. Everyone froze and stared wide-eyed at the six masked men who jumped out holding machine guns. Thinking it was some vice squad or task force authorities, no one wanted to move.So, they stood their ground.

O-Dawg was the only one who didn't jump out of the caravan; he stayed put in the driver's seat. His heart raced from the adrenaline rush as he watched his little soldiers put in that work. He sat back, observing the surroundings and making sure no one came from an unexpected place.

The Young Gunz did not hesitate to let off rounds. Bodies jerked from the impact of the large bullets pumping out of the machine guns. The large-caliber rounds tore through flesh like a hot knife cutting through butter as bodies began to drop. Arms and torsos were torn apart, ligaments shredded. Blood violated the air space and the walls. The dirt had turned onto a wine color from the massive amount of red fluid on the ground. Every intended target was mortally wounded as the clips ran out of ammunition. Before they could reload their weapons, O-Dawg shouted for the young boys to get back inside the vehicle.

"Close the doors!" he screamed while driving away with tires screeching.

Reaching into his fatigue pants pocket, O-Dawg pulled out one of the grenades. Pulling the pin out with his teeth, he tossed the small green projectile out of the window. The powerful grenade hit the concrete floor, its impact severely strong—shattering nearby windows and sending the remaining body parts into the air and onto neighboring walls.

O-Dawg raced through the bumpy alleyway, making a right turn out the back. He then punched the gas pedal to the floor, running through stop signs about 100 mph through back roads. He had no mercy for the law and other drivers; he was not going back to jail.

CHAPTER 16

Months had gone by since Sam first started laying low, and no one had heard a peep from him. He called no one and severed all contact with his family members and friends. Sam would stay cooped up inside his Florida Beach mansion all day, inhaling the fumes from some exotic weed. His wife and daughter were not allowed to leave the premises or have friends over. The man was a nervous wreck and feared his family would get hurt. He faithfully carried an AK-47 assault rifle on a shoulder strap. He would even sleep with the weapon next to him in the bed. Sam would stay up throughout the entire night and only sleep when his wife and daughter were awake. He knew it wouldn't be much longer before Juice discovered his whereabouts. Money ruled, and people loved money.So, people would talk.

There were only two men who knew about Sam's mansion in Florida—Will and Junior. Even with them being long-time associates, Sam knew people would turn their back on their own mother for the right price. He was growing tired of living a paranoid lifestyle and would give anything to live a normal one again. He longed for the day when he would be able to walk the streets without a care, take his family shopping, and wine and dine in an exquisite restaurant without watching over his back every second of the day.

Sam decided it was time to move to a smaller place. With no money coming in to support the family, he had to use up the only savings he had. He wanted to find a place somewhere in the mountains where he and his family would be able to roam freely and not have to look over their shoulders constantly.

After a week of searching and with the help of his real estate agent, he found the perfect house. The small rancher was located in the mountains of Boulder, Colorado. It was nothing compared to what he was accustomed to, but it was as far away from any civilization as possible. One had to travel a mile up a bumpy dirt road before reaching the residence.

Sam left the Florida mansion just in time. The next day, after the last pieces of furniture were moved, a team of assassins stormed the luxurious beach house in search of him and his family. Their helper, Maria, who decided to stay behind had a key to the place and was removing the last bit of her clothing, when she felt someone behind her watching her every move. She turned around and dropped the shoeboxes she had been holding in her hands. She was terrified at the sight of the masked gunman pointing a gun in her direction. Maria could only think of one reason this man was here. She had a clue that Sam ran some sort of illegal business but did not know exactly what kind. All the years she had worked for him, and not once did it cross her mind that something like this would one day happen. She wanted to scream, but the sound would not escape her vocal cords.

"Where is Sam?" asked the masked gunman.

"I don't know. He moved out a couple of days ago," she answered in a quivering voice.

"I can see that. I'm not stupid. Where did he move to? I want an address."

"He didn't tell me where he was going. He just told me that he was moving."

Fearing for her life, Maria would have told this man anything he wanted to know.

"I tried to ask him, but he wouldn't say where. All he said was that I would be hearing from him. He left me his private number in case I was to need anything."

She was indirectly pleading with this man to spare her life.

"Who are you?" the gunman asked.

"I used to be his maid, but I quit about a week ago and was just stopping by to grab the rest of my stuff."

"Give me that phone number he left you!"

Reaching in her pocket, Maria removed the white piece of paper and handed it over.

"You should learn more about your employers before agreeing to work for them."

He thought about letting the poor immigrant live but remembered what his boss said: *There are to be no survivors left alive*! He could not bear to look into her eyes. "Turn around and face the wall!"

As soon as they lost eye contact, he squeezed the hairpin trigger, letting loose a barrage of gunfire that tore through the back of her cranium. Blood and brain fragments splattered across the floor and walls. The bullets entered through her skull and exited through the front of her face. Matone turned around and walked out of the room, shaking his head from side to side. He somewhat felt a little remorse for taking the beautiful young girl's life. The sound of someone speaking into the microphone grabbed his attention.

"Is all clear?"

"Yes, the upstairs is clear."

"What was that about?"

"A fucking cat came out and scared me!" lied Matone. "There's no one here. Let's move out!"

***

Sam almost jumped out of the recliner chair when he heard his private phone line ring. Only a handful of people had the number, so this definitely got his undivided attention. The last time that phone rang, he didn't receive good news. He hoped this wouldn't be the same kind of call. He answered on the fourth ring.

"Hello! Who is this?"

"Hello, my friend, Sam. Sorry we missed you today at your Florida Beach mansion. It would have been pleasant to have found you there."

"Who the fuck is this?!" Sam shouted into the phone's receiver. "How did you get my private number?"

"Let's just say your young beautiful maid volunteered that information to us."

"Where is she? What have you done with her? She has nothing to do with this! I swear that if you harm her in any way or my family, I will personally kill you all!"

"That's not a very nice thing to say, Sam. The bossman will not be happy about that," responded Matone. "You can run, but you can't hide. No matter where you run to, I will eventually find you, than awaken you and your family out of a nice deep sleep."

"Fuck you, whoever you are! You don't even have the balls to tell me your name! Come for me, if you have the balls. I'll be waiting! I got something special for you motherfuckas, especially your man Juice!"

"Don't be surprised by how fast we move; this is your warning. I will find you just like I found that maid bitch inside your estate. That was fast, wasn't it?"

"Fuck you! See me when you see me!" yelled Sam before hanging up.

Sam was at a point where he didn't care anymore as long as his family would be safe. He thought about Maria and cursed himself for not protecting her the way he should have.

"Just when I thought these people were gonna leave me alone and let me be. They had to come and fuck shit up."

He could only think of one man who could surely take care of this ongoing situation between him and Juice. Unclipping the cell phone from his waistband, he made the overseas call. He paced back and forth through the living room as the phone played its sixth ring.

"Hola, who am I speaking to?"

Sam was relieved when the call was answered and quickly said, "Juan! It's Sam. We really need to talk."

"Sam, this better be important. By the way, is this a secure line you're calling me from?"

"I know better than to call you on an unsecured line," lied Sam.

He knew this could cost him his friendship with the cocaine cowboy, but all he cared about was getting Juice off his back.

"Well, what is it? Speak your mind, and make it fast! You know I'm a busy man."

He sounded agitated because Sam interrupted a head job session with a young beautiful Mexican call girl.

Sam explained the entire situation between him and Juice. When he finished, he added, "This asshole even killed my maid who was like family to me! If I hadn't moved from my Florida Beach house, I wouldn't be talking to you right now. I would be dead by the same hit squad he sent to my house! I've busted my ass for twelve years to build that empire. I took you up on your proposition for my retirement, and *this* is how I get treated in return. I don't want anything to do with the organization. I don't want to collect any rent from you guys either. All I ask is that you get Juice off my ass so I can live a peaceful life."

"Sam, my friend, I've never known you to act this way. If this is really bothering you, I'll speak to Juice personally and try to come to a conclusion about the situation. I cannot make you any promises, though."

"Juan, this is not only bothering me; it's destroying my life. I hope you can fix this problem for me and my family. I would really appreciate your help."

***

The federal investigators finally got the break they had been patiently waiting for. After all the years of investigating Sam and his corporation, they finally caught him slipping. They could not believe their luck as they eavesdropped on the entire conversation between the drug kingpin and drug baron. They even had the conversation between Sam and Maria's killer on tape. Now, all they had to do was put a face to the murderer's voice. The Feds already knew who Juice was and his entire background.

What they were skeptical about was this Juan character. From the conversation Sam held with Juan, it seemed as if Juan was a well-respected man who controlled a lot of people. Hearing Sam mention he had handed over the organization, the Feds figured Juan was also dealing drugs. This entire case revolved around Sam and all the information he knew. They could not afford to have him killed; it would destroy the investigation they had been working for so many years. They would use this information to their advantage and see if Sam would flip. They were not yet ready to bring him into custody without first finding out more about this Juan character.

***

Duce felt some type of way for killing his long-time friend, Andy, but the closer he got to collecting the hit money, the less stressful the situation became. Money made people do some ruthless things. Knocking on the apartment door to the address he was given, he waited patiently for someone to answer.

Matone opened the door and greeted Duce.

"What's up? You came to collect that money, huh?"

"Yeah, I need that money right now," responded Duce. "My stash is running kinda low."

"Come inside. The man is waiting for you in the living room," said Matone as he stepped aside, letting Duce walk through the door.

As Duce walked into the living room quarters, he noticed Juice smoking an expensive cigar on the sofa. Duce's heart raced as the realization of being alone in a room full of assassins hit him. Not wanting anyone to pickup on his nervousness, he took a seat on the opposite couch.

"Duce, my friend, it's good to know you came through for an old man!" Juice said. "I want to show my appreciation by offering you a full-time position in my organization as one of my hitmen. That was a magnificent job you did. Now tell me how it all went down while we sip on some expensive cognac."

Although the offer sounded enticing, Duce did not know what to say. Picking up the shotglass that Juice had poured for him, he swallowed the brown substance in one gulp. After setting the small glass down on the coffee table, he told Juice how he had killed Andy, explaining step by step in great detail. When he finished, he gulped down another shot, after which Juice poured for him a third one. Juice was trying to get Duce drunk so the man would continue running his mouth.

Feeling the effects of the alcohol, Duce let his impaired judgment do the thinking for him and agreed to become one of Juice's hitmen. He was determined to show Juice that he could do exactly what he and his men were capable of doing, and maybe even more.

"I'm in, and if there's anything you need me to take care of, just let me know…and it's a done deal. He'll be murdered, his body disposed of, and they'll never find the murder weapon nor the suspect."

"Everything is cool as of now, my friend," said Juice. "But you'll be the first to know if anything comes up, I promise. Now, let's not waste anymore time. Your fifty thousand dollars is in that bag over there."

He pointed towards the black gym bag sitting in a corner by a closet door.

"Take it and be on your way. I will contact you when the next job is lined up."

Duce was anxious to get his hands on the money so he could immediately start balling. He was already thinking of ways to spend the Benjamins. Walking over to the black gym bag, he crouched down and unzipped the bag. His eyes grew wide from the excitement of seeing all the bundles of cash. Zipping the bag back up, he slung the strap over his shoulder and proceeded to turn around.

"Yo, Juice, good looking…"

He froze in place, shocked to see the large-caliber pistol pointed at him.

"What the fuck is this?! I thought we had a deal?"

"My friend, I do not trust you men here in the United States. You men do not live by the code of honor. Therefore, I cannot risk the chances of you running off at the mouth about my business."

"Juice, how can you judge me and say I'm like the rest of them? Look at what I've done for you."

"You did not do it because I said to do it. You did it because I paid you to do it. Money talks while bullshit runs a marathon," snapped Juice.

He was tired of talking and wanted Duce silenced.

"I'm finished talking with you, my friend. Matone, *matalo!*" Juice shouted, ordering the killing of Duce.

Matone, who had been standing guard at the door, pulled out the .357 hammerless Magnum from his waistband and began approaching his victim. Cocking the gun loaded, he pointed the barrel at Duce's head.

"Juice, please don't let him kill me! I'll do whatever it is you want me to—"

The last words didn't get the chance to escape Duce's mouth as the six shots entered through his face, leaving holes the size of a quarter and exit wounds the size of a walnut. When the body hit the floor, most of the face was missing. Huge chunks of tissue and blood had splattered onto the walls and floor. As his lungs took in a final breath, he thought about Andy,whose life he took and how he would now be joining him.*What goes around comes around!*

"What do you want me to do with the body, boss?" asked Matone.

"Get rid of it, you damn fool! Throw it into the river but make sure to tie cinder blocks around him. I don't need a body popping up somewhere along the Delaware River. Do it the right way, or it's your ass!"

***

While Juice focused his attention on Duce, he had no idea what had just transpired inside the organization. He had given O-Dawg too much time and underestimated his power. He did not know the man was as ruthless as him or anybody else; his only soft spot was children.

Leaving Matone to take care of Duce's body, Juice climbed into his Range Rover and made his way towards the house of a friend named Yalonda for an incredible head job. He always kept his phone turned off whenever taking care of an important situation. Remembering the device, he reached into his pocket, retrieved the iPhone, and turned it on. Glancing at the display screen, he saw that he had ten missed calls and four voice messages, some marked urgent. Dialing his voicemail's number, he switched the phone's feature to Bluetooth and listened as the message played through the SUV's speakers. The second message, which was marked urgent, made him swerve towards oncoming traffic. Regaining control of the vehicle, he placed the phone down on the passenger's seat while he thought about what he just heard.

His comrade, Ralph, who had taken over Ruben's position as chief in charge, left him a message concerning the dramatic events within the empire.Wondering what had to be so urgent by the sound of Ralph's voice, Juice skipped the rest of the messages and dialed his chief's number.

Ralph answered on the first ring. He already knew who the caller was and didn't give Juice the chance to speak.

"Boss, stop by my place as soon as possible. What I have to tell you cannot be said over the phone, and you're not gonna like what happened."

"Enough said. I'm on my way!"

In Juice's mind, he was not prepared for the outcome of this tragedy.

Ralph lived a few blocks over from the empire. Before reaching his residence, Juice realized the police had a barricade established so no one could get through. Many law enforcement agents were surrounding the area, about half-square miles of the perimeter. FBI agents, along with ATF agents, were among the many forces at the scene. No vehicles were allowed access through and instead had to follow a detour put up by the police.

Juice made a left towards the detour and was shocked halfway through the turn. He could not believe his eyes. Half-mile down the road there were ambulances, paramedics, and a host of other authorities in front of the empire. It looked like a scene out of a movie. Juice was furious but did not have a damn clue what happened. Many reasons as to what took place crossed his mind, but not one of those thoughts was about O-Dawg.

Juice hated that he had to park the Range Rover a few blocks away from Ralph's house. With most blocks barricaded by the police, he had to walk about a quarter mile. Reaching the house Ralph was already outside, along with every other nosey person in the neighborhood. Walking through the front gate, Juice approached his comrade with an extended hand.

"What the fuck happened?" he asked as they shook hands.

Juice was paranoid; he hoped the police were not there for him.

"I've been trying to contact you since the shit first went down, but I kept getting your voicemail. Come inside, and I'll explain everything to you. There are too many nosey-ass people out here."

Anxious to find out what was going on, as soon as Juice stepped foot inside the house, he asked, "What the fuck happened? Get to the point!"

Ralph explained every detail to his boss of what went down—from the color of the van, description of the assailants and driver, how many rounds were fired and even about the grenade being tossed.

"How do you know for sure it was O-Dawg who pulled this stunt?" asked Juice.

His subconscious kept telling him that he shouldn't have slept on an enemy. He also thought that American-born Hispanics didn't have the balls to orchestrate something of such a severe nature.

"The front lookout saw him entering the alleyway in the caravan and yelled *esta bien*. Can't blame the man. He was not aware of the situation with O-Dawg."

"How many bodies we have, and who were they?" asked Juice.

"We know it was six people who got killed, but we don't yet know all of their identities. I do know for sure that one of the bodies was Marco and another was Bert."

"The man killed some of my men *and* put a stop to my operation!" Juice shouted. "I swear on my mother's grave that when I find him, I'm going to cut him into pieces. But first, I'm gonna kill every living thing he loves! Find out where his family lives. Pronto!"

The fear people felt for Juice always got him what he wanted in record time. Within fifteen minutes, Ralph had the information ready for his boss. All it took was a simple phone call and some bribe money.

"Boss, we can't locate his mother, but I have the address to his father's place."

"That's good enough for right now," responded Juice.

He removed his cell phone from its case on his waist and dialed his number one assassin's phone number.

"Matone, are you done taking out the trash?"

"Yes, boss. I'm now on my way to wash up."

"Forget about washing up! I need you over here at Ralph's place right now!"

Matone rarely heard his boss yell the way he did because Juice was not the type to let his anger get the best of him. So, he knew that whatever it was, it had to be serious. Rushing out of his apartment, he climbed into his Jeep Cherokee and pulled into traffic. Within ten minutes, he had arrived at his destination.

Juice and Ralph were standing outside on the porch, inhaling a blunt of exotic potent Kush. Juice passed the blunt to Matone as he approached the porch and gave the guys some dap.

"*Que pasa? Estas bien?*"

"Nah! That man O-Dawg done signed his own death certificate and his family's!" Juice responded. "I have his father's address, and we're going over there right now. When we're done at his father's place, I want the both of you to find out where the rest of his family lives. I doubt he's at his residence at this time, and he doesn't have a wife or kids, which narrows down our search. Bring a hammer with you and a few guns. Let's go!" Juice said, than turned to Ralph. "We'll wait for you in the car."

***

O-Dawg's father lived in a two-story row house located on the city's borderline, which connected the city and the suburbs. As the sun hid behind the horizon and darkness started to fall, Juice and his men waited patiently parked across the street inside of a tinted SUV. Once total darkness fell, all three men quietly stepped out of the truck and walked towards the house. Ralph was a pro-locksmith and was a professional at picking locks. As he worked on the locks, Matone and Juice listened for any noise coming from within the house. The lights were on inside, but it looked as if no one was home.

O-Dawg's father sat in his favorite rocking chair, watching *Sabado Gigante* on the television. He had been watching the Hispanic TV game show since his early teens. He even remembered his mother watching it every Saturday morning. He dozed off into a light sleep. The two half-pints of rum he drank earlier had him feeling drowsy. The television's volume was blasted, and he had the headphones connected to the TV. So, the old man couldn't hear lightning if it struck.

The three men entered the house through the back kitchen door, undetected. Matone headed upstairs while Ralph checked the basement and Juice checked the first floor. As the three men split up, Juice made his way into the living room and noticed the old man in the rocking chair asleep. Only weighing in at a buck twenty, his featherweight body made no noise on the hardwood floor as he approached the old man.

Placing the barrel of the gun on the man's temples, Juice said, "Don't move, or I'll blow your fucking brain on the walls!"

139

Due to the loud volume of his headphones, the old man did not hear a word said but felt the cold steel against his head. Turning his attention away from the TV and focusing it on the pressure point, he noticed the short, slim Hispanic male with the gun. O-Dawg's father was an original gangster in Puerto Rico back in the late 60s. So, the man in front of him with the gun did not intimidate him one bit.

Removing the headphones, he said, "What are you doing inside of *mi casa?*! How the hell did you get in?"

Less than a minute later, Ralph and Matone arrived in the living room and surrounded the man. Matone walked over to the television and turned it off before searching for some tape and rope. Ralph searched around for any signs of family members' whereabouts. He rampaged through the drawers and cabinets, looking for an address book or any other resourceful information that would lead them to O-Dawg.

Looking at the old man, Juice finally answered his question. "Your son got way out of line and is the reason why we're here. We want to leave him a message and show him who he's fucking with! But, first, I need you to tell me where he is."

"I don't know where he's at nor do I give a shit! That boy comes around here when he feels like it! I don't get involved with his personal life nor do I ask questions about it!" replied Francisco.

He loved his son dearly but disapproved of his dangerous lifestyle. But no matter what, he would not volunteer any information regarding his son, even if it meant laying down his life.

Juice knew the man wasn't telling the truth. He could see right through the bold lie.

"Tie him up to that chair over there," Juice ordered, pointing toward the dining room.

"Get the fuck up, you old fart!" Ralph snapped as he shoved the man towards the dining area.

After Francisco's hands and ankles were secured to the chair, Juice said, "This is your last chance! Where does your son rest his head at night?"

"I told you I don't know, and my answer ain't gonna change! Do whatever it is you came here to do, and let's get this over with!"

Juice could not believe the old man's bravery; he definitely had the heart of a lion. It was the first time in all the years he had been in the game that he heard a man speak of death without fear, and for that reason, Juice would respect him even after his death.

Making his way into the kitchen, Juice grabbed the biggest butcher knife he could find from the cabinet drawer. Opening another cabinet, he removed a pound of salt from the shelf before making his way back into the living room.

"Gag him."

Ralph shoved a piece of cloth into the man's mouth and tied another piece of cloth around his head, holding the gag in place. Juice then approached old man Francisco and cut off his shirt with the butcher knife. He continued by cutting small incisions into the man's arms, back, and chest area. The small incisions hurt like hell, but the old man looked Juice in the eyes with no fear. When Juice reached the count of fifty incisions, he stopped, turned around, and grabbed the pound of salt from the floor.

Francisco was sweating bullets, but he already knew what was about to take place. He once used this same technique on several victims back in his gangster days. So, he prepared himself mentally for the outcome of this torture.

Juice poured half the bag of salt into the old man's wounds. The salt seeped through the small openings, producing a powerful stinging sensation. Muffled screams could be heard as the old man shook violently against the restraints. Juice poured the rest of the salt into the wounds and watched as the incisions absorbed the small sand-like pebbles.

Francisco was exhausted but still showed no fear against his torturers. There wasn't anything that was going to break him into releasing his son's whereabouts. He was prepared for whatever they had in store for him. He knew this wasn't the only trick they would have up their sleeves. His gag was removed, and once again, the same questions were asked, but he would not give in. This made Juice even angrier.

"I will continue to torture you, then find and kill your entire family until I get the answer

I'm looking for!" Juice threatened while looking the old man directly in the eyes.

"Fuck you and the boat you came in!" shouted Francisco. "Hurry up and kill me because you're not getting that answer from me, you bastard!"

Stuffing the gag back into the man's mouth, Juice grabbed the hammer from the floor and began repeatedly whacking him over the head with it. The first few blows immediately knocked Francisco unconscious, so he did not feel a thing from then on. Juice continued hitting the old man with the hammer all over his body, breaking almost every bone. His skull caved in from the powerful blows, and his nasal bone was punctured.

Exhausted, Juice was now prepared to leave.

"Matone, would you do the honors of finishing the job? We'll be in the car waiting on you."

In less than a minute, Matone had emptied the entire extended clip of the TEC-9 semi-automatic handgun, leaving Francisco with over thirty bullet wounds—many of them to his facial and chest area.

CHAPTER 17

Kenny was starting to fall in love with the state of Texas. The topless bars and rave nightclubs were where he spent most of his nights. Things were now beginning to fall into place financially for him. With the squad of Texas Hood Stars on his team and a strip bringing in massive amounts of blood money, he was again back on his grind. Everyone in Texas knew him as Alex. He kept a low profile and would tell anyone he met that he was from California. Kenny was careful not to mention the state of New Jersey. He feared if he did his past would catch up with him.

Everyone knew him to be an out-of-towner because of his swagger, which was much different than everyone's swagger in Texas. Many guys disliked and hated on him due to his style but didn't dare test his patience. The crew he kept around him from Texas had much respect and was feared throughout the entire state. The fear and respect people held for this crew rubbed off on Kenny, making him feel untouchable.

He would keep in constant contact with his uncle in Philadelphia, who kept him up to date on the U.S. Marshals and when they would drop by searching for him. So, all in all, he felt like he had the upper hand.

On this particular day, Kenny decided to go to the mall to buy the new pair of Jordans that had just dropped in the stores. During the ride, he carefully steered the platinum-colored Cadillac Escalade on the highway towards the city of Houston while he thought about how good life in Texas had turned out for him in the past six months.

Arriving at his destination, he parked the expensive SUV in a tight parking space and prayed no one would hit his vehicle. Climbing out of the truck, he was amazed at all the single females surrounding the area.

Damn! There are mad bitches out here today! I'm guaranteed to bag me one to take to the motel tonight, Kenny thought to himself as he made his way into the mall and straight to the Foot Locker store.

Not waiting for an employee to help him, he approached the first person he saw wearing a Foot Locker T-shirt and said, "Yo, fam, do y'all have the new Jordans that came out today?"

Kenny must have been the fiftieth person to ask for the new sneakers, so the employee knew exactly what he wanted.

"Yes, we have them in stock. What size do you need?"

"I need a eight and a half, and can you bring me a pair of tan Timberland boots in the same size?"

As the sales-man went for the boxes, Kenny suddenly heard someone say his name.

"Kenny? I know that ain't my boy all the way out here in Texas," Justice said.

In a state of shock, Kenny's jaw dropped upon laying eyes on the disfigured face. His first thought was Justice might be out to get him. It crossed both men's minds that one was there to kill the other.

Playing it cool, Kenny replied, "What up, my boy? What brings you out here? And in the same store as me? And what the fuck happened to your face?"

"I've been out here for a few months, visiting my wife's family," Justice said. "I've been thinking about moving out here. It's a long way from home, but I like the atmosphere here much better. What about you? What brings you out here?"

"I live here now...been out here for six months now," responded Kenny. "Damn, this is a small world we live in."

Both men knew there was more to the reason they were in Texas than what was said. Neither man had a clue on why the other was so far away from home. Noticing that Justice did not answer the question about his face, Kenny left well enough alone.

"What are you doing in the mall?"

"I came to buy them new Jordans that hit the shelves today," Justice said.

Both men broke out in laughter.

"What are you getting into tonight? I know this nice titty bar in downtown Houston we can check out."

"Shit, that sounds good to me. We can catch up on things while we're at it, but I'm gonna have to pass on tonight. I have dinner plans with the wife," lied Justice. "How about this weekend?"

"Whatever day suits you better. Put my number in your phone, and give me a call whenever you're ready."

When Justice finished saving Kenny's number, he said, "I was wondering if you had any of that exotic bud with you. Since I haven't learned my way around here yet, I haven't been able to smoke."

"You know I keeps that sticky icky in the pocket of my dickies," replied Kenny, spitting a verse from Sheek Louch of The Lox. "I have it in my truck. I got you when we're done here."

Both men paid for their sneakers and then made their way out of the mall. On the way towards the truck, Kenny could not stop staring at Justice's disfigured face. He could not shake the thought of what must have happened. He was anxious to find out what took place, but his better judgment told him to wait until they went out to the strip club to ask again.

"This is you right here?" asked Justice, pointing to the Escalade.

"Yeah, this is just one of the rides in my collection. You know I gotta go hard or go home," Kenny mocked before handing Justice a Ziploc bag containing an ounce of exotic purple haze weed.

The green vegetation's odor was so strong that Justice could smell the weed before it even exchanged hands.

"How much do I owe you for this?"

"You don't owe me shit! That's on the strength of who we are and where we come from."

"Good looking! Best believe I'm gonna get up with you this weekend for that titty bar thing. Bring me another one of these Ziploc bags when we meet up this weekend. I'll pay you for the next one cause I know that one won't be free."

"Why wouldn't it be?" replied Kenny. "Shit, we go back to lunchbox days," he added as he switched on the ignition, bringing the powerful engine to life.

***

On the way home, Justice smoked on the Philly blunt filled with the exotic weed Kenny gifted him.

Retrieving his cell phone from his waistband, he dialed the out-of-state area code and number.

"What's good? Can you talk?"

O-Dawg did not recognize the number, but he recognized the familiar voice.

"Oh shit! What it do, cuz? How's Texas treating you?"

"Everything is everything. I kinda like it out here. But, yo, I called you because some funny-ass shit just happened while I was at the mall."

"You alright?" asked O-Dawg, starting to worry about his little cousin.

"Yeah, I'm good. Ain't nothing bad happened, but while I was inside Foot Locker, I ran into Kenny from the east side. Yeah, you're probably thinking the same thing I was thinking. What the fuck is he doing out here?"

"Oh shit! Word! So, that's where he's been hiding out. I bet they can't wait to find him."

"Why? What the fuck did he do?

"You ain't heard?! That man killed Fat-Chop."

"When did that happen?"

"A few months back. The shit was all over the news."

"How did the police find out he was the one who murdered him?"

"Homicide came to the hospital to question Riddles, who was with Chop when the shit popped off, and he ran his mouth to the police. You know that man is not built for this game. I don't know why Fat-Chop ain't just call his cousin Andy instead"

After hearing this, Justice relaxed. His wild thoughts were no longer fucking with him.

"I thought it was some funny shit going on since I'm on the run from Jersey, and I bump into a dude from Jersey."

"Stop being all paranoid you're good out there. Nobody knows you're in Texas, but me…and, of course, your man Kenny. Shit! After this, that man is probably gonna bounce from Texas. He might put in a little work, but he ain't 'bout nothing," continued O-Dawg. "We all bleed the same colored blood. Picture me being scared of another man who breathes the same air as me."

Justice noticed O-Dawg had quoted Biggie Small's lyrics.

"You want me to kill him?" asked Justice in a dead-serious tone. "Just say the word."

"Fallback, homie. I ain't got nothing against that man. Fat-Chop was my peoples, but you know as well as I do that it's survival of the fittest out here in these streets.We have instincts of a savage, so we gotta do what we gotta do to eat. That's just how I see things," added O-Dawg. "If you see things differently, then do you. Just don't go getting locked up. Bail money ain't the problem, but with them high-ass bails, it's not easy finding someone who will co-sign and be willing to lose their house or property…because we know your ass ain't going to court."

"The next time I get in some shit, there won't be bail. I'm a menace to society in their eyes. So, best believe I'm gonna be very cautious about what I do and the company I keep."

"You need any money?" O-Dawg asked, putting an end to their conversation.

"Nah, I'm good," lied Justice.

He didn't like to depend on anyone and felt some type of way taking money from a family member. However, he needed the cash. So, Justice decided to put his pride to the side.

"Actually, I do. Western Union me like nine thousand."

"Say less. It'll be there tonight. Just give me the address."

O-Dawg was going to mention the beef between him and Juice to his cousin but decided against it. Justice had too many problems going on in his life to be worried by more.

***

Justice had developed a plan; he just hadn't decided on going through with it or not. He juggled with the idea in his head for a couple of days before coming to a conclusion.

"Fuck it! Why not!" he said outloud. "I always thought of him as a clown anyway."

He had to first observe Kenny's movements and his daily routine before putting his plan into motion. By Wednesday, he had already gone through the ounce of Haze and decided to give Kenny an early ring for some re-up smoke. Kenny agreed to bring him the weed but said it had to be the next night, which was fine with Justice. It would give him another day of observing and planning. He wanted things to go accordingly and hoped the man would come alone. It didn't take him long to have Kenny's daily routine down to a tee. First thing in the morning after waking up, he would go to the store for a cup of coffee. Kenny then chilled on the block with the fellas for most of the day before heading to some female's house, where he would stay until around 3:00a.m. and then head home.

The following night after leaving the block, Kenny phoned Justice to let him know he was on his way. Justice had everything set and ready. While calmly waiting outside for Kenny to arrive, he noticed a dark blue BMW X5 pull up to the front of his crib.He was amazed by the beauty of the luxurious vehicle.

"This you right here?" he asked as Kenny stepped out of the vehicle.

"This shit belongs to my girl. I bought it for her on her birthday."

"You must be doing big things!" responded Justice, approaching him with an extended hand.

Kenny shook his hand and replied, "Money ain't about nothing. It comes, and it goes. Just like this right here." He handed over a large Ziploc bag containing a pound of Cush weed. "That's some fire right there."

Justice took the weed and was surprised at how leafy the buds looked.

"This shit looks a lot like cabbage. I've never seen no weed like this before. How much do I owe you?"

"You don't owe me shit, and I ain't taking your money! We from the same hood. That little bit of weed was out of my personal stash and didn't even put a dent in it. But, yo, I gotta get going. Make sure you get up with me on Friday night. I hope you ain't forget about our titty bar night out."

Having second thoughts about his plan, Justice decided to wait until Friday when he was sure they would be alone. He could not see inside the vehicle because of its dark-tinted windows, but he had a feeling someone was inside.

***

Friday night came around, and this time, Kenny pulled up in a candy-apple red, drop-top Jaguar.

Tonight is the night, thought Justice as they made their way towards downtown Houston.

Passing the blunt to Justice, Kenny said, "Taste this shit right here! This is that middle east Afghanistan chronic."

"Damn, you got all kinds of names for your weed."

"Wait till you get a hit of that Swedish Skunk I'ma bring you next time. That shit is gonna put you on your ass."

Justice could not help but laugh. He wondered how Kenny had managed to survive as long as he had in this grimy game. The man had the character of a clown and was as soft as cotton. Justice sat in the passenger's seat and gave as less feedback as possible during the ride.

Arriving at Supreme's Top Notch Strip Club, Justice felt some type of way for having to pay the forty-dollar cover charge. He was surprised and disgusted when he walked in and saw girls giving guys blowjobs and others bent over in the doggystyle position, getting banged from behind. The atmosphere smelled of stale cigarettes and sex. Justice could not believe the nerves of these trifling individuals. The sight and stench turned his stomach, almost making him throwup his evening meal. Not wanting to spoil their night, he promised himself to make the best of it.

"I love this place! You don't see shit like this back home!" shouted Kenny over the loud music as they took their seats in the VIP lounge and placed their drink orders.

Justice noticed that all the girls were on top of Kenny ever since they walked through the entrance doors.

"I see they love you up in this place," Justice commented.

"Shit, with all the money I spend in this place, they don't have a choice but to love me. We all know they don't *love* me love me; what they love is my money. Pick any of these girls in here, and I'll guarantee you'll fuck tonight—everything paid for by me."

Ever since the car bombing took place, Justice started wearing hooded sweatshirts to hide his disfigured facial features. He had lost all of the confidence he had with women and stayed away from them as much as possible. The only woman allowed next to him and in his bed was his wife. The titty bar was part of his plan to win over Kenny's trust. So, he was left with no other alternative but to participate in this event.

"I'll take that one right there in the blond hair, but she would have to shower first," he said, feeling uncomfortable.

Feeling the discomfort vibe coming from Justice, Kenny changed the subject.

"Drink up! It's on me tonight."

The liquor had Kenny's tongue loose. He spoke about the ins and outs of his operation but was careful not to mention vital details. Justice listened with much interest, taking in all the useful information.

The two men stood at the bar until three in the morning, when the lounge officially closed. Justice was ready to rob Kenny, but once again, he put a hold on the jux. Upon hearing Kenny say that the two should go out clubbing the next night, he agreed with the drug kingpin. He would wait it out until he knew everything about Kenny's operation.

***

The next night, both men went out to a rave nightclub and another titty bar the following night. In each place they visited, Kenny received the same respect from everyone as the last place. This same routine went on for a few weeks, and every time the two were together, Justice learned more and more about the man's operation.

It was a great feeling for Kenny to be able to show off his luxurious lifestyle to someone from his hometown. He wanted people in New Jersey to know he still had his freedom and was balling at the same level—even after committing a murder. He liked Justice, even though the two never hung out together back home. He was starting to build a trust bond with him, and as time went by, he let him in on the entire ins and outs of his operation. Kenny even disclosed his drug connection to Justice, which no one ever did because it violated the street code.

On this night, they were out to yet another stripbar.

As both men sat at the VIP lounge Kenny asked, "Have you made up your mind about moving out here permanently?"

"I've been in Texas for a while now, and my wife actually likes it out here.So, yeah, I'm gonna stay."

"So, you ready to get this money with me?"

Justice was surprised Kenny wanted him to join forces with him. He had only known the man for about a month, and not too many drug lords would let that happen. This spelled out *"Kenny is soft"* right across his forehead.

"Shit, the way you're balling, why wouldn't I wanna be your right-hand man?"

Justice used the term "right-hand man" to demonstrate what position he was only willing to take.

By the following week, Justice had everything in the operation down to a tee. Winning Kenny's trust was like taking candy from a baby, and it was now time to put his plan in motion. He stayed as far away as possible from the rest of the team. He did not want to draw attention to himself since he planned on staying in Texas. Once he got rid of Kenny, he did not want his crew members coming after him. So, the less they saw and knew about him, the better of a chance his plan went smoother. To stay out of the limelight, he gave Kenny $10,000 of his own money to invest. Justice knew he would see his money back plus a hundredfold. He wasn't planning on having their friendship last this long, but things were working out for the better.

The right moment presented itself. Kenny phoned Justice to ask him if he wanted to come along with him to re-up.

"I have to meet the connect out in Cali. It's a long ride, but if you want, you can relax in the back of the truck and watch movies."

"Yeah, I'm wit' it," Justice said. "Just come pick me up whenever you're ready."

"I'll be there in a few, and bring your ratchet along. I ain't never have a problem out there, but we play for keeps in this game. Anything can go wrong."

Justice waited patiently for Kenny's arrival. He was as excited as a kid on his first day at an amusement park. Kenny moved a few kilos of heroin and cocaine each week. So, Justice knew there had to be at least a couple hundred grand riding on this move. Since he always wore a hooded sweatshirt, one could not tell he had a Kevlar vest underneath. He was prepared with twin .45 caliber automatics—one in a shoulder holster and the other in the pocket of his sweatshirt, a seven-shot .380 pistol in an ankle holster, and extra clips in his fatigue pants pockets. He also brought along a razor-sharp Rambo knife as a precaution.

Half an hour later, Justice heard a horn blaring in front of the apartment building. He knew it was Kenny as soon as his phone started ringing. Without answering the device, he quickly made his way outside. Approaching the Cadillac Escalade, he noticed someone sitting in the front passenger seat.

Fuck! I thought he was coming alone. Now, I gotta catch two bodies, he thought to himself as he climbed into the backseat.

"What it do, fool?" greeted Kenny, giving Justice some dap. "You remember my man T-Roc from McClain Housing Projects?"

"Yeah, what's good?" said Justice, giving the man some dap while fingering the .45 caliber he had in his sweatshirt's front pocket.

"Roll this up for me," Kenny ordered, handing Justice a blunt and a bag of weed. "That's some Jamaican Chocolate Thia. You ever see the movie *Shottas*?" he asked.

"Nah. Why you ask?"

"That's what I just put into the DVD player. You gotta see this shit!"

Justice had already seen the movie but played dumb. *You and your peoples are about to be part of my movie,* he thought to himself.

Twenty-five minutes into the ride towards California, T-Roc was into the movie while Kenny diverted his eyes back and forth from the DVD monitor to the road. Justice wasn't going to wait until they were across state lines to do what he planned. It was too risky to do it in unfamiliar territory. He did not care about the kilos; what he wanted was the money.

It's now or never, he thought as he reached in his sweatshirt pocket and shoulder holster to retrieve the powerful .45 caliber handguns. In one swift motion, he pointed both weapons to the back of each man's head.

Feeling the cold steel pressed against their heads, both men turned around.

"What the fuck—"

Kenny's words were cut short as Justice smacked him across the face with the gun.

"Shut the fuck up and keep driving! Get off on the next exit, turn this truck around, and go back in the direction we came from!"

"I told you not to trust this man!" shouted T-Roc. "I knew he was a snake from day one when I first laid eyes on him!"

"Since I'm a snake, you're gonna lay with the snakes."

Boom!

A single bullet sent T-Roc's brain fragments splattering all over the passenger side window and dashboard. Blood squirted from the half-dollar-sized hole in the back of T-Roc's head. Since his seat belt was on, his body did not slump forward, but his head did.

"Now, if you don't wanna end up like your boy, I suggest you keep your hands on the steering wheel and drive to your crib!"

"Justice, I thought we were bigger than this. How you gonna cross me like this?"

"You just said the keyword—*thought*. It's survival of the fittest in these streets. So, stop acting like a bitch and roll with the punches. Better it be me who robs you than one of these Texas clowns."

"There's 230,000 thousand dollars stashed underneath the backseat. Take it and let's forget this ever happened. I'll take care of T-Roc's body."

"Do I look stupid to you? I know you got more money at your spot, and I want it all. Now, shut the fuck up and keep driving!"

Due to the dark tinted windows, no one could see the limped body in the passenger's seat or the blood splattered on the windows.

Arriving at Kenny's residence, Justice was surprised at the sight of the expensive house. One thing Kenny did not disclose to anyone was where he rested his head at night.

"Damn, homie! Big things are definitely poppin'!" said Justice as he eyed the massive structure with its luxury vehicles lining the driveway. "Who else is inside?"

"My wife, but she's probably still sleeping. I'm gonna give you all of the money. Just please don't kill me or my wife."

"You don't have a choice but to give me all the money. And I haven't decided if I'm gonna kill you or not. You got some balls asking for mercy when you didn't give Fat-Chop any!"

"So, that's what this is about? He shot up my crib and tried to kill me. How the fuck was I supposed to react?!"

"This ain't got shit to do with Chop! This is about me needing to feed my family while I'm on the run from Johnny Law," replied Justice. "Now, open the fucking door before your neighbors have to pick up your body from the pavement!"

Once they were inside Kenny's house, Justice immediately said, "Take me to the stash, and don't try no funny shit if you wanna live."

Upon entering the master bedroom, the beautiful naked creature lying across the bed asleep was the first thing to catch Justice's eye.

"Honey, I'm home!" he shouted, imitating Kenny's voice.

At the sound of what she thought was her husband's voice, Tamika opened her eyes. She let out a near-piercing scream when she saw the scary-looking intruder holding her man at gunpoint.

"Scream again, bitch, and I'm gonna put a fourth hole in your body!" Justice threatened. "Go sit your ass in that chair," he ordered Kenny, pointing towards the recliner in the far-right corner. "Now, get your sexy ass up and tie your man up. If you leave the knots loose on the rope, I'm gonna let some of the bullets fly from this gun."

After Kenny was secured to the chair, Justice asked, "Now, where's the stash?"

Kenny looked at his wife and gave her a look as if to say, *Don't try anything*. He knew she was a ride-or-die chick, but he would rather them give up the money than risk losing their lives.

"It's behind that picture," he answered, pointing at the expensive artwork hanging on the wall. "The combination to the safe is 23-14-64-79."

Justice knew better than to turn his back on them.

Looking over at Tamika, he said, "Bitch, what are you waiting for—an invitation? Open it!"

Walking up to the bed, he removed a case from one of the pillows and tossed it to her.

"Put all the money in here!" he ordered.

Tamika was deeply in love with Kenny and would do anything to protect him. She wasn't trying to go out like a chump, and she damn sure wasn't going to let this man rob them of all their life savings. She debated with herself on what to do as she fingered the gun inside the safe. When she finished stuffing the bundles of cash inside the pillowcase, she swiftly turned around, holding a 9mm Beretta in her left hand.

"Drop your gun!" she ordered.

Justice started laughing. He watched as her hands trembled uncontrollably.

"Shoot 'em, baby!" Kenny cheered.

Tamika hesitated a second too long, which gave Justice the chance to squeeze the trigger. The thunderous roar from the powerful pistol echoed off the walls, leaving everyone in the room deaf. Kenny looked on in shock at his wife's body falling to the floor—two large holes in her chest.

Approaching the corpse, Justice grabbed the pillowcase full of money next to the body and turned his attention towards Kenny.

"Thanks for the money, and when your soul transitions, let my boy Chop know I said what's up."

Boom!

Justice took the steps two at a time as he rushed to get out of the house before authorities arrived on the scene. He knew the rest of the money was inside of the Escalade, so he quickly climbed in the truck and sped away.

Looking over at T-Roc's lifeless body, he thought, *Homie, I bet your dumb-ass wishes you would've stayed home today. Now, look at you!*

D.N.A. was a culprit in crime scenes, and the smallest piece of fiber unseen by man's eye could leave a person with a life sentence or worse, the death penalty. Knowing this, Justice made a right turn into a wooded area not too far from his home, parked the Escalade, and climbed out. Opening the rear passenger door, he removed the pillowcase, which he had placed in the backseat, then retrieved the rest of the money hidden underneath the seat. He now had two bags of cash, which he set down on the ground. Retrieving a piece of cloth from the rear compartment, Justice stuffed it into the gas tank, pulled out a lighter from his pants pocket, and set the cloth on fire.

Justice watched from a safe distance as the truck went up in flames. He would not leave until he was sure all of the evidence had been destroyed. Five minutes later, he heard the loud explosion, which was like music to his ears. Now satisfied, he carefully made his way out of the wooded area. He glanced in all directions, making sure no passersby spotted him as he made his way to the main street.

Unclipping the cell phone from his waistband, he dialed his home number. After giving his wife directions to his location, he patiently waited for her.

When she arrived, the first words out of her mouth were, "Boy, what the hell is inside those bags?"

"Money be the rule to all evil! Now, let's pack our bags when we get home, and I'll let you decide our destination."

As his wife pulled off, Justice reclined the passenger seat and zoned out, distracted by thoughts of what just took place.

CHAPTER 18

Sam knew he had to keep him and his family moving. He had a bad feeling something was going down. Regardless, he wasn't going to let anything stop him from catching a flight the following morning to the Dominican Republic. Sam had received a call from the mayor of the city where he had built his empire warning him that he was under investigation by the Feds. He knew this was not a game. He had been friends with the mayor since middle school and hung out with him on many occasions. Back in the day, the mayor would help bag up cocaine to help pay for his college tuition. Between Sam and Junior, these two powerful connected hood figures donated more than five million dollars to the mayor's campaign. Without their connections and money, Mr. Melendez would not have won the election.

Sam felt he had no time to pack, so the furniture and the rest of their belongings would have to be left behind.

"Babe! Hurry up!" he yelled upstairs to his wife, wanting to get out of the house ASAP.

"Hold on! I'm looking for my purse!" she shouted in return. She hated when he acted paranoid.

When she got downstairs, the whole family quickly made their way into the garage. After securing his daughter into the car seat of the CL 500 Benz, Sam climbed into the car, pushed the small button on the garage remote, and put the vehicle in reverse. When the garage door fully opened, he pressed the gas pedal with his foot and slowly backed the car out. Before Sam could reach the end of the driveway, a team of FBI agents in unmarked sedans swarmed on the scene, blocking the exit.

"Shit!" he yelled, knowing this was the end.

Sam knew this day was bound to come but did not think it would be today. He was too busy running and hiding from Juice, which occupied most of his thoughts. With nowhere else to run and with twenty federal agents pointing their government-issued Glocks in his direction, he made the choice of not putting up a fight and surrendered.

"Turn off the car's engine and put your hands in the air!" shouted the agent in charge.

Sam did as he was ordered and was immediately yanked out of the car. He was forcefully thrown to the ground face-first—his face smacking against the pavement.

"Samuel Vargas, you are under arrest for the continuance of a criminal enterprise and trafficking narcotics across state lines. You have the right to remain silent. You have the right to an attorney. If you cannot afford one, the courts will appoint one for you..."

"Babe, call my lawyer and tell him what happened," Sam told his wife while being escorted to an unmarked car. "I'll be at the county jail waiting for him."

"Your wife will not be giving your lawyer a call because she will be coming along for the ride. She is a suspect in this case and will also be charged with conspiracy to manufacture, distribute, and traffick narcotics. Agent Stevenson, could you read her rights?"

Sam was stunned; he could not believe what was happening. His kids would be put into foster care or released in the care of a family member. He had to put a stop to this; he couldn't let his family down or see his wife behind bars. On the ride downtown towards the federal detention center, Sam thought of a solution to his problem. If he testified against anyone the authorities wanted him to, Sam was sure he and his wife would go free.

When they arrived at the FBI headquarters, Sam and his wife were placed in separate rooms. He knew they would question them. She knew nothing about his drug-dealing lifestyle, so there was nothing she could comment on or contradict him about. His legs were shaking terribly; no matter how hard he tried, he could not keep them still. One good thing was he taught his wife never to break under pressure.

I wonder how much these motherfuckas know, he thought to himself. *Shit, they probably know everything, and...*

His thoughts were cut short by two bulky, white federal agents entering the interrogation room.

"Mr. Samuel Vargas, I'm Senior Agent Howard, and this is my partner Agent Polowski. We are the two agents in charge this case. As you may know, the charges brought against you are very serious—"

"Don't I have the right to have my attorney present before answering any of your questions?" interrupted Sam.

"Yes, you do, Mr. Vargas, and if that's your wish, I'll be more than glad to grant it. However, I will advise you to at least listen to what I have to say."

"Speak. I'm listening," responded Sam.

"We have been on your trail for almost a decade," Senior Agent Howard continued. "We had several opportunities to arrest you in the past, but instead, we waited things out, letting you sink your own battleship."

Sam was shocked to hear they had been investigating him for so long. He had no clue, which meant Juice and the others were probably also under investigation.

"We've known about your organization for quite some time now. You moved swiftly and carefully, making all of your phone calls through a secured line. You even had your house and cars swept monthly for tracking devices or wiretaps. However, lately, you've been slipping and making your calls from your private line, which we're sure you knew was tapped. We also know about your associate, Junior, who launders the money through his businesses for your empire; lets not forget Mr. Big Shot himself Columbian Juan. And how about your little problem with your friend Juice? Yes, we know all about that and how he sent a hit squad after you and your family in Florida. You fled just in time. Instead, your cleaning lady was murdered to send you a message."

The agents had Sam in a corner; there was nothing he could deny because they knew just about everything. He knew he was facing a lot of time and was not prepared to face that.

"So, correct me if I'm wrong. With the power and connections Juice and Juan has, your ass is doomed. Now, if you comply with us, we will work with you. I can guarantee you and your family full protection if you give us your full cooperation. Let me remind you that you're facing a life sentence without the possibility of parole. Think of your family and how much harm you'll be costing them," agent Howard said, figuring he had thrown in the last worm.

Sam was shit out of luck; he knew this was a no-win situation. He was a dead man if he talked, and if he didn't talk, he was still a dead man. Sam couldn't see himself in a jail cell, let alone locked up behind prison bars for the rest of his life. With the people who were out looking for him and the bounty on his head, he doubted he would last five years in prison or out in the streets. Sam grew up in one of the roughest, poorest neighborhoods in the country and was always taught not to snitch. Breaking one of the street codes meant instant death. Once labeled a snitch in the streets, it stuck with the person. He hated to take that route but felt he had no other alternative. The chips were stacked high against him.

"What about my wife?"

Those were the first words Sam had spoken in thirty minutes. He was concerned about her, knowing they were drilling her with questions.

"If you comply with us, all charges against her will be dismissed, and she'll walk away scot-free."

"And what will I be getting out of this?"

"Mr. Vargas, we cannot promise you anything until we've heard what you have to tell us. If and only if the information you tell us is worthy, then we will talk to the prosecutor in handing down a light sentence," Agent Polowski informed him, speaking for the first time. "After you've served your sentence, we will secure you with a new name and social security number and put you and your family under our Witness Protection Program. But first you have to wave your right to an attorney."

"Fuck an attorney I wave my rights and believe me, the information I have is damn sure worthy of less time," said Sam.

"Well, Mr. Vargas, let's hear what you have to say," Agent Howard chimed in. "We will also be recording this conversation. So, if I may."

He clicked the play button on the tape recorder he had been holding.

"This is Senior Agent Howard with the Federal Bureau of Investigation. In the room, we also have Agent Polowski with the Bureau of Investigations and defendant Samual Varges Today's date is the eleventh day of May 2006. This is operation Golden Block, the investigation of a drug empire ran by Samuel Vargas, multi-millionaire and founder of this illegal drug business. Mr. Vargas has agreed to work with the Federal Bureau of Investigations as a star witness in this case and will be testifying against former associates. He has also agreed to give us a full statement and explain his version of how the operation is ran. Could you state your name for the record?"

"Samuel Vargas."

"Would you explain to us how this organization came about and what year it began?"

Sam told everything to the Feds, from the day the empire came into existence to the names and ranks of everyone involved. He commented on Justice's attempted murder/car bombing and how Justice retaliated by murdering four of Juice's men. He discussed Juice's involvement in the operation, how he took over his retirement and how all their current problems came to light.

"So, who is this Colombian guy named Juan?"

"He was my Colombian connection until my retirement."

"How many kilos of cocaine was he shipping to you by boat?"

"I would call him whenever I started to run low on product. We would never speak about drugs over the phone. He would always know how many kilos I was calling to buy. It would always be the same amount: 350 hundred kilos. Our meetings always took place in different countries."

"Mr. Vargas, are you willing to testify about everything you've just said in front of a jury in open court?"

"Yes, if it will benefit me in anyway."

Ending the recording, Agent Howard said, "Thank you, Mr. Vargas, for your cooperation. All we have to do now is continue our investigation on the people you mentioned. If everything checks out, you'll be looking at a very light sentence, I promise. In the meantime, you and your family will be placed under our protection. One more thing, Mr. Vargas. We have pictures of all the men involved in this operation, except for Juan. If you don't mind, could you point out and name each individual?"

"Only if I sign an agreement form."

"No problem, but remember, no promises," Agent Howard said, waving at the two-way mirror for someone to bring in an agreement form.

The agents went through three sixty-minute cassette tapes full of Sam squealing. His tongue was so loose that the agents were surprised it didn't fall off.

***

Product was running low, and Juice was too damn greedy to let even a dollar slip by him. Picking up the payphone from its cradle, he dialed the international number.

After the man on the other end of the receiver answered, he said, "This is Juice. When and where?"

"Canada. Tomorrow evening. Nine o'clock sharp at the airport. One of my drivers will be there to pick you up and escort you to my place."

Juice could not let his problems interfere with his business. Business came first, but he was beginning to slip because of all the drama he was mixing himself in lately. He had plenty of men who were paid to do his dirty work but he was too caught up in the thrill of torture. He hadn't even checked up on his drug empire in Puerto Rico for months. He wondered if things were fine back home. He had not received a call from the island lately, so he quickly erased the thought from his mind.

Juice's trip to Canada was in a few hours; he had no problem leaving the organization for a few days. His newly appointed capo and his chief of staff were doing a great job running things. He knew his US multi-million-dollar empire would be in good hands while he was gone.

Parking his Porsche Carrera in the city's downtown transportation center, he flagged down a cab and directed its driver towards the Philadelphia International Airport. On the flight to Canada, he thought about all the things that had been unfolding lately and felt it was time for a vacation.

The flight took six hours to reach its destination. As Juice disembarked the aircraft and made his way down the ramp, he noticed one of Juan's men waiting for him. The man went by the name of Lolo. Every time Juice arrived in a different country to meet with his connect, the same cold-stone face awaited him as he exited the plane. Without the slightest exchange of words, as usual, they just nodded. Juice followed the man to an SUV, where silence filled the air as the large vehicle made its way to their destination.

***

The Colombian waited patiently in the VIP section of the lounge, sipping a glass of expensive wine. Seeing Juice approaching the table, he stood up with an extended hand, welcoming his friend/business partner.

"Juice, I'm glad you could make it. It's always good to see you. Have a seat."

Before sitting down, Juice shook the Colombian's hand and said, "It's always a pleasure to see you, as well, my friend."

"Before we get started, I would like to announce that there will be a change in plans on how I deliver my product to you," responded Juan. "My sources tell me that your man, Sam, is working with the government. Let's not forget that he knows all about your operation and how I deliver my product to you. Things will now have to be done differently. I have a close friend who holds a position of power within the Newark, New Jersey, port terminal. I've taken care of things, and your next shipment will await you there. The sea box and load numbers are 4365 and 4399. When you get there, ask for a guy by the name of Mr. Watson. He will take care of the rest. In the future, when you need more product, give me a call and say tia Lidia passed we need you at the funeral, and I will have the shipment sent the same way as this one. Someone will contact you once the shipment has arrived at the port terminal. Remember to ask for Mr. Watson," he added.

"Tonight, I will text your private phone with the new Swiss account number," Juan continued. "The Feds are onto you, so I suggest from now on, you choose your steps wisely. I can't believe the nerve of that fool to call me the other day, pleading that I get you off his back."

"He did what?!" yelled Juice. "I always knew there was a soft side to him."

"That was before I found out about his cooperation with the alphabet boys. The blue eyes are on us like hawks. So, from now on, we will no longer be meeting in person. And, Juice, do me one last favor. Find Sam. I don't give a rat's ass where he's hiding. Find him!"

"I'm already on that, my friend," answered Juice. "We missed him the first time, but I now have the location to his new residence in Boulder, Colorado. My men are on their way there as we speak."

***

Juice had never felt this frustrated in his life. He knew it wouldn't be long before his life came crashing down on him. After the meeting, he caught the next flight to Puerto Rico—this time under a different name using one of the many passports he owned. No one on the Island would know of his arrival, so he planned to catch his men by surprise. This time, when he exited the airport, there was no limo awaiting him. Instead, he caught a taxi to the nearest car rental shop and drove away in an Audi A4. Retrieving his cell phone, he dialed his top lieutenant's number.

"Tony, how is everything on the Island? It's been a long time."

Tony was surprised to hear from his boss. For a minute, he didn't know if his boss was dead or alive.

"Everything is fine, boss. Just a small problem that we've been having lately, but I'll handle it as soon as I come up with a solution."

These men will never be able to run a business like I do, thought Juice. "Tony, no problem is to be taken lightly. Explain this small problem to me when you get to my mansion. I'll be there waiting, and bring the dirty clothes with you."

When Juice arrived at his mansion, he quickly took a shower and put on a comfortable robe. Hearing the doorbell, he asked his live-in maid to answer it.

"Señor, it is Tony at the door," said the maid upon returning. "Would you like for me to escort him in?"

"Yes, Gloria, please."

Tony walked into the living room and immediately covered his nose with his shirt upon smelling the weed burning. He was one of the few who didn't smoke. Because of this, Juice had

164

much respect towards the man.

With a muffled voice, Tony said, "What's up, boss? Shit, I can't remember the last time I heard from you!"

He set the duffle bag full of money on the floor, next to the recliner chair where Juice had been sitting.

"Have a seat," responded Juice. "Explain to me this small problem you mentioned over the phone."

"Lately, money has been coming in slowly, and after investigating, I found out we have a rival by the name of Orlando at the San Juan housing projects. We've tried numerous times to take care of the problem," continued Tony. "We've shot up his house, blown up his cars, and even killed most of his corner workers. But these little bastards keep coming back—posting up on the block and selling his shit. For some reason, we can't seem to find this Orlando guy. It's like he vanished off the face of the earth. Last week, he retaliated and killed four of our men. Now there's a war going on between us, so money has been coming in slow. Buyers are scared shitless to come buy our product for fear of getting shot and killed."

"So, this guy Orlando...where is he from?" asked Juice.

"He grew up in Ponce. That much I know."

"I will call my sources; they will know who this guy is and where to locate him. In the meantime, make sure not even a nickel bag gets sold on his turf. Spread our men out on a wider perimeter and notify all of the customers that their safety is guaranteed."

Juice was exhausted and wanted nothing more than to relax, but since this situation had something to do with his residual income, it could not wait and had to be taken care of immediately. After contacting his sources, it took less than five minutes before he had all of the necessary information gathered on Orlando. He knew the man would not be at the location given to him until that night. So, he decided to get a few hours of much-needed sleep until then.

***

Juice awakened at 2:43 a.m. Noticing the time, he quickly got out of bed and made his way into the bathroom to wash up. Afterwards, he called Tony and ordered him to get the men ready and be at his residence as soon as possible. While he waited on their arrival, he got dressed and prepared himself for the anticipated adrenaline rush.

Twenty minutes later, his living room was at full capacity with armed militant men.

"My friends, how are we all doing this early morning?" announced Juice. "I apologize for waking you at such an early time, but our situation with our friend, Orlando, calls for an urgent outcome. Armed men heavily secure the place we will be storming, but I have come up with a solution, and this is what I have in mind."

Juice laid down the entire plan to his crew. When he finished, they immediately headed out, making their way towards the destination.

Arriving in Carolina, Puerto Rico, the four black Cadillac Escalades came to a halt in a secluded spot about two hundred feet from the residence. Orlando's house was located deep in the woods, surrounded by trees and bushes. Juice and his sixteen-man crew, equipped with silenced sniper rifles, slowly crept their way through the wooded area as quietly as possible. Speaking into his headset microphone, Juice ordered all of his men to form an outside perimeter around the house. The night-vision, heat-sensor goggles the men wore made it much easier to see in the dense darkness and spot their heavily armed targets. Each man chose a different location to position themselves within one hundred feet of the house. When they were ready to fire, each one radioed their boss.

Orlando had twenty of his men stationed outside of the house and five more men inside guarding him. Some of the armed men outside sat in chairs fast asleep, while others stood guard conversing with each other.

"Most of these motherfuckas are knocked out," someone softly spoke into their headset.

"Alright, fellas, on the count of three, take out the ones who are not sleeping," Juice ordered into his mic. "Then go for the deadbeats. *Comprenden*? One, two, three..."

The hit went smoothly. Each guard took a bullet directly to the head. It took less then a minute before all twenty corpses laid lifeless on the ground.

Juice watched from a distance, astonished. He did not know his men were such accurate shooters.

After about two minutes of silence, he spoke into his receiver, "Are we clear?"

"Clear."

"Clear."

"Clear."

Juice waited until all of his men checked in before continuing.

"Okay, gentlemen, lets get ready to move in. I want eight of you to form a perimeter around the house, four of you to follow me. We're going through the rear entrance. Tony and the rest of you make entry through the front door," he ordered.

Orlando was in the master room on his bed, naked as the day he was born, fast asleep with an American tourist by his side. He had faith in the men who guarded his home. So, every night, he would fall into a deep sleep like a baby. The only noise heard throughout the house was Orlando's snoring and the downstairs television. The remaining five guards were watching TV in the living room, unaware of what just took place outside. While two of the men were asleep on the couch, the other three stared at the tube.

Juice retrieved a silenced .40 caliber from his shoulder holster, aimed and fired a single round into the doorknob. The powerful slug tore the knob out of its resting place, sending the door swinging quietly open. Simultaneously the rear door was breached; the teams quickly and noiselessly rushed inside the house, split up in pairs, and started their search for any occupants.

Juice and his team of hit- men took to the living room. He could see the back of the heads of two figures sitting on the couch and carefully aimed his weapon. His men followed suit and raised their rifles, as well. Using his fingers, Juice counted to three. When done, all three men fired their silenced weapons in unison at the heads of their targets. The powerful slugs made the bodies of both men sitting on the couch fall forward, landing face-first on the carpet.

Juice and his men turned the corner, now having a full view of the living room, and noticed three more men sitting on another couch. Aware that the house was being invaded, the men reached for the weapons on their waists. Before Juice's handgun could let off a slug, his team of killers had already riddled the bodies on the couch with a barrage of bullets.

Hearing the commotion coming from the living quarters, the other four men quickly turned around and hurried to join their boss.

"Is everything clear?" asked Tony.

"Yes, everything is clear," Juice, said into his mic. "We're making our way upstairs."

Juice led the way towards the second floor, taking the steps two at a time slowly. Reaching the top of the stairs, he held up two fingers, indicating for two of his men to go and check the other room. He then proceeded with caution towards the door straight ahead. Noticing the bedroom door was slightly ajar, Juice pushed it all the way open with his gun's barrel. Searching for the lights, he flicked on the switch located on the right side of the wall.

The couple lay asleep as the men surrounded them.

"Is this him?" asked Juice, pointing towards the naked male figure on the bed.

"Si," replied Tony.

Approaching the sleeping figure, Juice raised his right hand and immediately brought it down, smacking Orlando on the mouth.

Orlando awoke quickly as if from a bad dream and looked at the man standing over him with a confused expression on his face. He did not know who this man was, and he wasn't thrilled in the least about having a team of militant men around him.

"What the fuck are you doing in my house?!"

He could not believe he did not hear any noise. He wondered where his men were that he paid to protect him.

"Don't play stupid. You know why we're here!" said Juice.

The young man in front of him looked to be no older than twenty-five. Juice wondered how he could be so young and hold such a position of power in Puerto Rico.

The commotion awakened the American girl. Hearing her lover's voice, she opened her eyes.

"Eeeeeeeeeee!" She quickly grabbed the sheets and covered herself. Looking over at her lover, she said, "What's going on?"

Juice diverted his eyes from Orlando and glanced at the woman. Raising his pistol, he fired two rounds—one striking the woman in her chest and the other bullet striking her in the neck.

"Get the fuck up and get dressed!" he shouted at the naked man. "I'm taking you to The House of Death!"

***

Orlando wondered where the hell they were taking him. They had been driving for over an hour, and for the past twenty minutes, the roads were nothing but bumpy terrain. He had found a way to get the handcuffs to the front part of his body, which gave him the chance to get his phone from his pocket and text his girlfriend. He could not provide his location, but he let her know who had kidnapped him and that they were possibly going to kill him. Noticing the car finally coming to a stop, Orlando put the cell phone back in his pocket and prepared to attack the first person who opened the trunk of the car. He was not going out without a fight.

Benito, the driver of the vehicle, hit the button inside the glove box to pop open the trunk. Because of his stupidity, some of the men had to chase down Orlando. The man jumped out of the trunk like a jack-in-a-box and had to be tackled to the ground. Juice was furious because of this and decided a couple of strikes across Benito's face with his pistol would teach him a lesson.

Orlando took in his surroundings; the deserted barn had no nearby neighbors. It was miles away from civilization and surrounded by fields of crops. Once ushered inside the barn, Orlando scrunched up his nose at the smell of death lingering in the air. There was blood splattered on the walls and torture tools spread neatly on top of a gurney.

Taking in the horror scene, Orlando stopped in his tracks. A hard shove from behind brought him down to his hands and knees. He felt a sharp pain explode on the side of his ribcage from being repeatedly kicked.

Juice left his men's side and went to grab a chair to try a new technique on Orlando. It was something he had never done before and had thought about the entire process during the drive to the barn. Cutting out the cushion to the chair, he left the middle part hollow.

"That's enough, gentlemen!" he shouted. "Bring him over to me. Sit him down and secure him to the chair. I want you to duct-tape his legs and thighs, too."

While his men duct-taped Orlando to the chair, Juice taped a pool ball to the end of a rope. This swing-like weapon would be his new torture tool. His men looked on in bewilderment, wondering what the hell was he going to do with such a device.

"You should all take notes on what I'm about to do. This can be any of you sitting in this chair if you ever decide to cross me."

Swinging the rope in circles at full speed, he aimed for under the chair.

The pool ball found its target. Orlando let out a scream that echoed off the walls of the barn as the ball came into contact with his testicles. Never in his life had he felt pain of this severity. His nutsacks felt like they were on fire. He continuously let out screams of agony while being repeatedly struck with the pool ball.

"So you think you can do as you please!" yelled Juice in his face. "This is my island, and what I say goes around here! You will be an example for anyone who thinks they can come against me!"

Juice dropped the tool on the floor and retrieved a sharp knife from the metal gurney. Approaching the victim, who shook uncontrollably from the pain, Juice rested one of his hands on top of Orlando's leg. Then he bent down and reached under the chair with his other hand, which held the sharp knife, and numerously stabbed his victim in the groin area.

Orlando's body was left duct-taped to the chair, inside of the barn, bleeding to death.

CHAPTER 19

A week had gone by before O-Dawg's father's decomposed body was discovered inside of the house. The neighbors could no longer tolerate the awful stench coming from next door, which finally caused them to contact the authorities. After getting no response to their knocks on the door, the police had no other choice but to kick it down. When the first officers on the scene entered the residence, their stomachs immediately let loose from the rancid-odor of death. The gruesome sight of the man with half his face smashed in made most of the officers turn and walk out of the house. Most officers in their thirty-year-old careers had yet to come across a crime scene of this nature.

O-Dawg was informed of his father's death and asked to stop by the city morgue to identify the body. He had yet to find out the cause of death and was not prepared for the news to come. The detective who stopped by O-Dawg's house to deliver the news only said that his father was murdered and would not elaborate further on the ongoing investigation.

O-Dawg immediately knew who was behind this daring and gruesome act. On the way towards the city morgue, his hands would not stop shaking as he tried to keep a firm grip on the steering wheel. Arriving at the morgue, he quickly made his way over to the coroner's office. Entering the cramped confinements of the office, he rudely interrupted the doctor, who had his eyes glued to the paperwork on his desk.

"Excuse me, sir. I was told to stop by here so I can identify the body of my father, who was brought in a couple of hours ago."

Startled by this man, who had barged into his office without first knocking on the door, Bob Caligan looked up and said, "Yes, I was just finishing up the paperwork on the case."Getting up from his desk, he added, "Follow me. I have to warn you, though. The body has massive amounts of trauma to the head."

"What do you mean by that?" asked O-Dawg. "What was the cause of death?"

"We have yet to come to a conclusion, so the official cause of death has not been determined. However, from my many years of experience in this field, I can say there was blunt force trauma to the cranium caused by a heavy object, such as a hammer, followed by multiple gunshot wounds to the body and facial area."

As they entered the morgue, the coroner continued walking to a wall filled with small refrigerator-like doors. Opening one of the doors, he pulled out a metal gurney, which held a body covered in a white sheet.

Pulling back the white cover off the deceased, the coroner asked, "Is this your father?"

The sight of the badly battered body brought O-Dawg to his knees, making him throw up the food he had eaten earlier. The coroner tried to console him, but O-Dawg wasn't accepting any of it.

"Get ya hands off me!" he shouted as tears streamed down his cheeks.

His father's face was almost unrecognizable from the severity of the beating. He could not believe Juice would do something like this.

"We had to identify him by dental records. However, he did have his driver's license in his wallet."

O-Dawg didn't say another word. Instead, he stormed out of the coroner's office. Climbing into his SUV, he raced towards his storage shed, not caring if the police spotted him. The way he was feeling, he would not pull over for anyone. Arriving at the storage shed, he stocked the back compartment of the truck with all kinds of artillery before making a phone call.

"Nate, I need you to meet me at the spot in an hour and bring the rest of the crew with you. Oh yeah, and another one of those stolen caravans, too."

"I got you, dawg. I'll be there. Are you alright?"

"I'll explain everything to you when I get there. Right now, I'm in a rush."

Ending that conversation, O-Dawg dialed another number.

When that person answered, he said, "Will, are you at the crib?"

"Who's this?"

"It's O-Dawg!"

"Oh shit! What's the deal? Why you sound all freaked out?" responded Will, having never heard his friend sound like this.

"I need to holla at you. This shit is urgent! I'm on my way to your crib right now!"

Will had yet to hear the news about O-Dawg's father. So, when his friend arrived at his house looking agitated and angry, he was anxious to find out what the hell was going on.

"Come in, dawg. What the fuck is going on? Last I heard, you were blowing shit up inside the organization."

"So, you already know about the beef between me and Juice. I can't believe that man took things to another level!" O-Dawg said, teary-eyed. "The motherfucka killed my pops. Not only did they murder my dad, but they tortured him, too! I almost didn't recognize him when I went to identify his body."

"Oh, shit!" Will exclaimed. "He's bringing the pain to our loved ones. Fuck that! We gotta put a stop to this! This man is getting way outta hand!"

"I need for you to tell me where he rests his head at night."

Will knew the consequences if Juice were to find out he was the one who gave up his whereabouts. For a minute, he thought about what would happen to his loved ones if he disclosed this information. He had much love for O-Dawg's father, though. Now that he had gained Juice's trust, it would be the perfect opportunity to get back at the man, who had been murdering his friends one at a time. Will knew it wouldn't be much longer before he ended up a victim. He knew what it felt like to have someone close to you get murdered. Someone needed to put a stop to Juice's madness, and if things were planned right, it was possible.

"Alright, I'll tell you what you want to know, but I want in on the action. O-Dawg, if we do this, it has to be done right. No fuckups! There are no second chances! Our families' lives are on the line, so we'll do it my way or no way at all."

"I'm listening," responded O-Dawg. "Let me hear what you have to say."

"Juice is in Puerto Rico as we speak, so we'll have to save the best for last. We'll start by picking Ralph and the rest of the crew off one at a time. I've gained these men's trust, so best believe we'll use it to our advantage."

Will went on laying the plan down without any interruptions from his friend. When he was done, he added, "How many men do you have that are willing to ride with us without asking questions?"

"I got a whole crew of young guns. They are waiting on my orders as we speak. They're ready and willing to bust their guns."

"Those same little motherfuckas who was with you the day you decided to start this war?"

"Yeah."

"I gotta give it to you. Those young boys are about that action!" cheered Will. "I was told they were lighting shit up like the Fourth of July. Look, do whatever it is you gotta do and meet me at the Mobile gas station in half an hour."

O-Dawg quickly left Will's house with his adrenaline pumping as he made his way to meet the crew. When he arrived at the housing projects, they were already waiting. This time, they stood next to a money-green Chevy Suburban, dressed in all-black army fatigues.

Stepping out of the vehicle, O-Dawg said, "What the fuck is up with this big-ass Suburban?"

"This is the fastest whip we could find," responded Nate.

"Fuck it! Beats that cramped-up caravan!" O-Dawg replied.

Even though it was a time of grievance for O-Dawg, it brought a smile to his face knowing these loyal young boys were ready to ride with him.

"So what's going on?" asked Nate.

"Same guys from last time, is what the fuck is up! They killed my pops!"

The entire crew was stone-faced at what they just heard—each one trying to imagine how they would feel to be in those same shoes.

"I see they ain't learn their lesson from the last time," Lil Moses said. "We definitely playing for keeps this time! Let's murder their whole family!"

"We're gonna show them how we get down in the dirty Jersey!" said O-Dawg. "Now, come and help me unload this shit outta my car and into the Suburban. I'm ready to get this over with before my pop's funeral."

***

Will sat in his Ford F-150 anxiously waiting for O-Dawg in the gas station's parking lot. One hundred and one thoughts raced through his brain. He wanted to change his mind, put the truck in drive, and head towards Arizona with his family, where he would be safe and out of harm's way, but his conscience would not let him leave. Noticing the dark Chevy Suburban pull alongside his vehicle, he almost drove away until he heard a familiar voice.

"Hold the fuck up, dawg! It's me!"

Seeing it was O-Dawg, he put the gearshift back in park.

Climbing out of the truck, Will said, "There's too much shit going on for you to pull up alongside me the way you did. You're lucky my first instinct wasn't to shoot."

"Get the fuck inside!" said O-Dawg. "Let's get this shit poppin'!"

After getting in the Suburban, Will was introduced to the entire crew. He was amazed at how young the boys were.

"Fellas, this here is one of my childhood friends. We call him Will."

"So I finally come face to face with the little terror squad! I heard you all be putting in that work. You!" Will added, pointing at Lil Moses. "I've seen your rascal face around before. Ain't your momma's name Fatima?"

"Cut that shit out, dawg, and let my little man know what time it is," interrupted O-Dawg.

Will explained the entire plan to the crew. When he finished, it was time to put the plan into motion.

Nate and Lil Moses were dropped off around the corner from the apartment that held four of Juice's men. They were given detailed instructions on how the plan was to be executed. Dwayne and Leafy were also dropped off at their location with clear instructions. O-Dawg then proceeded with Will and the rest of the crew to put the plan's third phase in effect.

***

Nate and Lil Moses had no problem getting into the apartment unnoticed.

And they call themselves assassins, thought Moses, chucking to himself as he climbed in through the open downstairs window.

"Damn, these boys are trifling," he said outloud while looking around at all the empty beer cans and spilled blunt guts that littered the floor.

The flashlight he carried helped him find his way to the front door without knocking anything over. Unlocking the door, he opened it and let Nate inside.

"Hurry up before someone sees us," whispered Lil Moses.

Both boys knew there wouldn't be anyone home for at least the next hour. They were willing to wait all night long if that's how long it took for them to accomplish the mission. Moses was first to start looking around for any valuables, while Nate followed behind bitching.

"Come on, dawg. We ain't got time for this shit. What if they show up and catch us slipping?"

"We're not gonna get caught slipping. I know these fools have some money stashed around here somewhere. They don't run around doing all this hitman shit for nothing."

Since it was a one-bedroom apartment that all four men shared, it wasn't long before Moses found what he was searching for.

"Jackpot!" he shouted happily. "I knew I was right!"

He pulled out the bottom drawer to the dresser, and seeing massive amounts of money wrapped in ten-thousand-dollar bundles, he ordered, "Go get a bag to put this shit in!"

***

Dwayne and Leafy had a little trouble getting into the other apartment, but it was nothing they couldn't handle. The windows to the apartment were locked, so Dwayne kept an eye out for any nosey neighbors while Leafy looked for something to bust out the back window. The boys knew a sparkplug was the perfect tool to use. Once the plug came in contact with the window, there would only be a shattering noise.

Leafy pushed on the shattered glass with a gloved hand, and it fell inward on the plush carpet, making minimal sounds. Removing the rest of the broken glass from the windowsill, he then climbed inside. Quickly finding his way to the front of the house, he quietly opened the front door for Dwayne.

"Hurry up inside!" said Leafy.

"You check that side, and I'll check this side," said Dwayne. "Whatever we find, we'll split in half."

***

O-Dawg parked the stolen Suburban in front of Will's house and climbed out.

"Alright, this is it. Remember, no fuckups!" said Will as they all proceeded up the steps and into his house.

Picking up the house phone, he made the call.

"Ralph, it's Will. I have to speak to you about something I just found out. It's very important," he lied. "Meet me inside my basement in ten minutes and bring every man that's available from your team. What I'm about to tell you is only meant for certain ears. My men cannot know about this. I fear they will leak this information to its source since the person happens to be a close associate of ours."

"I'll be there in a few," answered Ralph. "I'm gathering my men now."

After terminating the call, Will sang, "This is it, baby! They are on their way over. Let's head down to the basement and wait for them."

"You're sure he didn't pick up on our scheme?" asked O-Dawg.

"No, he didn't. I told you...they trust me now. If I thought this shit wasn't gonna work, I wouldn't have gotten us involved."

"I still think we should've done things my way," replied O-Dawg. "It would've been much faster and easier to kill them all at once."

"Thank me when we're finished. Right now, hurry up and get your ass inside the bathroom before they get here," joked Will as they all entered the basement.

"What if someone needs to use the restroom?" asked O-Dawg.

"This won't take long at all. It should all be over in matter of minutes as long as all you mofos watch who you're shooting at." said Will.

Everyone assumed their positions, heading straight towards their assigned area. O-Dawg hid inside the bathroom, which consisted of a toilet and a small sink. Will tuned in the television to the sports channel, and two of the young boys hid inside a closet by the pool table. While the third youngin Ray-Ray hid behind the washer and dryer machines.

Everything needed to look normal when Ralph and his men arrived. Will took a seat on the recliner and stared at the television, calming himself. Looking nervous in front of these men trained to pickup on such things was not an option. A knock at the front door made his heart race ridiculously fast.

Still trying to calm himself, he shouted, "Come in! It's open!"

Ralph, Matone, and a few other guys from Juice's crew piled into the basement. It was the first time Will called on a meeting; it was out of the ordinary. So, they were all curious as to why they were there. Everyone stood there in total silence.

Breaking the ice, Will said, "Gentlemen, have a seat." Gaining control of himself, he continued. "What I am about to reveal to you all should not leave this room. It has to be handled immediately and cannot in no way come back to us."

"Get to the point," Matone said, growing impatient.

Brushing off the ignorant comment, Will continued, "We all know Vic didn't take his termination from the empire lightly. A dependable source told me that he is going around recruiting men to get at Juice. He also has a thirty-thousand-dollar bounty for the murder of your boss."

"I'm gonna kill that bastard!" Matone yelled. "Where the fuck is he?!"

"He'll be at his house within the next hour. He doesn't know this information has been leaked. So, since he thinks everything is gravy between us, we will befriend him. I say let's pay him an unannounced surprise visit. Go home, put on an all-black outfit, and grab your most precious gun. Bring it with you and meet me back here in half an hour. Is that enough time for everyone?"

"Will, I think we can manage without your help," said Ralph. "Just give me his address, and we'll take it from there."

"What do you mean without me? I want in!"

Will was doing a great job acting.

Crouched in the closet, O-Dawg chuckled to himself and thought, *He could win a Grammy for Best Actor.*

"Trust me. My presence would make things a lot easier on all of us. He has known me for a long time, but he doesn't really know you guys."

Ralph knew Will was right. Without Will's presence, Vic would just get paranoid, which would end up making things worse.

"Well, if you insist. We'll meet you back here in half an hour."

"You and Matone should stay here so I can go over the plan with the two of you," Will suggested before they could exit the basement. "If you don't like what I planned, then we can rearrange things before your men return."

In case Will's plan didn't work, O-Dawg was prepared to come out of the bathroom busting his gun. He kept his finger wrapped tightly around the trigger and was seconds from letting bullets fly. When he heard Ralph give in to Will's demands, he released the pressure his finger held on the trigger.

"Gentlemen, go ahead without me. I'll be here when you return. Remember half an hour. Don't be running late, or your ass will be left behind and dealt with later," Ralph warned the men.

O-Dawg and his crew were prepared to launch their attack; they were waiting for the cue. Hearing the front door close, they began double-checking their weapons.

"So, what do you have in mind?" asked Matone.

He didn't trust Will and kept his eyes open. He took in his surroundings, looking for anything out of the ordinary.

"Take a seat, gentlemen," Will insisted while he relaxed in the recliner. "You might disagree with my plan, but I think it's the best solution."

This was the signal for the fellas to spring into action. O-Dawg was the first to come out of the bathroom unnoticed and approached both men from behind.

"Good evening, gentlemen."

At the sound of the voice, both men turned around at the same time. Matone wasn't surprised to see O-Dawg. He knew the man would retaliate and was prepared for it, but he didn't think Will would be involved.

Looking at him directly in the eyes, he said, "You've just signed your death certificate. Juice will extinguish the life of every living creature you love."

Ant and Bucky emerged from their hiding spot inside the closet with guns drawn as Ray-Ray did the same.

Matone looked at the three young bloods and began to laugh, "You guys are that desperate to recruit soldiers? What did you do? Go to an elementary school and pick the two most rebellious kids?"

"Shut the fuck up!" shouted Will. "You spics think you can come into our country and do whatever you fucking want. Kill my friends and walk around these streets like shit is sweet. If it weren't for Sam's scary-ass letting you wetbacks play mind games with him, none of you would be here right now! But guess what?" he added. "We're not Sam, and you motherfuckas bleed just like we do! See, your problem is," he continued. "That y'all do shit cowboy status, while in the United States we wait patiently for the right opportunity. As soon as your boss exits that plane, he's gonna feel the wrath just like you two. We are taking back control of this organization, and nothing's gonna stop us!

"Fuck you!" said Matone. "I'm not scared of death! Have you forgotten? I invented death!"

Cutting to the chase, O-Dawg said, "Were any of you involved in my father's murder?"

Both men glanced at the AR-15 assault rifle in O-Dawg's hand and then looked at each other before shrugging their shoulders. They were not going to say anything.

"So, now you're deaf, dumb, *and* stupid? I promise not one of you will have an open casket for your family to mourn."

Walking up to Ralph, O-Dawg placed the barrel of the rifle on his kneecap.

"You feel like talking now?"

"Death before dishonor!"

"Loyalty. I like that in a man."

Boom!Boom!

The large-caliber bullets tore both of Ralph's kneecaps from their joints. He screamed from the excruciating pain.

O-Dawg then made his way over to Matone and asked, "Are you willing to tell me?"

"Fuck you!" shouted Matone before spitting in O-Dawg's face.

Matone would not give him the satisfaction he wanted. Instead, O-Dawg emptied the clip across Matone's legs, then slit his throat from ear to ear.

Ralph looked bewildered as his partner's blood splashed on his clothes and face. He could not believe how fast the tables had turned.

Aiming the rifle at Ralph, Will said, "Now it's up to you whether you live or die. Who killed old man Francisco?"

"Look, do whatever it is that you're gonna do. Death before dishonor."

"We're gonna see just how honorable you are to Juice," said O-Dawg. "Ant and Bucky tie his ass up and let's carry him to the truck; but first check him for weapons. I have something special planned for his ass."

After tying Ralph up and putting a gag in his mouth, he and Matone were then carried out to the SUV and placed in the back compartment of the Suburban.

"What do you plan on doing with them?" Will asked as they pulled away from the front of his crib.

"You'll see," was all O-Dawg said.

Silence played the role between everyone inside the Suburban as O-Dawg drove towards an isolated wooded area. Will knew he had already played his part in the mission. It was now up to O-Dawg and his young crew to finish the job.

Arriving at the wooded area, O-Dawg jumped out of the truck and said, "Help me get these fools out the back."

Will was lost in his own thoughts as he helped unload the bodies from the truck. Both bodies were placed by a huge tree and then tied around its trunk. Wondering why O-Dawg was going back to the Suburban, Will began to follow him. His question was answered when he saw his friend exit the SUV juggling two green hand-grenades.

O-Dawg walked past Will and headed straight for the two bodies tied to the tree.

"Didn't I say you were going to have a closed casket viewing?"

Ralph saw the grenades and began pleading for his life. The muffled *mmm* sounds could be heard, but the gag kept any words from escaping his mouth.

Feeling merciless, O-Dawg approached Ralph first and said, "You should've answered my question. Now I don't want to hear the answer."

He pulled the safety pin off with his teeth and shoved the live grenade inside Ralph's drawers. Quickly making his way over to the dead body, O-Dawg then rammed the other grenade inside Matone's pants before making a run for it.

"Run! Run!" he shouted to everyone. "Get as far away as you can! Hide behind the truck!"

A smile crossed his face as he glanced back and noticed Ralph shuffling around, trying to shake the grenade loose.

Boom! Boom!

The loud explosions sent the guys off their feet and in the air before colliding back on the ground. Getting up, O-Dawg wiped the dirt off his clothes.

Will made his way over to his partner and said, "You alright?"

"Yeah, I'm good."

Noticing the young boys also approaching, he added, "Ray-Ray, grab that trash bag from inside the truck."

When Ray-Ray returned with the bag, he almost puked. The sight of the two heads that O-Dawg held in his hands looked like raw meat.

***

Moses held the bag containing the money tightly in his hand, and with his other hand, he clutched the AR-15 assault rifle. He was not leaving without the money. Nate watched his friend as he sat on the opposite side of the living room behind the couch, patiently waiting for the men to arrive.

"What the fuck is taking them so long? We've been here for over an hour."

Nate hoped everything went well on O-Dawg's end. He would be furious if something happened to the man who put him under his wing and took him off the streets. He looked up to O-Dawg as a father figure, and the thought of something going wrong had him on edge. Hearing voices and footsteps approaching the residence brought him back to his senses.

"Here they come. Get ready," said Moses in a low tone.

Juice's assassins hurried to get home to change their clothes. Miguel was the first person to reach the front door. The other three men waited behind him as he pulled out the set of keys and inserted the proper one into the keyhole. It was pitch black when all four men stepped into the apartment. The only light came from the outside hallway, which only lasted a few seconds before the last man inside shut the door behind him, leaving them in total darkness.

"Why the fuck did you do that?" snapped Miguel as he searched for the light switch.

Locating the switch, he flicked the lights on. All four men were caught off-guard and startled by the two baby-faced teenagers standing by the couch, aiming military assault rifles at them.

"Surprise!" said Nate. "Welcome home!"

"Is this some kind of joke?" responded June.

"Does this look like a fucking joke to you?" replied Moses, feeling offended for not being taken seriously.

"Come on, kids. Be real," chimed in Miguel. "You two aren't even old enough to buy alcohol, let alone stand the recoil force of that weapon."

"Who wants to find out first?!" shouted Nate.

"Do you know who we are?" responded June, making the mistake of reaching for his gun.

Boom!

A spray of bullets from both Moses' and Nate's gun riddled the body of the loud-mouthed man.

Seeing these young boys were about that action, the remaining three men froze in place.

"Now that you all know we can withstand the forces of these weapons, I will proceed with my duty," said Nate. "I'm sure you all have heard of a man by the name of O-Dawg." Not giving any of them a chance to speak, he continued, "Let me refresh your memory. Your boss, Juice, murdered his father! Does that ring any bells?"

All three men looked at each other. They knew what the young boy was talking about but had no involvement in the actual murder.

"We didn't have shit to do with that!" answered Miguel.

"Whether you did or not, all who work for Juice or are affiliated with him must suffer the consequences. Blame yourselves for letting the puppet master pull your strings. I am only here to deliver a message."

All three bodies jerked before tumbling to the ground. As the bullets tore through their flesh, blood and pieces of meat traveled across the room, staining the walls. When the shooting ceased, loud ringing could be heard in the atmosphere. Swinging the rifles' straps over their shoulders, Nate and Moses stepped over the deceased bodies before making a run for it.

***

Dwayne and Leafy kept a close eye out for their victim's arrival. As Dwayne peeked out the living room window, a pair of approaching headlights caught his attention. He noticed the car pull over in front of the apartment building. When the three Hispanic males exited the vehicle, he immediately knew it was his awaited guest. His theory was confirmed when they began approaching the building.

"Here they come. Take your positions."

Leafy was a little upset they didn't find any valuables during their search. Taking his position on the opposite end of the room by the broken window, he wasn't ready to kill these fools yet. He wanted them first to lead him towards the stash before murdering them. He knew men of such caliber had to have a nice amount of cash stashed away someplace.

As the men made their way towards the apartment, something caught their attention.

"Hold on a second, guys. Did any of you come back to the apartment during the day?" asked Domingo. "I know I was the last one out, and I swear I left the lights on. It's a habit I've had since I was a kid."

"No wonder the light bill be so fucking high!" joked Santos. "We left the crib this morning! How the fuck do you remember if the lights were on or not?"

It was more of a challenge than a question.

"I'm serious, man! This shit ain't funny!"

"You're bugging, man. We only have half an hour to do what we gotta do. We don't have time to be stalling or playing games," Jamie complained.

"Nah, I'm not bugging," responded Domingo. "I have a gut feeling that something isn't right. Santos, go check the back while me and Jamie check out the front."

When Santos reached the back of the apartment and noticed the broken window, his instincts told him that Domingo's gut feeling was right. Reaching in his waistband, he pulled out the .38 revolver and carefully peeked through the window.

I can't see shit! he thought to himself; the streetlamp barely illuminated the room.

Domingo unholstered his gun and held the weapon in his right hand. He inserted the key into the doorknob with his left hand and carefully pushed the door slightly open. The light from the hallway helped him partially see the living room quarters as he slowly stepped inside.

Santos watched his partners from the back room's broken window. He could see them carefully walking into the living room. He looked on as Domingo searched for the light switch.

Dwayne felt a cold chill run through his body as he watched the two men slowly enter the apartment with their guns drawn. Not seeing the third party that was supposed to be tagging along with his comrades, he knew right away something was wrong.

I think these motherfuckas know we're here, Dwayne thought.

From where he was positioned, he could see them, but they could not see him. Before Domingo got the chance to hit the light switch, Dwayne wildly fired at the two figures.

Domingo and Jamie didn't stand a chance. The last thing they saw were flashes from the powerful gun muzzle as they were both cut down by a barrage of bullets.

Leafy stood by the broken window, not noticing the man squatting two inches to his left. Neither did Santos see the figure squatting two inches to his right side. Both men were unaware of each other's presence. Leafy dove towards the right side of the wall when he heard the mighty roar of a .357 Magnum in his left ear. The flame that escaped the gun's barrel gave up Santos' hiding spot as he fired aggressively at the guys who had just murdered his comrades.

The shooting that came from the broken window caught Dwayne and Leafy off-guard. Before Dwayne could turn towards where the shots were coming from, an unexpected slug went right through his throat.

As he dropped his gun and raised his hands to his neck, his last thoughts were, *Where the fuck is Leafy?*

Seeing the sparks coming from the opposite side of the broken window, Leafy aimed his rifle at the window and fired endlessly. His reactions weren't fast enough, but he hit the target. However, he was seconds too late to save his friend's life. When the shooting stopped, he was the only man left standing.

***

"Damn! Where the fuck are those young-guns?!" spazzed O-Dawg. "I told them to meet me at the spot as soon as they got done!"

Just then, his phone rang. He hoped it was the call he had been expecting.

"Who dis?"

"It's Nate. I'm at the spot waiting on you."

Hearing that voice took a huge burden off O-Dawg's shoulders.

"Damn, you had me worried. I passed through the spot a few times and didn't see anyone. I was starting to think something happened to y'all. Where's the rest of the crew? Are they there with you?"

"Lil Moses is here with me, but I haven't seen Dwayne or Leafy yet."

"Stay right there. I'll be there in a minute."

O-Dawg had never been so quick to react to anything; he desperately made a U-turn and headed for the spot. The Suburban tilted on its side, almost tipping over as he struggled to straighten the steering wheel while pushing down on the gas pedal. In less than five minutes, they arrived at the spot.

"How did it go?" O-Dawg asked as soon as Nate and Moses jumped inside the Suburban.

"Shit went accordingly. You should've seen the look they gave us when they walked in and saw our young faces. They thought it was some kind of joke 'til we popped they asses. I gotta give it to them. They went out like true soldiers!" Nate said cheerily while Moses sat in the back of the truck, quiet as a church mouse. The only thoughts on his mind were how to begin spending the money he had taken.

"What you got in that bag?" asked O-Dawg curiously.

"A little something we came across on our mission," replied Moses, wearing a huge smirk on his face. "Best believe I wasn't leaving out of there empty-handed."

"I bet. I had a feeling y'all was gonna ransack that entire place before they arrived. They had plenty of dough, so I know y'all must've came off with a few hundred grand. Here's something extra y'all can put with that little stash, as well," added O-Dawg.

Reaching in his pocket, he retrieved two bundles of cash; each bundle contained ten thousand dollars.

"There's more in the long run. Let's just call this a bonus gift."

O-Dawg handed each man a bundle.

Hearing his phone going off, O-Dawg quickly reached for the device while focusing his attention on the road ahead.

"Who dis?" O-Dawg said into the receiver, then paused to listen to the caller. "Hold on. Slow down. I can't understand a word you're saying!"

Leafy was speaking at least a hundred words per minute. Shaken up by the event, his words were coming out tongue-twisted.

"Dwayne's dead! They shot and killed him!"

"Where are you now?"

"I'm at the spot."

"Damn! We just left from there! Stay right where you are. I'm on my way."

O-Dawg quickly busted another illegal U-turn and raced down the back roads, hoping to avoid any oncoming traffic and the police's radar gun.

"What's going on?" asked Nate.

"I'll let Leafy tell y'all."

Noticing the Suburban approaching, Leafy came from behind the car where he had been hiding and flagged down the stolen SUV. As he climbed inside, he was still shaken up from witnessing his friend's murder.

Seeing Leafy's blood-stained shirt, Nate asked, "What the fuck happened? Where the fuck is Dwayne?"

"It's my fault! I should've been on point!"

Leafy stuttered from nervousness while trying to explain to them what happened. By the time he finished telling the events, tears were running down his cheeks.

O-Dawg felt bad for losing one of his soldiers. Pulling up alongside his BMW, he climbed out of the stolen Suburban and said, "Will, drive this thing and follow me?" Looking back at Leafy, he added, "You, come ride with me."

Will was grateful for completing the mission. As he sat in the driver's seat, he prayed their final phase would go accordingly.

"I know how it feels to lose someone close to you, youngin'," O-Dawg told Leafy as he drove towards his house.

It was the first time he would be bringing someone to his home. Not letting anyone know where he rested his head at night was a rule he took seriously.

"Look inside that glove box and take what's in there for you."

Leafy opened the compartment and was amazed at the five neatly stacked bundles of cash.

Picking up the bundles, he said, "All this right here?"

"Yeah, that's fifty G's. Take it and start a new life. Get away from all this shit while you're still young. If someone would've given me this same opportunity, I wouldn't be here talking to you today."

Leafy took in the advice and planned to do just that. He wondered why O-Dawg was being so generous.

"Why are you giving me fifty G's like it's nothing?"

"Look, son...I gota feeling shit is gonna hit the roof. I see a lot of potential in you and want you to do something with your life. Dwayne once told me that you're nice with the mic. Think wisely. We only live once."

O-Dawg didn't know what got into him, but something or someone was putting thoughts in his mind. Today, his thoughts told him to pull over and drop the kid off—not to take him along for the last phase. So, that's what he did.

"What are you doing?" asked Leafy, noticing the vehicle pull over at the bus station.

"Get out, youngin. This is your stop. Jump on that bus and don't look back."

Leafy looked at O-Dawg with a bewildered expression.

"You know what, you're right!" he said before getting out of the car.

***

Juice was scheduled to return the following day. O-Dawg was more than willing to put his life on the line; he had a surprise for the drug lord. Arriving at his home, he pulled into the garage and waved for Will and the youngins to follow him inside. After making sure all the doors were locked, he set the alarm and outside sensors to the home.

"Fellas, make yourselves at home," O-Dawg said as he turned on the large plasma television. "*Mi casa es tu casa*! Open bar tonight! I have anything and everything you guys wanna drink."

The bar and the selection of liquor were equal to what one would see on a downtown strip. Mirrors aligned the back wall, and stools were the choice for comfort. Two professional pool tables also held their grounds in the large living room quarters. The party lasted throughout the entire night. Only when the sun started to rise did the boys take it down for the day.

CHAPTER 20

Juice had been trying to contact his men in the United States the entire night; he wanted to notify them of his arrival. The following day, he picked up the hotel's phone from the nightstand and made the international call, but again, no one answered. Many thoughts ran through his head, one being that something must've happened to his men. Juice was a man of confidence like no other man; he knew many men feared him. They all knew the consequences of crossing a man like him, so he quickly erased that thought from his mind. The thought of his men partying and binge drinking also crossed his mind.

"Maybe they were in a drunken stupor and didn't hear the phone ringing."

Since this thought made the most sense to him, he went along with it. Finally frustrated, he decided to dial the number to the man who would know what his men were up to.

The vibration on his hip woke Will up from his sleep; for a second, he didn't recognize his surroundings. The crazy events from the night before ran through his mind as he reached for his cell phone, which he had placed on the couch's armrest before falling asleep. He almost had a panic attack once he noticed the number on the Caller ID. Taking a deep breath, he pushed the button to answer the call.

"Yes, Juice, what can I do for you?"

"Have you heard anything from those fools of mine? I've been going crazy trying to contact them all night. I bet the fools are probably too drunk to know their right from left."

Hearing Juice make that statement immediately gave Will an idea.

"They were over at my basement last night. The championship game was on, and I had the surround sound on full blast. We got drunk as a skunk, which reminds me... Ralph owes me five hundred dollars for the bet he lost. They left my place around five this morning, but if I happen to see any of them, I'll let them know you're looking for them."

"Please do. My flight departs soon, and I will be expecting them to be there when I arrive."

"Juice, you know as well as I do that no matter what, they will be there."

"You know something, Will? You're right. They know better! I always thought you were different from your other friends. That's why I took a liking to you from the very beginning."

Ending the conversation, Will immediately got up in search of O-Dawg. Making his way up the stairs, he followed the thunderous snoring, which led him into the master bedroom.

"Wake the fuck up!"

O-Dawg woke up feeling groggy and hungover from last night's drinking binge. The shots of taquilla didn't stop until 3:45 am, he had only gotten four hours of sleep.

"Damn, what time is it?" he asked, rubbing the crust from the corner of his eyes. "What the fuck are you doing waking me up so early?"

"Juice just called my phone."

O-Dawg was fully awake now.

"What did he say?"

Will shared the details of the phone conversation he had with Juice. When he finished, he added, "I'm ready to get this shit over with. This fool's in the way!"

"Shit hasn't been the same since that man took charge of the organization," responded O-Dawg. "Shit has changed drastically, so he definitely gotta go."

"When this shit is over, I'm taking my family to Arizona and never looking back," said Will. "Things will never be the same, so ain't no need to stick around. I need a change in scenery and environment."

"Did he mention what time his flight is landing?"

"No. All he said was he would be here tonight. I don't care if we have to stake out that airport all day and night. When Juice finds out what happened to his men, he will use every resource possible to wreak havoc on every single one of us. I don't know about you, but nobody, especially a man who's not even from this country, is gonna chase me out of my city. If and when I decide to leave, it'll be voluntarily."

"What are we gonna do about his men not being able to show up at the airport?"

The same thought had crossed Will's mind earlier; he even had a plan laidout. Juice's power was growing rapidly in the U.S., and the originals from the organization could not allow this virus to continue to spread. Many of his close friends had already lost their lives to this madman. If Juice continued to be in charge, there would be no man left in the empire. Will knew if his plan failed, all hell would break loose. No matter the consequences, they could not let this opportunity slip by. He was willing to lose his life before allowing an outsider to have total control of the empire or city.

"This is what I planned," continued Will. "We rent a limo and be the ones to pick him up from the airport. We'll have Felipe, who he's never seen, wait for him near the baggage claim area, holding a sign with Juice's name. Felipe will then escort him to the limo, where the biggest surprise of his life will await him. We kidnap his ass and take him to your basement to begin our physical scientific experiment. A second crew will need to tail us and keep a close eye on our surroundings. This is where your young boys play their part. To be on the safe side, we'll bring a third car along just in case he tries to make a scene for attention, and we have to switch vehicles."

The plan sounded solid; O-Dawg just hoped everything went accordingly. He no longer cared for the empire; however, he was thirsty for revenge.

"Contact the limousine company and let the young dudes know what time it is. I'm gonna head home and suit up. I wanna be at the airport as soon as it gets dark out."

It had been quite some time since Will last put work in but tonight, he would put the gloves back on one last time. Making his way out of the house, he said a silent prayer.

Reaching the bottom of the steps, O-Dawg was surprised to see the crew up and ready.

"Tonight's the night we take our city back!"

All the young boys sat up at attention and listened to their mentor speak. Lil Moses still clutched the bag containing his share of the money; he hugged the bag as if his life depended on it.

"Juice will be arriving at the airport tonight, and he will be expecting his men to pick him up. But we all know that's not gonna happen," continued O-Dawg. "We're going to rent a limo and provide our services to this man, which means we will be picking him up. He will be thinking it's his men who are picking him up, but his surprise will be waiting for him once he gets in the limo. I need you guys to keep a close tail behind me in the stolen Suburban. We will be taking him back to my place, where he will slowly and painfully meet his fate. Remember, anything can go wrong, and our plan can go sour. So, stay on point! I need you guys to be my other set of eyes and ears. Now take y'all little asses home and do whatever y'all gotta do, but meet me back here at five o'clock sharp. Nate, you can take my car, but don't go crashing my shit or getting pulled over. You'll be hustling on the corner for the rest of your life if something happens to my bitch!" O-Dawg joked.

"I got you, dawg. You know my driving skills are superb. You've witnessed them firsthand."

"Your little crazy ass is right about that,"laughed O-Dawg. "I'll never forget that night. Matter of fact, Moses, take the Suburban and burn it. Get rid of all the DNA. Steal another one or a caravan. Before you go, take the garbage bag in the rear compartment and put it inside the garage. I gotta warn you, though. It smells really bad."

Nate and the boys departed, leaving Will and the O-Dawg alone.

"Yo, Will, did you take care of that?"

"Yeah, Felipe will be here with the limo at five-thirty. I'm glad to be getting this shit over with finally. Now I can move to Arizona and live in peace with my family."

"You know you don't have to move all the way out there to be in peace. You can be the new of the new person in charge of the organization once everything is done."

"Nah, I'm good. I'll take my chances in Arizona. I have a nice sum of cash put away in an offshore account. It'll be enough to get me and the family through a few rainy seasons. I'll probably open a construction business on the West Coast. I think it's about time I leave the game alone. There's too much drama, and it won't be long before the Feds come crashing down on all of us. I'm not tryna throw dirt on us; I just don't wanna be around when the shit hits the fan."

"I feel you on that one, bro. I might bounce out of Jersey myself and leave my operation to the crew. Those little youngins done put in enough work for me. I think it's time for them to shine like the star they are; they deserve it. I'm pretty sure they won't have a problem holding shit down on their own. They're tryna outshine the next man, so taking food off their plate will be like trying to take food from a dog's plate."

"So, do you have any place in mind where you wanna go?"

"I was thinking about joining Justice in his run-around-the-world tour," joked O-Dawg.

"I always wondered where he ran to after that shit with Juice went down," Will responded. "He came to my crib right after being released from the hospital and wanted me to ride with him. Since it wasn't a good time back then, I tried to talk him out of it. I wasn't with all that cowboy shit and wasn't gonna make a move on Juice until we had a solid plan that wouldn't blow up in our faces."

"You should've called me when he left your place!"O-Dawg said.

"I thought since I didn't ride with him that day, he was gonna holla at you next."

"I wish he would have come to me that day before he pulled that stunt. We would've both been on the run, but Juice and his men would've been wiped off the map a long time ago."

***

Moses grabbed the garbage bag from the rear compartment of the Suburban while Leafy waited for him in the passenger seat. The awful stench coming from inside the bag made him gag. Pinching his nose with his fingers, he carried the bag to the garage with his other hand.

What the fuck is in this bag? he thought to himself.

Letting curiosity get the best of him, he set the bag down in the garage and peeked inside. Its contents made him hurl last night's liquor as he shockingly stared at the two heads.

He knew O-Dawg could be ruthless at times but never thought of him pulling a stunt like this. The man he had looked up to, he now feared more. Moses quickly closed the bag and hurried back to the truck.

Noticing the paleness on his friend's face when he climbed inside the truck, Leafy said, "You look like you just saw a ghost. You alright?"

"Let's hurry up and get rid of this truck," was all Moses said before driving away.

***

Nate was feeling himself as he drove around in O-Dawg's BMW, stunting like he owned the vehicle. Glancing over at the bag on the passenger seat, he knew some of that money was going into a new car, maybe even one like his boss's. He now knew how O-Dawg felt like when he drove around the city in his expensive car. He had a few hours before he had to go back to the house, so Nate was going to make sure everyone in the hood saw him driving this luxurious sedan. He thanked O-Dawg for giving him the opportunity to come up at such an early age.

***

Will and O-Dawg sat on the recliners in the living room, sipping on the remainder of last night's Remy Martin. They reminisced about the good ole days and talked about what the future held for the both of them. The effects of the alcohol had their mouths moving a mile a minute. The conversation's topics went from one to another in seconds. Five o'clock came around unnoticed until a knock on the front door brought both men back to the moment at hand.

Glancing at his diamond-encrusted Rolex watch, O-Dawg said, "Oh shit! It's five o'clock!"

Quickly getting up from the recliner, he made his way to the front door. When he opened the door and saw his crew was on time and on point, a smile appeared on his face.

"Y'all sure ain't playing no games," he joked.

"For you, dawg, we'll ride or die," said Nate.

O-Dawg felt those words and knew his crew meant every word spoken.

Stepping to the side, he said, "Come inside. We still have half an hour before the limo gets here. I want to talk to y'all about something."

The crew walked inside and situated themselves on the couches. Seeing the serious look on their boss's face, the guys wondered why.

"Guys, I was doing some thinking and thought about leaving the state once this shit is over. Before y'all get rowdy, let me finish," continued O-Dawg. "I love y'all like family, and y'all have been extremely loyal to me. I doubt if anyone will be able to put a stop to the come-up y'all on. I can't promise that I'll come back, so I decided to leave y'all with the block. I've already spoken to my connect about the transaction, and he trusts my judgment and word."

Handing Nate a piece of paper, he added, "Here's his phone number. He would like to meet with you as soon as possible. I still have a few kilos left, so whenever you run low on product, you already know where to re-up."

"Thanks, dawg. I don't know what to say," said Nate.

"Don't say anything. Just don't start getting sloppy. You can move into this house if y'all want—"

A car's horn blared outside, interrupting O-Dawg.

After peeking out the window, he told them, "That's us. Let's go!"

The limo was out front—right on time.

"Remember what I said. Follow the limo."

Everyone stepped outside, and Will immediately climbed inside the limo, sitting in the back on the passenger's side. O-Dawg quickly turned around and made his way to the garage. Grabbing the garbage bag that he told Moses to put in the garage earlier, he then made his way back to the limo and placed the bag inside. Climbing into the backseat, he watched as the crew of young boys piled into the stolen caravan.

Nate followed closely behind the limo, not letting any traffic get in between them. Forty-five minutes later, they arrived safely at the airport's parking terminal.

The sun was beaming, and gas was starting to run low. Still, there was no sign of Juice.

Rolling down the middle divider that separated the chauffeur from the passengers, Felipe said, "we've been parked here illegally for an hour, and the police have already asked me to move. I don't want to get a ticket, plus we're dirty—"

"Look, I will pay the fucking ticket! Let's just give it a couple more minutes.The man is about to arrive," snapped Will, growing impatient himself.

"Go in there and wait for him.Carry his bags when you see him."

He described how Juice looked to Felipe and then sent him on his way.

***

Juice tried again to contact his men during the flight, but the call would not go through due to reception failure. Juice thought about what Will had said and agreed with him. His men would show up and be waiting for him out front of the airport in a limousine as usual. He looked at the two men he brought along with him and considered where to place them inside the organization. They were powerful men and killers.

Juice was feeling good. He had money to burn and a solid establishment in the United States. As he relaxed, for some odd reason, Sam crossed his mind. He had men all over searching for this man, but no one could locate him. The last crew he sent to look for him found a furnished apartment with no occupants. It was costing him a pretty penny to locate Sam, but it was worth every dime spent.

The three-hour flight to the United States had him feeling exhausted, but he still planned on celebrating, tonight. After retrieving his bags from the baggage carousel, Juice turned around and saw a chauffeur holding a sign with his name.

"I'm your driver for today, Sir Juice. May I take your bags?"offered the older-looking man while approaching him, his gray beard and slim build giving him the appearance of a senior.

Since the man addressed him by his name, it made Juice feel at ease. A smile appeared on his face; he knew his men would come and not let him down. Handing over his bags, he continued towards the exit with his two companions in tow.

"Where are my men?" he asked the gentleman

"They're waiting for you inside the limo, sir."

This was not unusual since his men never entered the airport due to weapons being prohibited on the premises, instead a chauffeur was always sent inside.

O-Dawg's heart skipped a few beats when he noticed the two men following Juice. They had not planned for this. It was a good thing the men would not be armed coming out of an airport—or so O-Dawg hoped.

"We have some uninvited guests," he announced.

"Don't worry about them. They aren't strapped unless they're cops, and even if they are police, they'll get it just like their partner," responded Will, cocking his weapon.

Felipe was the first to reach the limo. Opening the trunk, he placed the men's luggage in the back. Juice took it upon himself to open the back door, but before he noticed what was going on, O-Dawg seized the opportunity to grab him by his business suit and yank the small man inside.

"Shut the fuck up," he said, shoving the silenced 9mm in Juice's face. "Open your mouth, and I'll have your brain all over this window."

Juice tried to speak, but with the weapon inside his mouth, his words were muffled. His two companions, who were placing their bags in the trunk, did not notice what was taking place inside the vehicle.

Hearing the trunk shut, O-Dawg removed the gun from Juice's mouth and sat on the opposite seat facing him. While pointing the weapon at his opponent's head, he warned him to keep his mouth shut.

"I always thought you guys here in the United States were soft, but you, O-Dawg, have proven me wrong. Will, my friend, I knew you would one day cross me, but I didn't figure it would be this soon in the game."

Juice was heated he could not believe he had fallen for this trick. He did not know what was going on, but everyone involved—including their loved ones—would be tortured if he somehow made it out alive.

"Haven't I proven how far my hands can reach by killing your father, O-Dawg?"

O-Dawg lunged forward to strike Juice with the butt of his gun, but Will held him back just as the rear door opened. Juice's two companions climbed into the backseat and sat next to their boss. Everyone fell silent as both men glanced at the gun and then at Juice.

"You've jumped into the wrong limo. You should've stayed home instead of following this piece of shit," said O-Dawg, raising his silenced gun and firing a single shot into the face of one of the men.

Pulling a handkerchief from his jacket pocket, Juice wiped the blood and brain fragments from his face.

Felipe felt the blood come into contact with his skin. Scared, he turned around in his seat and said, "What the fuck, dude?"

Will knew they had no time for games. Pulling out his .50 caliber Desert Eagle, he aimed it directly at Felipe's head.

"Turn around and drive back to New Jersey. And don't say another word!"

Felipe immediately turned back around and pulled away from the illegal parking spot. Juice's other companion looked on nervously, not knowing the outcome of his situation. He kept his mouth shut in hopes they would let him live.

Felipe attempted to roll up the middle divider so he could try to place a call to Sam, but his plan was shattered when O-Dawg noticed what he was doing.

"Leave that shit rolled down. I ain't ask you to close it!"

Having just witnessed a man die, he was not trying to be next. So, Felipe reversed the divider's direction, lowering the window back down.

"Pull over when we get to North Philadelphia," ordered O-Dawg.

Looking at Juice, he had not forgotten the comment he made earlier about his father. Juice felt the cold eyes staring at him and stared right back.

"You gotta problem, my friend?"

O-Dawg did not respond. Instead, he swiftly lowered his gun and fired a shot into Juice's left kneecap.

Juice screamed and then started laughing maniacally. The pain was excruciating, but he refused to show it by continuing to scream like a bitch.

"So, you think it's funny?"

Juice continued laughing in O-Dawg's face, but deep inside, he wanted to choke the life out of him.

Feeling disrespected, O-Dawg fired another round—this one striking his victim in the groin. Juice screamed from the excruciating pain and threatened to kill every living creature, but continued laughing maniacally. Fifteen minutes later, they arrived in the North Philadelphia section of the city.

"Pull this motherfucker over," snapped O-Dawg. "Will, take this man to the youngins and tell them to handle that," he added pointing to the gentleman sitting next to Juice.

When Will stepped out of the car, O-Dawg continued his assault on Juice pistol-whipping him across the face numerous times, breaking his jaw, and shattering his teeth.

From inside the vehicle tailing the limo, Nate wondered why they pulling over in North Philly. Seeing Will holding a man at gunpoint as he climbed out of the limo made things even crazier.

"What the fuck is going on?" Nate asked as he rolled down the driver's window.

"O-Dawg said, take this fool with you and handle that."

"Say no more! Throw his ass in the back, but first, make sure he ain't got no weapons on him."

Will searched the man, and after not finding anything, he tossed him headfirst into the back seat of the stolen caravan.

"He's good."

***

The crew held their captive at gunpoint as Nate navigated the caravan through the streets of North Philadelphia. He headed towards the Benjamin Franklin Bridge, which crossed into Southern New Jersey.

"Do you know where you're going?" asked Lil Moses. "Don't be getting us lost out this bitch."

Nate didn't want to say anything, but he was lost indeed. He wasn't good at finding his way around Philadelphia and had gotten them lost a few times in the past.

Moses could tell by the look on Nate's face that they were lost.

"Pull over. I'll drive."

Once Moses jumped in the driver's seat, it didn't take long to find their destination. Five minutes later, they pulled over by a deserted spot next to a junkyard.

"Get out of the van!" ordered Nate.

The man looked at the gun's barrel, pointed directly at his face, and immediately did as told. A stone-cold killer, he never imagined being the one looking down the barrel of a gun. He prepared to let himself out but was kicked from behind with much force. He fell face-first into the dirt, eating the sand-like material. Getting up, he dusted off his clothes and spat out the dirt from his mouth.

Nate walked up to the dirty, well-dressed man and fired two rounds at his chest. The remainder of the crew climbed out of the caravan and joined in on the shooting frenzy. Feeling hurt by Dwayne's death, they all walked up to the corpse one at a time and emptied their clips into the dead man's body.

***

Entering the state of New Jersey, O-Dawg ordered Felipe to pull the limo over again.

"Pop the trunk," he added.

Exiting the limousine, he quickly made his way to the trunk and removed the garbage bag he placed there. Shutting the trunk, he made his way back inside the limousine.

"Here's your surprise. Take a look inside."

Juice hesitated before grabbing the bag. The weight was heavy, and the bottom of the bag felt slimy. Juice placed the bag between his feet and opened it. He quickly turned his face away from the awful stench that escaped the black plastic bag.

"They belong to Ralph and your best friend Matone," said O-Dawg." If you're wondering where the rest of your men are, let's just say you'll be joining them soon."

"Very impressive," responded Juice as he closed the bag containing the body parts. "You wouldn't have breached my team and got as close as you did without the help of your friend Will. Regardless, if I live or die tonight, you two, as well as your families, are as good as dead."

"You're a funny dude, Juice, but the only one dying tonight is you!"

Felipe arrived in front of O-Dawg's house and pulled the vehicle over by the curb.

"Pull this shit into the garage," Will told the chauffeur.

When the limo came to a complete stop inside the garage, O-Dawg put a bullet in the back of Felipe's head before ordering Juice out of the car.

"You read my mind," said Will. "I wanted to shot em so bad. He was acting like a bitch the entire time."

"Hurry up!" O-Dawg shouted, ushering Juice through the garage and in the door, which led to the kitchen.

I can't wait till this shit is over, O-Dawg thought to himself.

Inside the house, Juice was escorted downstairs to the basement and bound to a chair with duct tape.

Juice didn't believe all of his men were dead; he thought they would come to his rescue somehow. They were trained to handle situations like this and taught to go out and look for him if they didn't hear from their boss in a day. He didn't fear death but was not ready to die just yet.

As the minutes continued to tick by, O-Dawg started growing impatient. He hoped nothing had happened to his crew.

"They should've been here by now," he said to no one in particular.

He wanted to get started but also wanted his youngins to witness this torture. It would be the first time they would see something like this in person. He planned to have each one of the crew members chop off one of Juice's fingers. It would be their initiation into his world.

After an hour, the frustration grew too intense. Approaching Juice, O-Dawg began pistol-whipping him again across the face.

"Chill dawg!" Will interceded. "You're gonna kill the man before we get a chance to torture his ass."

O-Dawg stopped the vicious beating and walked away. He paced back and forth, anticipating his crew's arrival.

Juice sat unconscious from the brutal attack; he sustained multiple injuries and was losing a massive amount of blood. If he did not get to a hospital soon, he would go into shock and possibly die.

O-Dawg could not help but to get one last hit off. Approaching Juice, he forcefully backhanded him.

"Wake your ass up! I'm not gonna make it that easy for you!" he shouted, smacking Juice again.

O-Dawg finally grew tired of waiting for his crew and decided to continue without them. Grabbing his cigar cutter from inside the cigar box he kept on a basement shelf, he approached the unconscious man and picked up his right hand.

"This little piggy went to the market..."

Gaining consciousness, Juice screamed at the top of his lungs as the sharp blade cut through his flesh and dissected his bone. He tried to yank back his hand, but the powerful duct tape wouldn't let him move an inch. Blood squirted from the amputated finger like a leaking faucet.

O-Dawg put a piece of tape over Juice's mouth. He had a way to go before he finished and didn't feel like hearing anymore screaming, but before he could continue.They heard a loud noise coming from upstairs. It sounded like someone had kicked in the front door. O-Dawg's theory was correct.

"FBI!"

Will ran towards the miniature bar to grab his rifle as footsteps were heard rushing down the basement stairs.

O-Dawg's future flashed right before his eyes. Without hesitating, he desperately fired his weapon at the figures approaching. The first agents down the stairs were caught by surprise. The bullets ripping through their vests sent them tumbling towards the bottom of the steps.

"Ceasefire! Drop your weapons!" yelled the remaining agents from the top of the staircase. "Get on the ground!"

Three agents followed behind the first ones but were met with the same resistance. Bullets ricocheted off the concrete, striking two of the three men. Debris flew in all directions, sending the last man behind them scurrying back up the stairs.

Looking at Will, who stood frozen in place as if this was not happening, O-Dawg said, "How the fuck did they know we were here?"

"How the hell am I supposed to know?!"

When the shooting stopped, the thought of Will setting all this up crossed O-Dawg's mind. He truly believed his long-time friend had burned him to the Feds. How else did they know where to find them?

"You set me up?"

Will could not believe what he just heard. How could his best friend accuse him of snitching?

"Are you out of your fucking mind?"

As O-Dawg raised his gun at Will, a bright flash blinded him. He instantly knew the bright light was a flash grenade. A strong odor burned his nostrils as he inhaled the scent, sending him into a coughing fit. His mind quickly registered that it had to be a canister of tear gas. Holding his breath, he shut his eyes and squeezed the trigger of the AR-15 assault rifle.

Bullets whizzed by Will's head as he dove for cover behind the miniature bar. Cocking his weapon, he returned fire wildly in hopes of striking O-Dawg. He was not going out without putting up a fight, and if he lost, he hoped to take his opponent down with him.

"You fucking snitch," yelled O-Dawg, continuing to fire his weapon until he ran out of rounds. "I'm gonna fucking kill you!"

***

Nate finally reached the block to O-Dawg's house. As he made the left turn onto the street, he automatically slammed on the car's brakes.

"What the fuck!" he shouted.

Patrol cars and unmarked police vehicles surrounded the house. Quickly putting the gearshift into reverse, he made an illegal U-turn and pressed down the gas pedal.

"God does work in mysterious ways, because if I hadn't gotten us lost in Philly, we would've been dead in the middle of that shit," said Nate as they sped away from the scene.

He wanted to take full credit for them not being in jail.

"Fuck that!" shouted Lil Moses. "Let's go back and show them pigs who they fucking with. We can't leave O-Dawg in there for dead or in jail. We have to save him!"

"This ain't no motherfucking cartoon movie!" snapped Nate. "That will be like going on a suicide mission! Listen to yourself. You sound crazy!"

"Yeah, what good are we to Dawg if *we're* dead or in jail?" chimed in Bucky.

"You're right," replied Moses.

"Look, let's just get the fuck away from here and go to the projects," Nate told them. "We'll figure out what we're gonna do when we get there. Right now, shit is hectic. We don't know what the fuck is going on inside that house. I say we chill out until later tonight and then try to contact Dawg. If I don't get an answer from him, we'll come over here to his crib and see what's good—do our own investigation. He'll call me from the county jail or from wherever they take him, and he'll let me know what's the deal."

The crew knew Nate was right. O-Dawg was the hand that fed them. Without him, there was no income, which meant they would probably starve and would have to start doing their own thing to survive. O-Dawg was the man with all the resources. Regardless of the outcome, they would remain savages and strive to survive. For right now, there was no other alternative but to wait it out and see what would be O-Dawg's fate. Each crew member had their own thoughts regarding the outcome, but each knew if O-Dawg fell from his throne, there would be disagreements within the crew about who would be taking charge—maybe even bloodshed over the rights.

***

Back at the house, O-Dawg fell to his knees while still clutching his assault rifle.

Click, click, click, click.

O-Dawg squeezed the trigger to an empty chamber. He searched nearby for another clip, but the tear gas was becoming unbearable—burning his throat and squeezing the life out of his lungs.

It was impossible for anyone to see in the smoke-filled room, but he knew he hit his target when he heard someone tumbling down the stairs.

The agents filled the room one at a time, stepping over any dead body. Not wanting to come in contact with friendly fire, they each stood close to the wall. The twenty or so masked agents fired their weapons in search of their prey.

O-Dawg let out a loud cry as the excruciating pain from a bullet ripped through his left leg, tearing his flesh and shattering his bone. He knew there was zero chance of him making it out of there alive. Still, a smile appeared on his face from knowing he had taken a few alphabet boys, the name he used when referring to federal agencies, along with him to the grave.

Another flash grenade was tossed into the basement—this one giving away his hiding spot. The agents fired at the crawling marine-like figure on the floor and didn't stop until they heard the commanding voice yell, "Ceasefire!"

O-Dawg's body jerked from the many bullets that tore through his flesh. The bulletproof vest he wore did nothing to protect him from the huge rounds. While taking his last breath, his final thought was about Will setting him up with the Feds. He never thought a lifelong friend and OG would have violated the code of the streets.

Stay tuned for my upcoming book

Consequences To The Game.

See next few pages for a peek inside.

PROLOGUE

"Let me get two bundles of rock (crack cocaine)," said Solo, approaching the corner hustler. "I'm a get this fool," he thought to himself. What he did not realizing was that today things were not going to go as planned. Robbing the cities corner drug dealers was an everyday task for the youngster and his cousin. They had been going at it since their early teenage years and not a soul had yet to figure it out. Letting greed supersede his judgment he decided that today he would go at this mission alone without his partner in crime. Not inviting his cousin along for the journey would be a mistake he would come to regret.

As the addict approached, Mack who had been hustling crack since 7 o'clock that morning felt a funny vibe. He left the burner (Gun) stashed in the abandoned building across the street and was not prepared if something were to go down. The young man in front of him look to be no older than 16 years old. Since there were females and males ranging from all ages using drugs, these days. Mack shook off the odd feeling upon noticing the baby-face and went along with the normal routine of serving the everyday fiends.

"I only have 14 bags on me, wait here and I'll go get the rest," said Mack before turning around and quickly sprinting towards his stash. Crossing the street Mack thought about going into the abandoned building to grab the gun for safe measures, but the early morning blunt once again clouded his better judgment. Instead, he made his way over to the stash and picked up the drugs. Glancing left and right, he observed the entire block in search of any suspicious activity. Not seeing anything out the regular, he crossed the street and made his way back to where the customer awaited.

Solo knew exactly where Mack kept his stash. He also knew from past surveillance that the Block Boyz kept the remaining drugs and the daily proceeds, hidden somewhere inside the abandoned building across the street. Noticing the dealer approaching, he prepared to react at the right moment. He did not want this act to take on the wrong turn towards violence. Pulling the money out of his pocket, he acted as if he were counting the green paper.

"Here you go fam," said Mack handing the drugs to the young addict.

Solo quickly took the drugs and handed over the money. Putting the drugs inside his hoodie pocket, he pranced on the perfect opportunity as Mack focused his attention on counting the money. In one swift motion, he pulled out the small .38 caliber pistol from his waist. "You already know what time it is," he said, aiming the weapon directly at his opponents head. "I'm not here for games! Run everything you got stashed in the building!"

Mack looked up in astonishment. He could not believe this was taking place. He now wished he would have listened to his gut feeling a few minutes ago and grabbed the gun. Not being one to take losses, his mind raced for a solution as he lead the way to the abandon structure. Entering the dimly lit building, the smell of urine and feces saturated the atmosphere. Mack knew that even if he gave up the drugs there was still a chance he could lose his life. "There's nothing in here," he lied, hoping the young boy would believe his words.

Feeling played, Solo snapped. "I told you I ain't got time for games!" Squeezing off a warning shot into the building's rotted floor. "Play with my emotions again and the next one will be to your dome," he added. "Now hurry the fuck up, I ain't got all fucking day!"

Seeing that the stick up kid was serious as a heart attack, Mack weighed his options and decided that the money and drugs wasn't worth his life. "A'ight... A'ight," he nervously said, reaching for the stash. Handing over the drugs and money, he looked Solo directly in the eyes and said, "I never forget a face!"

The smart remark made Solo furious, as he took the threat very seriously. "Remember my face, but also remember this," he said letting off two rounds striking Mack's in both kneecaps.

Mack let out a loud scream of pain and terror as he watched the young boy who just robbed him exit the abandoned building

****

 A block away officer Harold sat inside of his patrol car, drinking a cup of coffee and reading the newspaper. *Boom!* The loud noise caught him off guard making him spill his coffee. "What the fuck," he said outloud tossing the cup out of the window. Circling the block a few times, he wondered what direction the shots had come from. When all of a sudden…*Boom! Boom!* Two more rounds fired. This time he was damn sure the shots came from the next block over. Racing to the crime scene, he arrived just in time as he noticed the young black male racing out of the abandoned building…

www.ingramcontent.com/pod-product-compliance
Lightning Source LLC
Chambersburg PA
CBHW030316180626
46810CB00003B/1112